About the Author

Moitrayee Bhaduri loves reading crime thrillers as much as she enjoys writing them. A content specialist, Moitrayee discovered her love for books and music early in life, in her hometown Kolkata. After graduating with History Honours from Loreto College and studying M.A. at Jadavpur University, Moitrayee joined the corporate world as a technical content writer. Thereafter, she has worked with leading IT organizations in various writing and people-managerial roles. Moitrayee also started book clubs and newsletters in most of the organizations she worked with.

Moitrayee loves animals, especially dogs. She enjoys singing, travelling, and watching cricket. Currently, she resides in Mumbai with her husband Sagnik Ghosh. *The Sinister Silence* is her first book.

To know more about Moitrayee, visit www.moitrayeebhaduri.com. Connect with her on Facebook at www.facebook.com/thesinistersilence or tweet to @moits04. You are welcome to send your feedback on this book to moitrayeebhaduri@gmail.com.

THE SINISTER SILENCE

Moitrayee Bhaduri

Srishti
PUBLISHERS & DISTRIBUTORS

SRISHTI PUBLISHERS & DISTRIBUTORS
Registered Office: N-16, C.R. Park
New Delhi – 110 019
Corporate Office: 212A, Peacock Lane
Shahpur Jat, New Delhi – 110 049
editorial@srishtipublishers.com

First published by
Srishti Publishers & Distributors in 2015

*In loving memory of my guardian angels
who left this world a little too soon…
Dipak Bhaduri, my father
and
Malabika Ghosh, my mother-in-law.*

*In fond remembrance of my beloved friends
who loved me unconditionally:
Badshah, Begum, Rupi, Bagha,
Lalu, Bhulu, and Poppy.*

Acknowledgements

❦

Thank you *reader*, for investing your time in this book. Hope you enjoy reading it.

A big 'Thank You' to team *Srishti*, my publisher, for believing in this book and for helping me debut as an author.

My family – It is tough to find words to thank the people who stick with you, no matter what. A hug is simpler! Nevertheless, *thank you all!*

Deepa Bhaduri – my mother, my inspiration and my best friend. My world revolves around her and she is the reason that I write.

Sagnik Ghosh – the first reader of this book who also meticulously reviewed all the drafts. My biggest critic and greatest support, this book would not have been possible without him.

Kushal Bhaduri – for motivating me to write a crime thriller, and for being my constant support.

Rajeswari Ghosh – for her positive feedback on the book, especially because she is a voracious reader, and for being there when it matters the most.

Anubhuti Bhaduri – for her fresh ideas and spontaneous feedback on the story and book covers.

Rathindra Nath Ghosh – for his inputs on storytelling, comments on the manuscript, and for encouraging my creative endeavours.

Samidha Bhaduri and Abhipriti Bhaduri – for their enthusiasm and overwhelming support.

Priyanka Singh – for inspiring me with her 'go-getter' approach and 'never say die' attitude.

Aneeta Razdan – for being the rock-solid motivating factor in my life over the last five years.

Jalaj Bhaduri and family, K.K Bhattacharya and family, Satyaki Ghosh, Abonty Banerjee, Sudeshna and Soumitra Banerjee, Pradip Majumdar, Ajoy Ghosh, Atashi Seal, and all other family members.

My Teachers from school, college, and university – I will always be grateful to each one of you. Thank you for everything!

My friends and well wishers – thank you so much!

Nancy Louise Stevens – for being the angel who continues to bless me from God's home.

Raja Thirunavukarasu – for conceptualizing and creating the book covers and my website.

Mitrajit Bhattacharya, Mona Sen Gupta, Sharmila Ramnani, Arnab Mitra, and Erika Banerjy – for guidance with the publishing process, events, and feedback on the manuscript.

Sudarshan Banerjee, Sthubanta Mukherjee, and team Utopeia – for the overall marketing support.

Nachiket Dighe – for conceptualizing, storyboarding, and creating the book trailer.

Mona Sen Gupta, Sushroota Sarkar, and Ahava Communications – for the enormous support and guidance as my launch partner in Kolkata.

Sumathi Mohnani, Anand Srivastava, Nancy McTavish, and Janet Rich – for being exemplary leaders who encouraged me to follow my dreams.

Harigopal Nj Dasa – for sanctioning my long-leave request to help me complete this book.

Dipen Ambalia – for the enthusiasm, motivation, and guidance at all times, and for believing in this book even when it just had the first two pages! *Thank you so much!*

Shreya Upadhyaya, Anupama Ambika, and Ipsita Bhattacharya – for the insights on editing, and for the eagerness to see this book published.

Payal Bose, Venkat S Iyer, and Asha Deshpande – for going out of the way to help me with research on this book, and for being a huge positive influence.

Jeevan Gaikwad – for instilling the faith in me that every moment has a story waiting to be told.

Saibal Banerjee, Bhavna Sanghvi, Aparajita and Kaushik Sengupta, Sreelekha Chatterjee, Rudra and Indrani Chaudhuri, Sourav De, Somenath Dey, the 'Khush Raho' WhatsApp group, Brindha Seshadri, Alka Singh, Dr. Sharmila Majumdar, Maneet Bhavnani, Suresh Iyer, Rukmini Roy, Bahnishikha Chatterjee, Anita Singh, Renu Kakkar, Suparna Sengupta, Nilanjana Kar, Rucha Phatak, Karan Singhi, Bratati Sengupta, Varsha Khatri, friends from IBM, RS Software, Apeejay House, Carmel School, Loreto College, and Jadavpur University: *Thank you!*

Finally, thank you God – for everything!

Prologue

Alibaug, 1996

Enakshi believed in her dreams. The sixteen-year-old swimmer had been working hard. Her goal was to win the 1996 Inter-College Swimming Championship.

'A month from now, the gold will be mine,' Enakshi announced as she continued to swim in the fresh blue-green waters.

"This is not your swimming pool Kashi. Don't go further," her boyfriend Ritesh commanded from the beach, while clinging on to Kashi's slippers and sunhat that the flirtatious breeze continued to tease.

"I cannot be swimming inside the pool all my life, Ritz. The sea is fun. Join me," Kashi aka Enakshi yelled back.

Tired of the futile counselling effort, seventeen-year-old Ritesh walked towards his friends, hoping to find someone who could convince Kashi. The lifeguards were blowing neon-coloured plastic whistles as a warning to keep people away from the sea. The sun was on its way home. Its fiery redness created a beautiful reflection in the sea before fading into the horizon.

Ritesh spotted Kashi pleading with a lifeguard for a last swim. Just like the setting sun, her feisty demeanour seemed to wane away with the guard rejecting her request with a whistle that went 'puuuuuurrr'. Even though away on the shore, Ritesh shuddered at its piercing sound.

"Good girl," Ritesh shouted as he saw Kashi walking towards the beach. She waved at him and he flung the sunhat towards her with all his might. It landed on the sand in front of Kashi. She picked it up and signalled a thumbs up to Ritesh. He waved back and then quickened his pace to join his friends who were having an intense argument over dinner plans.

Kashi was in no mood to return. As soon as the lifeguard she was pleading with turned around to alert other people, Kashi jumped back into the water, further away from the shore. She realized that the sunhat was still in her hand. She didn't bother throwing it back to the beach. Instead, she let the sunhat float freely on the water.

"Where's Kashi? I doubt if she will like the crab idea," Kashi's twin brother asked Ritesh.

Ritesh grimly glanced at his watch. Twenty minutes earlier Kashi had been walking towards the beach. "Where did she go now?"

The disturbed teenagers rushed towards the sea, now dark and cold.

Suddenly, a girl who was running frantically towards the shore bumped into Ritesh and fell down. She sprang up almost immediately.

"I...I did not do it," she said, pointing to a hat trapped in the inescapable grip of the ruthless waves.

Ritesh and Kashi's brother reluctantly followed the girl's eyes that wore a fear-coated guilty look.

"Tai, you didn't do anything. Let us go and tell Papa," the younger girl consoled her. "Chalo, run!"

"Look, Kashi's hat," the brother screamed and dashed towards the water.

The lifeguard pulled him back. "The currents are unforgiving. Not a step forward, boys."

"But my sister..."

"The rescue team is at work," the lifeguard assured them.

The two boys restlessly paced up and down the beach. Soon, their friends joined them.

Almost three hours later, the rescue team returned from the sea. The weary look on their faces said it all.

"We are really sorry, we tried our best. She was caught in strong currents. The sand is slippery and dangerous. We are constantly warning people. It is impossible to resist the current."

Kashi's brother looked at the lifeless body of his sister. The sound of the sea was deafening. He cried into the darkness until the pain in his voice overpowered the sea.

Ritesh looked at Kashi's pale, peaceful face and hugged the wet sunhat tightly.

Kashi would never be the swimming champion now. She was dead.

Part - 1
Mumbai, 2014

Saahil Kerkar

❧

Mumbai, 4 July 2014

The residents of Mumbai had been greatly inconvenienced by incessant rains for two days in a row. On the 4th of July, the third day, the sky was unexpectedly clear. As drowsy-looking trees witnessed their shrivelled leaves lazily clinging on to the branches, the gloomy afternoon got ready to welcome a passive evening. However, the calm did not last long. Soon, darkness enveloped the sky and the increasing intensity of beastly winds created a ruckus in the city. Finally, the rain gods descended, resulting in uninterrupted rains.

Highways were jammed and train lines in the western suburbs became dysfunctional. Auto-rickshaws and taxis disappeared from the streets. Buses could not squeeze in any more people. The bus stops were stacked with people and stray dogs, each looking for a dry, temporary shelter. The Bandra-Worli sea-link looked precarious; the irascible winds and the tidal waves had entered into a dangerous competition that threatened to jeopardize Mumbai.

Cellular phone networks went haywire due to the sudden upsurge in the number of calls. People on the streets were in a rush to go back home, mostly dreading a 'July 26' like calamity.

For Mumbaikars, hard-hitting rains were reminiscent of the black day of 26th July, 2005 when torrential showers had ravaged Mumbai, claiming thousands of lives.

"The weather department reports that the storm won't last long. Our business continuity back-up site at Philippines will pick up client requests in case servers get jammed. Otherwise, it is business as usual. Our Mumbai office will be functional. Please do not panic!" Vikrant Sharma's low-pitched voice reached all his 785 Mumbai employees through the central announcement system.

"The CEO never sees any reason to panic," retorted Gopal, Information Architect at Zarine Software.

"Why don't you go to his cabin and convey the message?" winked Srishti, Technical Writer with the Usability team.

Among the top three IT firms in the country, Zarine Software was a name to reckon with. Headquartered in Mumbai, the company profits had doubled in 2014 and Vikrant Sharma, the Chief Executive Officer had been honoured with the 'Entrepreneur of the Year' award. This was a big achievement, considering Zarine was a young company, barely in its seventh year in business.

"We must leave immediately," added Preeti, the IT Support Engineer. "My driver has already called twice."

"It is just 3.30 p.m.," said Gopal.

"Oh yes, I do not want to be stuck here until 3.30 a.m.!"

Amid all this tumult, Saahil Kerkar, a thirty-something employee with Zarine was unperturbed. He continued to play games on the Internet while the CEO's announcement kept his colleagues on their toes!

Senior Project Manager Saahil was an ace performer with an enviable delivery turnaround time and an eye for perfection. Since he was managing a US project and the fourth of July was a public holiday in America, Saahil had no project closures that day.

"Are Americans as emotional about their Independence Day as we are?" he thought.

A bit of blogging, some net surfing on the 4th of July celebrations and multiple online chats later, Saahil decided to pack up.

"What are Friday evenings for?" he smirked and brushed off some imaginary dirt from his brand new laptop.

This new electronic device with a superfast processor was Saahil's lifeline. He was addicted to the virtual space and unusually possessive about his gadgets. Ever since this laptop arrived, Saahil was devoted to it just as he would dote on a new girlfriend. At times, Saahil found it difficult to divide his time between his laptop and his guitar, the other love of his life.

A gifted singer and guitarist, Saahil sometimes went on abrupt leaves with only his guitar for company. He created magic in the office cafeteria with his guitar. Pretty management trainees would swoon over Saahil and Zarine Software would suddenly look like a college campus. However, Saahil enjoyed it the most when he played alongside Morena.

Saahil's good looks and gifted voice made him popular among women, both online and offline. The 'hits' and 'likes' on his music videos kept him upbeat and gave him the confidence to launch his own album. He was looking at making his debut in August 2014.

Today, Saahil's status on FriendMe, the popular social networking site, simply read 'Happy :)'. Happy he was as he hit 'Enter' for the final time today. He had met Neha only once but had been chatting with her for the last seven days. An aspiring model, Neha was attractive, petite, and witty. Saahil thought she would be fun to hang around with for a while.

While locking his workstation, Saahil's eyes fell on the stapled bunch of old e-mails. Most of these were from Morena Dave, his friend and confidante for the last four years. On the

10th of December 2011, Morena had said something funny and Saahil had almost fallen off the chair laughing. He had promptly stated, *'I love people who make me laugh'*.

But how different things were today!

"This formality coffee makes no sense to me anymore." Morena's words were fresh in Saahil's mind.

Saahil wondered why he was still preserving these printouts, which were the mouldering remains of an unpleasant relationship. He briefly glanced at Morena, who was sitting on the other side of the bay.

"Thank God it is over," he murmured and unnecessarily slammed the workstation drawer before locking it.

He looked at Morena again and thought she looked reasonably decent in pink. Her cheeks reflected the colour of her dress when she wore pink, red, or any other happy colour. For a split second, Saahil had an uncanny urge to speak to Morena. His eyes were moist but he collected himself immediately. Simple, dignified, and caring – that was the Morena Saahil had befriended; not this pretentious, self-absorbed hypocrite in front of him.

Saahil peeped out of the corridor through the smoke-tainted glasses at the open sky. The rains had been overtaken by thunderous lightning and the evening ahead looked dangerous. He glanced at the washroom mirror to ensure that his hair was perfect.

As he trudged down the corridor, Saahil noticed a fly stuck outside the windowpane. It flapped its wings for a while; then gave up the fight against the plump raindrop that overpowered it by the sheer strength in its suddenness. Saahil felt suffocated for a moment. He closed his eyes and took a deep breath. He did not want to stay trapped in his mental battles anymore.

Regaining his composure, Saahil whistled out to his colleagues. "Anyone interested in a lift? I can accommodate three people comfortably."

"Saahil bhai, wait for me," shouted Rounak Arora, his friend and team member.

"You are coming by default, bro," Saahil replied with a childish cheer.

"How do you manage to stay cool even on such a horrible day, Saahil?" asked Ram, the next bay neighbour and Project Manager for e-learning deals.

"I don't have a wifey back home yet, Rams. Are you coming?"

"Ah…no! You guys carry on. I will wait till the storm calms down."

Ram focused on his excel spreadsheet, discomfort evident in his tone. The whole office knew about his domineering wife. Ram did not mind if the world perceived him as henpecked. He loved his Mira and that is all that mattered.

"Okay then, peeps," Saahil looked at Morena again through the corner of his eyes despite deciding against it. She was so absorbed in her laptop that Saahil wondered if she were watching porn!

"What else could be so exciting that she cannot take her eyes off the laptop?" he thought.

Saahil failed to read Morena's body language. The pink dupatta was very distracting. The colour complemented her cheeks and the radiance reflected in her delicate silver earrings that brushed against her earlobes each time she adjusted the dupatta. He sped past Morena, waved at the people he met on the way and jumped into the elevator.

Rounak took the stairs as somebody had told him that the best way to lose weight was by using the staircase. At ninety-five kilos, Rounak had been trying this method since the past two weeks. On the way, he met Farzad Mistry, his friend from the Opulus project. Farzad was looking for a lift to the local railway station and Rounak invited Farzad to accompany him.

Saahil drove his car out of the parking lot and honked. "Come on buddies. The weather is real sick. It is just 5 p.m. but looks like past nine already!"

"Sorry sorry... let's go. I thought you would be packing your guitar Saahil bhai," said Rounak as he took his seat beside Saahil and closed the door.

"Good that I didn't get her today. Had my baby got wet, I'd have a tough time drying her up."

"You bet," said Rounak immediately.

"You comfortable, Farzad?" Saahil asked while adjusting the mirror in front of him.

"Err yes Saahil, am perfect. Thanks!" Farzad smiled back at the mirror.

"Farzad, did I tell you that you look like Ashton Kutcher's brother from another mother?" Saahil said as he started the car.

"You must have said that at least five times already Saahil," laughed Farzad. "I wish I could explain how it inflates my ego."

"Saahil bhai is perpetually finding similarities between people. The other day, he said, Arbaaz Khan looks like Roger Federer," added Rounak.

"Wow, that's actually true! Great observation Saahil," said Farzad, with a surprised look.

"And doesn't our CMO resemble Penelope Cruz?" Saahil continued, while driving towards the main gate of Zarine Software.

"Oh my God! Now I know why she always looked familiar," Farzad said instantly. "You are a genius, Saahil!"

"Hahahaha!" Saahil responded. "They say that each one of us has at least one more person in some part of the world who looks exactly like us."

"Hey, do any of you know Yuvika Patil?" Farzad asked gleefully.

Saahil suddenly pulled the brakes and the car screeched to a halt.

Rounak's head hit the dashboard. Farzad, who had been leaning forward while speaking, hit his nose against the driver's seat.

"Ouch! Careful Saahil," he said.

"Sorry man! That lazy cat! Rounak, how many times should I ask you to wear the seat belt?"

"We are not even out of the ZS compound, Saahil bhai. Am wearing it now," Rounak replied defensively.

"But where is the cat?" asked Farzad.

"Oh yeah, the kitty is waiting to say hello. Just shut up, Farzad. The weather is pathetic," Rounak blurted out furiously.

"Relax people," said Saahil.

The drive back home was Saahil's favourite journey of the day. The rains refused to stop. He hummed to himself before switching on the car radio. Ah, it was Arijit Singh again. Saahil loved this song *'Jo tu mera hamdard hain'* from the latest Bollywood flick *Ek Villain*. Each time Saahil heard this versatile singer, he remembered Morena. She was crazy about Arijit's voice.

Five hours later

The weather continued to worsen. Traffic had come to a standstill. The waterlogged streets and the power cut added to the misery of the Mumbai suburb. Saahil was tired of driving at a snail's pace. The last two hours had been worse than post-lunch office meetings! Finally, Saahil saw a blink of hope when two police officers sporting fluorescent raincoats started clearing the traffic knots. Saahil was about to accelerate, but instead slowed down his olive-green SUV at the adjacent bus stop. He spotted a familiar face there.

"Hey…you're all drenched. Get in, get in!" Saahil opened the front door of the car to allow his acquaintance to step in.

"Thanks," gulped the familiar face.

"You ought to be home, killer day today. Get in fast!"

"Hey, thanks a lot, Saahil," smiled the co-passenger and stepped in beside Saahil, quickly squeezing out the excess water from the black windcheater.

"No worries!" smiled back Saahil. Uttering these two words had become a habit, thanks to the last ten years in the Information Technology industry.

"Rather I should thank you! I was getting bored of driving alone," Saahil added.

Saahil's watch beeped. 10 p.m.

"Ah, missed it again," he said, blowing the horn in frustration.

"Huh?" the co-passenger reacted.

"My favourite sitcom. I miss all the episodes. I wish we could be programmed to leave office at 6 p.m. every day!"

There was no reaction from the listener. Saahil drove on slowly, trying his best to meander through the pothole-filled dark streets. His co-passenger was unusually quiet. The silence within the car made Saahil uncomfortable.

Ten minutes later, Saahil felt an acute pain on his left arm. His eyes got droopy and he struggled to keep them open. He turned towards his co-traveller with a confused look on his face. The person smiled and said, "Relax Saahil. It will not hurt. Trust me."

There was pin drop silence… a sinister silence.

▼

In the wee hours the next morning – 5th of July 2014 – Saahil Kerkar lay in a pool of blood inside his car near the Blue Lime Residential Complex on Yarawada Road, Mumbai.

There was no trace of the person accompanying him.

Mili Ray

❦

5 July 2014

At 5.30 a.m., when most of Mumbai was somnolent, Mili woke up to the moist fragrance of the fresh breeze.

"Thank God the rains have subsided," she yawned. The previous evening had been encrypted by rains. That is how Mili's technology-oriented brain would comprehend it.

As she stepped out of the bathroom and pulled out her yoga mat, Mili jumped at a screeching noise! It came from the road, just outside her building. She grabbed her housecoat and ran to the balcony. "Some drunken jerk early in the morning," she fumed.

"*Madamzee, zaldi nisse aaoo,*" cried Thapa, the building security guard, spotting Mili on her balcony. A car had hit the banyan tree opposite her house and halted. Mili picked up her mobile phone from the bedside table and hurried downstairs. The car kept honking, causing quite a cacophony.

Mili lost no time in running towards the car. The window shades were closed. There was someone in the driver's seat! Mili rushed for the door. Few people ran to the scene along with Mili. However, anticipating danger, Mili instructed them to stay away from the car.

Mili unlocked the door, trying to ignore the ear-splitting noise of the car horn.

10

A young man sat there with his eyes closed and head down on the steering. There was blood on his hands, on the steering, and all over the seats. His hands were in such a position that an onlooker would think he had been meditating. The engine was on. Mili took a hanky from her housecoat pocket, wrapped it around her fist, and turned off the engine. Next, she called the ambulance before touching the man. The man's right wrist was slit and he was bleeding profusely.

Mili leaned inside cautiously, put one arm around the man's neck and reached for his left shoulder. With her other hand, she held his right shoulder and slowly pulled him up from the steering. The honking stopped. She rested his head on the seat. He was not breathing.

There were multiple injuries on his forehead, cheeks, and left eye. The left side of his face was heavily swollen. Perhaps, he had been beaten up. The direction of the bruises on his right hand was from right to left and pointed upwards, more towards the palm. The police would suspect a suicide attempt, Mili inferred.

Mili quickly felt his left wrist, which was unhurt. No pulse. She left his hand in dismay and suddenly his index finger moved. Mili looked for the pulse again. *Yes*, he was alive.

The ambulance arrived. Mili instructed the staff to handover the patient to Dr Amit Shah at the Shreelok Hospital. Dr Shah had been helping Mili with emergency cases right from her early days in the Indian Police Service. Once the ambulance left with the injured man, Mili called the doctor.

"Okay, I will look at him."

"His name is Saahil Kerkar, Dr Shah," Mili said, looking at the driver's licence she had gathered from the man's wallet lying on the seat. "I don't know how long he has been unconscious."

"I will keep you posted," replied Dr Shah.

"I will inform the police. But please start your treatment. He must live."

"I will do my best, DCP Ray...I mean Detective Ray," assured Dr Shah.

Mili smiled. "Just Mili will do, doctor."

The victim's wallet had some money, a photo ID, and a visiting card. The driving licence was easy identification. Saahil Kerkar – 08/07/1979. Mili had no doubt that Saahil Kerkar was a handsome young man. The visiting card indicated that he was employed with Zarine Software.

"I hope he lives to tell the tale," she prayed.

Mili found a laptop bag in the car. It was not rocket science to figure out that it belonged to the victim. She handed it to Thapa and asked him to keep his mouth shut. She needed to examine the laptop before the police got hold of it. There was no mobile phone in the car. Perhaps it was stolen. May be destroyed, if the attacker wanted to kill Saahil. Mili ruled out the possibility of a techie not using a cell phone.

Mili informed the nearest police station about the attack on Saahil Kerkar. She thought about Saahil's face again. He sported a diamond stud on his left ear. Even with his face heavily swollen, he looked familiar. Mili took pride in her ability to remember people, even perfect strangers she may have chanced upon years ago. But she could not place him yet. She looked at his wristwatch. 10.45 p.m.

▼

The police reached the crime spot at around 6.30 a.m. The crowd grew bigger.

"Even residential areas in Mumbai are not safe anymore," an elderly jogger commented.

"Madam sir, good morning. Sub-inspector Shirodkar reporting."

"Morning Shirodkar! The name is Saahil Kerkar. He works with Zarine Software. Dr Shah is hoping he will survive. There are injuries on his face, possibly allergies or the result of a bad fight. His right wrist is slit. Inform his family immediately. The car was found exactly how you see it now. It hit the banyan tree but this was not an accident. There is no sign of vehicle damage – even the airbags are intact."

"Noted and thank you, madam. I will move the car once the tow-van arrives. Is that okay?"

"You don't need my permission, Shirodkar. I'd be interested in the fingerprints' story."

Shirodkar had worked with Mili when she was heading the Special Investigation Squad in 2010.

"Thank you, madam sir." Shirodkar replied before leaving. He continued to be loyal to addressing Mili the way he had done for over a decade. That she was his inspiration was a different story.

▼

Soon, the police cordoned off the site. Medical examiners and police photographers sprang into action.

"Oh my god, who do we have here? What more can a reporter ask for? What is the scene here, if I may ask, Ms Ray?"

"Err...nothing." Mili had not expected Ayesha Mathur at the crime scene. Ayesha was the chief correspondent with a leading TV channel in Mumbai. Known for portraying any crime news as sensational, Ayesha was not among the best journalists in town.

"Oh come on! We will not have ex-super cop Mili Ray take charge if there is nothing here! So tell me, does our firebrand debutant detective suspect a murder here?"

"I thought you had come here to jog, Ayesha," Mili reacted, looking down at the lanky Ayesha sitting cross-legged on the pavement.

"Sure, I did. But you are surely not jogging in your night suit, Mili!" Ayesha strode towards Mili, who suddenly felt dwarfed despite standing reasonably tall at five feet and four inches!

"Look Ayesha, I would appreciate if you do not highlight it in the media right away!"

By the time Mili completed her sentence, she regretted her futile suggestion to the tall woman infamous for her tall tales.

"Oh, but the people are saying someone has been killed. My team is already working on the story. Sorry, wish you had warned me earlier. Now, it is too late. It's Zarine Software, after all."

"Who told you?" Mili's otherwise confident face suddenly wore a question mark.

"Well, I overheard your conversation with the police officer. Part of my job, you see."

"Do you realize that this man is seriously injured? Just stop reporting rubbish!" Mili began to lose her temper.

"Oops! Sorry, super cop. But if we don't cover the story, someone else will." Ayesha stated, shrugging her shoulders. She was starting to enjoy irritating Mili.

"Just get out of here," Mili yelled back.

"Saahil Kerkar? Nice name to start with," Ayesha added sarcastically before walking off.

Zarine Software was a big name in the IT industry. However, Mili had not expected the news to spread so fast.

How she hated Ayesha Mathur!

▼

Mili needed keys to enter her home. Instead of waiting for her house-help, she walked across the road to her friend Gatha Trivedi's house.

"In a lawyer's home, there are no early risers," she thought. Funnily, the sound of Gatha's doorbell always reminded Mili of her college days in Pune.

Finally, the housekeeper answered the door. While Mili waited for Gatha on the ground floor of the kingly bungalow, she had only one question on her mind – "Why did Saahil Kerkar look so familiar?"

Gatha Trivedi walked down the palatial flight of stairs, rubbing her eyes. She looked like a queen with her gown sweeping the staircase as she descended. A successful criminal lawyer and Mili's close friend, Gatha was beautiful, fiercely ambitious, and perceptive. Everyone in her family, except her brother-in-law, was a lawyer.

"What brings you here at this hour?" Gatha spoke sleepily.

"Kwest just got its first case, Madam Secret Agent. Wake up!" screamed Mili and shook Gatha's hand vigorously.

Gatha returned a wry look and before she could speak, Mili blurted out, "I'll answer all your queries. For now, just get me my keys. I can't enter my home."

"But what are you doing outside so early in the morning in your pajamas?"

"I'll answer you later. Keys please!"

"Okay, okay," Gatha replied with her 'hands up' in surrender position, consciously avoiding another deadly handshake with the hyperactive ex-super cop.

Soon, Gatha was back with Mili's duplicate keys. Mili grabbed them and announced, "Meet me at my house in an hour from now. Get Anubhav along."

▼

Security guard Thapa had safely kept Saahil's laptop bag in his room. Seeing Mili walk towards him hurriedly, Thapa immediately fetched the bag before 'madam zee' could ask for it. Thapa took great pride in running errands for Mili. She paid him handsomely and was appreciative of his work. It made Thapa feel that he was part of the police force and doing a noble service to society. He was a loyal and efficient old man, guarding the Blue Lime Residential Complex for over seventeen years.

Mili gestured a thumbs-up to Thapa while collecting the bag and sprinted upstairs. She entered her room, threw the bag on the sofa and ran to take a quick shower. Her mind kept going back to Saahil, "Where have I seen him?"

Mili unzipped Saahil's bag carefully and poured out the laptop on her bed. Along with it emerged a LAN cable wire, a mouse, and mouse-pad with ZS written on it. The laptop was locked, something which Mili had expected. She thought for a split second, dashed to fetch her own laptop and curled up on her bed. She put her phone on silent and lit a cigarette.

Though a technology buff herself, Mili knew that getting into a techie's laptop would not be easy. However, much to her surprise, she did not need a Windows password to log in to Saahil's system! She hit 'Enter' and the system was unlocked. Mili doubted she would find anything useful in the machine.

Despite the office email window being open, Mili thought it was wise not to connect to the Zarine Software (ZS) server from Saahil's machine. ZS firewalls were highly secure and she did not want to risk a security breach. Browsing through Saahil's files and folders, Mili did not find anything that would help the case. All folders were work related. The one titled 'Personal' had his office pay slips, accounts, Form 16, records of online bills paid to cell phone services providers, internet providers, and his credit card statements. Mili copied the 'Personal' folder onto a pen drive.

The only important catch from the laptop so far was Saahil's mobile phone number. Next, she looked for Saahil's phone records. The bills since 2011 were neatly saved in a folder with payment dates mentioned against each one. Saahil had cleared all his mobile bills on time, Mili noticed. The 2013 and 2014 bills had been paid on the seventh of each month, except the bill for June 2014. The due date was the 7th of July. But Saahil had already paid this one on the day of the mishap – 4th of July 2014.

Mili could not help appreciate Saahil's taste in music. What an amazing collection, she thought! However, she did not have much time to go through Saahil's system. This was vital evidence she had 'stolen' and it had to be returned to the police at the earliest. Mili copied the entire data from Saahil's system into her personal laptop. She was not sure if someone had already tampered with the data. The system had been last accessed at 17:00:54 hours, on 4th July 2014. In all probability, this was when Saahil would have logged off, Mili thought. Only Zarine Software could now validate if anyone else had accessed the data from a remote desktop or server. However, Mili discovered that Saahil's laptop was not on remote sharing. If Saahil was attacked, why did the culprit leave Saahil's laptop behind?

The rains had stopped. Mili felt sleepy. Just the previous week, the doctor had advised her to get adequate sleep. But there was so much happening in the world all the time, where was the time to rest? Mili would sleep only when she could not stay awake anymore. In her childhood, when her mother tried lullabies to help her sleep, Mili insisted, "I will sleep with my eyes open." Her mother would nod at the preposterous demand and keep rocking the cradle until Mili could not stretch those big eyes any longer.

The doorbell rang. Anubhav and Gatha had arrived. Mili hid the laptop under her pillow. Her phone rang immediately.

"Hello!"

Morena Dave

A month ago

8 June 2014

"Oh, what a $$A#*," Morena exclaimed as she sipped her morning tea.

"I'm glad I got rid of him! I cannot believe I had been acting so dumb! Imagine the impact a narcissistic sadist can have on you!" she said, indignantly.

Trying to piece together a narrative of the incidents that had broken her heart was not easy. Morena tried to sound casual while recounting the facts, but her throat tightened each time she dug into the mug of piping hot Darjeeling tea. The aroma of first-flush tea, which was usually get-going therapy for her, was not working today, perhaps a result of the unruly memories lurking in her mind.

Varun chipped in, "But you invited trouble, Ren, and he obliged."

Thirty-three-year-old Varun Kulkarni was an architect with one of the topmost real-estate companies in the country. A name to reckon with in business circles, deals were often signed faster when clients learned about Varun's involvement. A good-natured, attractive young man with a flawlessly chiselled body, Varun was a perfectionist. A loving husband, he enjoyed pampering Morena.

"Remember your promise, Varun. If you chance upon that nerd ever in your life, you have to slap him across the face. Just the way you strike those perfect aces at the club every weekend!" winked Morena.

"Your command is my service, ma'am! But before we celebrate your grand victory, can you at least share the story with this lesser mortal? What was it that changed your opinion about your best friend overnight?"

She looked so beautiful when she smiled, thought Varun. She needed to do it more often and be her happy-go-lucky self – the chirpy, vivacious girl Varun had married four years back.

At thirty-four, Morena Dave was a successful Project Manager at Zarine Software with a bright career and a loving family. Helpful and appreciative by nature, Morena's face generated a radiance that made her likeable. Her mischievous eyes had a twinkle which was difficult to miss. Some people told her that she had a 'goodness halo' around her.

"Saahil Kerkar was never my best friend, Varun. Rashi will hate you if she hears you calling *him* her competitor! My opinion did not change overnight. You know that!"

Morena's best friend Rashi Singhi was aware of the uneasiness in Morena's life.

"Each wound comes with an expiry date and this too shall pass," *Rashi had comforted Morena.*

"All right, Ren. But at least I deserve to know the details, don't I?' asked Varun, pretending to show anger at Morena's dilly-dallying.

"Since I was feeling so claustrophobic with this hide and seek that was going on between me and you-know-who, I decided to meet him and talk to him. As colleagues, the least we could do was be civil with each other!"

"Why can't you take his name? I mean…ph-lease…gimme a break! Saahil is no Dark Lord that we cannot name him in a discussion! Be a Potter, show some character and name thy fiend with dissent," chuckled Varun. Then they both started laughing.

"Oh my god! You are just too funny Varun!" Morena grinned. Varun threw her a flying kiss.

"The moment I take his name," Morena added in a confused tone, "his contagious smile pops up in front of my eyes. Though I am happy that I screamed at him, I still cannot hate him."

"Drama queen! Story please," grunted Varun impatiently.

"So, like I said earlier, he was reluctant to meet me. I sent him a mail in the morning, almost begging to meet – such a fool I have been! He was hesitant and said he would confirm later. Towards late afternoon, he pinged to say he would not meet me. He has this new girlfriend and meeting some other woman would not be the right thing to do. I took some time to swallow that! You know Saahil, right? He always shared his 'date stories' with me. Now suddenly he was treating me like a 'girl'! As if, meeting *me* was equal to cheating his lover! That was a shocker!"

Varun burst out laughing! "So much for your friendship, Ren! Didn't I tell you long back that this guy is weird! Now when you talk about 'the end of your friendship', you almost make it sound like a 'break up'. Boy!"

"Break-up it was. Come on, friends break up too! Just that it was not the best of break-ups," added Morena.

"Whatever!" Varun playfully raised his hands above his head and then lowered his head and hands together, bowing down before Morena.

"When I tried to mend things, I thought, Saahil would be angry for a while and then he would laugh. After all, I had not committed any crime. He wouldn't send me to jail!" continued Morena, ignoring Varun's gimmicks.

"So, he doesn't want to meet you now that he has a new girl!" flecked in Varun, munching on the last chocolate cookie on his plate. Just as he was about to lick the molten chocolate left by the cookie on his finger, his cell phone rang. *Boss calling!* He signalled to Morena apologetically, requesting for a break in the conversation.

Morena nodded. Almost instantly, her thoughts drifted to Thursday, the 5th of June, 2014.

She had been unable to speak to anyone since the confrontation with Saahil. Varun was out of station that day. Morena replayed the chat transcript several times in her mind and still found it difficult to think Saahil could treat her that way. He had been by her side all the time since she joined Zarine in February 2010.

Morena : *I want to meet you for one last time.*
Saahil : *I already said NO. You are troubling me a lot these days.*
Morena : *I am troubling you?*
Saahil : Yes. *If you bug me again, I shall have to talk to Vicky about it.*
Morena : *You are humiliating me Saahil!*
Saahil : *I am done with this discussion. I will seriously complain.*
Morena : *I must talk to you.*
Saahil : *I am not meeting you. Call me if you want. Two minutes only.*
Morena : *Ok*

Varun was back!

"All good?" Morena asked hiding her tears.

"Umm, yes. With so many organizational changes happening every day, you know how it is! I will fix it first thing Monday morning. Dunno why the buggers had to escalate to boss. Anyway, let us get on with your story. Yes, Saahil and his new girlfriend. Boy, how many can that guy handle at one go?"

"Remember Varun, in school – whenever we fought with a friend, it never lasted more than a day. I was stupid to apply the same logic to my friendship with Saahil. I thought I would say sorry and he would laugh. Then we would do coffee and forget the fight. However, loving your friend doesn't mean that you swallow your self-respect, right?"

"What happened next?" Varun scowled, afraid that his unexpressed prejudice about Saahil would soon be substantiated with facts.

Morena took a deep breath and slowly narrated every bit of that chat transcript to Varun.

"You still called him up after that? Were you out of your senses?"

"Hate me if you want, but I had to make that call. He couldn't get away with humiliating me like that."

"I always thought you were so high on self-pride, Ren. You need not have done that."

"I should not have told you all this," retorted Morena.

"Ah…I deserve to know! Just that I cannot believe that he treated you like that. I have never talked to anybody like that… *ever*."

"Will you stop being judgmental? Do you want to hear me out?"

"Oh yes, I am dying to know how it ended."

"Now that's really mean!" Morena folded her arms and leaned against the refrigerator.

"Sorry sweetheart! R-E-A-L-L-Y sorry!"

"Saahil warned me on chat that he would complain to Vicky about my behaviour."

"I would have done the same, Ren. Coming to think of it, you were behaving obsessively. Weren't you?"

"Yes, I was and that's what I'm trying to explain. But I guess I shouldn't be discussing this with you!"

"No no... I just got a little carried away. Sorry!" Varun put his hand over Morena's and smiled.

"Saahil said he would complain to Vicky! Not Dipasree or Tanuj. He would complain about me to Vicky, the big boss. Especially after all that we have been through together with Vicky, this came as a rude shock!"

Varun's eyebrows cringed. He filled water in the electric kettle. Tea would be essential during this conversation. The open kitchen allowed Varun to make tea while still looking into Morena's eyes, as she sat down on the living room sofa.

"Finally Saahil agreed to speak to me. I felt like a cucumber," said Morena, flaring up.

"Hi Morena"

"Well Saahil, I apologized several times about what I told you in February. But you would not forgive me. Why was it so difficult? Why can't we be friends again? I swallowed all the insult only because you were my friend. But today, you crossed all limits! You want to complain to Vicky that I trouble you, I harass you? This is what you think about me? Please go ahead and tell Vicky all that you want. I can also go and speak rubbish about you. But I won't stoop to that level ever."

Saahil was breathing heavily on the phone.

"I considered you so close to me, Saahil. I loved you so much! I cannot believe you did this to me. I never knew someone as creative as you can be so inhuman! You humiliated me for one mistake I made. Were we really friends?"

Morena's voice was getting choked. She raised her voice,
"You are an insult to this institution called friendship. I regret my association with you! I wish you good luck in life."
There was uninterrupted silence for a while.
"That's all I wanted to say. Do you have anything to say?"
"…no, I wish you well too."

"I was so relieved after the conversation. I have no hard feelings for Saahil now. He cannot be a part of my life anymore. It is over and out."

"I guess it couldn't have ended in any other way," said Varun.

"I intend teaching him a lesson so that he dares not repeat this behaviour with anyone again!"

Varun added, "Forget it. Vengeance never gets anyone anywhere. See, when we are emotionally hurt, our minds stop thinking. If he was rude, you were outrageous too! Do not play the victim. Anyway, you are not even the revenge types!"

Morena jumped over her dashing husband and hugged him tightly. "Did I tell you that I married you for your intelligence?"

After the heart-to-heart talk with Varun, Morena was in high spirits.

A hot shower in the evening is refreshing, especially when teamed with the fragrance of rose. The water on her face felt good. Morena loved fragrances, especially while in the shower. A soothing vermillion sunset fragrance or a sandalwood soap always helped elevate her mood. Her visits to the spa also explained her strong affinity for aromas. While listening to music, she liked to create a tranquil ambience with scented candles or incense sticks. She had a fragrance collection that anyone would envy!

Why did Saahil cut off from Morena so abruptly? Varun shot a quick sideways glance to ensure his wife was out of sight. He grinned. Teaching that nerd a lesson was not a bad idea after all!

Kwest

❦

Dr Shah's report

8.30 a.m.
5 July 2014

"Is there any chance of survival?" Mili asked anxiously, while tilting her head to balance the mobile phone between her left ear and shoulder to open the door. She gestured to her associates to take a seat. Gatha and Anubhav took the wobbly sofa, which despite its dilapidated condition was very comfortable.

"I can confirm that only after forty-eight hours," replied Dr Shah.

"And this was not a suicide attempt?" Mili inquired, putting the phone on speaker.

"I think it is too early to make such conclusions. All I can say at this point is that the swollen face is an allergic reaction. He ate something that did not agree with his body. I found an anti-allergy pill in his pocket. Perhaps he didn't have time to take it."

"So someone slit his wrist after he fainted from the allergies?" asked Mili.

"That is for you to investigate, detective! But yes, an anaesthetic drug had been injected in his left arm – a mild dosage, enough to keep him unconscious for about twenty minutes."

"That's ample time to slit the wrists. So our culprit is medically sound!" reckoned Mili.

"Possible. These drugs are not readily available in medical shops."

"Sub-Inspector Shirodkar has arranged for security at the hospital, doctor. I am afraid, Saahil may be attacked again," said Mili.

"I concur."

"Thank you, Dr Shah. Please call me as soon as Saahil Kerkar gains consciousness."

"If he does, I will. His family has just reached the hospital."

"I can imagine their plight. I will be there soon," responded Mili.

"You are an impossible optimist, Mili. The victim is on life support. I hope we can save him," said Dr Shah.

"Thank you doctor," Mili disconnected the phone.

Why did Saahil need anti-allergy pills? Does he have a medical history of being allergy-prone? Did he eat the food he was allergic to deliberately or was he force-fed? Else, why would he eat what he did on a crazy rainy day? Or was it the office cafeteria?

Gatha interrupted Mili's thought process.

"Hello, we heard Dr Shah. Now, will you share what is going on inside your head?"

"Guys, just give me fifteen minutes, okay? I need a smoke," declared Mili and walked towards her balcony.

Getting into the groove

5 July 2014

While they waited for Mili, Anubhav asked Gatha, "How well do you know Mili?"

"Why?" asked Gatha, raising her brows.

"I've known her for less than a month and we already have this case. In our interactions, she comes across as tough and intuitive. I like plunging into action too. But I am confused about my role in this case. So, let me ask you Gatha – how do you expect me to contribute to this case?"

Gatha smiled. "I understand where you are coming from, Anubhav. Since we will be working together, we must be frank with each other, but Mili will always have her secrets. Do not freak out if you get some information late, even though you were with her all along! I do not know about expectations, but surprise her with your investigation. She likes surprises. However, most of the times, she will be the one surprising us. Besides, she will always be in action-mode and expects the same from everyone around."

"I have read about her laurels and was shocked that she quit the police. I remember the Latif Raza case where she had tracked down a gang of notorious drug peddlers. I was overjoyed that they were arrested," said Anubhav.

"Not all of them," added Gatha.

"Oh yes! I meant arrested or eliminated like the dangerous three - Latif, Sridhar, and Intikhab," explained Anubhav.

"I didn't know Mili at that time but I get goosebumps when I think of those days," added Gatha.

"Every time I read about Mili's cases, I felt an inexplicable thrill. Encounter killings were rampant in Mumbai between 2000 and 2003," said Anubhav.

"In the wake of blasts and other terrorist activities that were ripping the city apart, people thought encounter killings ensured instant justice! Unfortunately, innocent lives were also sacrificed in the process," said Gatha.

"If Mili was so passionate about encounters, why did she become a private investigator?" Anubhav asked.

"Not encounters, my friend. Mili always had a detective in her. True that initially she earned fame as an encounter specialist, but we cannot forget the impossible murder cases she solved as part of the Special Investigation Squad! She is an incurable optimist. Cracking the motive behind the crime is her forte. Between 2011 and 2013, she arrested over a hundred murderers, rapists, and kidnappers! In several instances, bureaucratic or political involvement made the cases trickier. She didn't care though!"

"Wow! What a shame that she left the police!" said Anubhav.

"They cut her wings! My best guess is that she resigned because of the transfer to the training department," said Gatha. "But now I think it was something deeper than that."

"Oh, what was it?" Anubhav asked impatiently.

"I wish I knew Anubhav. It is impossible to read her mind," sighed Gatha.

"But why this sabbatical for a year?" asked Anubhav.

"Mili does not talk about it and I have never asked."

"I hope she will not take too much time to spring back into action."

"Not a chance! You must know two things about Mili Ray. One, she hates liars! She has zero tolerance for them and she will not think twice before shooting one. Two, she is blessed with an exceptional memory. She stores faces, names, numbers, and incidents in her mind. She remembers lengthy speeches, poems, and songs by heart, and never misses important dates. She will remember your face, even if she had met you some ten years back in a fish market!"

"Whoa! Any vices, if I may ask?" said Anubhav, clearing his throat.

"Well, well…her only enemy is the cigarette. She never even tries giving it up! Now that she is a private detective, she will be in the Sherlock mode, am sure!"

"But the new Sherlock doesn't smoke," added Anubhav, quite seriously.

Gatha could not help laughing. "Well, Mili will sometimes go through months without a smoke. She says, '*Smoking is a habit that one can acquire and quit at any time. I control its butt. I can kick or kiss it as I wish*'. That's Mili Ray for you!"

"You guys discussing me?" asked Mili as she joined Gatha and Anubhav in her drawing room.

"Nooo," Gatha said, looking at Anubhav's unsettled body language.

"Oh, I was wondering why you have 'encounters' scribbled on my whiteboard," Mili winked.

Kwest – The inception

May 2014

After quitting the police service in 2013, Mili shifted to her parents' house. She travelled extensively, researched, meditated, and planned her next course of action. Mili was deeply inspired by her illustrious great-grandmother Mrinalini Debi, a freedom fighter and satyagrahi. Though Mili never met the braveheart, she felt a sense of responsibility and pride each time she looked at Mrinalini Debi's portrait that adorned the drawing room of the Ray household. A righteous rebel, Mili was proud of her virtuous lineage.

In her childhood, Mili learned about Mrinalini Debi's courageous undertakings from her father Dr Indranil Ray. A professor of history, Dr Ray loved reliving the golden days he had spent with his grandmother. Mili attentively listened to her father as he narrated accounts of Mrinalini Debi's dauntless deeds during the Indian freedom struggle, especially in the late

1930s. Mili was proud that her great-granny had a detective streak too and had sacrificed her life for her motherland. Mili was fascinated by the fact that she had been named after this revolutionary lady, whose nickname had been 'Mili'.

At fifteen, Mili's role model was Kiran Bedi, India's first woman IPS officer. After completing her post-graduation in Economics from a leading college in Pune, Mili joined the Indian Police Service as Superintendent of Police. She could have opted for the Foreign Services or the Administration Services owing to her rank in the national civil services exams, but she *wanted* to join the police.

Few weeks into her new role and people already had a name for her – Fearless Mili. Her passion for the uniformed job soon saw her handling complex and dangerous cases where she confronted notorious criminals head-on and did not think twice before knocking them down. Mili busted drug trafficking rackets, led anti-militant operations, and saw many encounters early in her career. With each operation, Mili's popularity soared higher. She was a terror for drug-peddlers. She received bravery awards from the government and international organizations.

In 2010, with the establishment of the Special Investigation Squad, Mili was summoned to head it and she fell in love with this role. She solved complex murder cases and high-profile kidnappings, exposed human trafficking gangs and became a people's cop in no time. Her mantra '*Crack the motive and you have got your murderer*' caught on with the new officers too. She received life-threatening calls and even survived a gruesome attack, but nothing could discourage her.

After serving in the police force for over thirteen years, Mili suddenly quit without any explanation. She did not appear in a single press interview after that. People wanted their Deputy

Commissioner of Police (Special Investigation Squad) back, but Mili stuck to her decision.

In May 2014, Mili started Kwest, her private detective agency, almost a year after leaving the police force. Soon, she was in need of an associate, two at the most.

Gatha Trivedi

"If you join me, we can start off tomorrow morning!" Mili proposed to her friend Gatha, who was older, taller, and calmer.

"Me?" an astonished Gatha stopped caressing the lone strand of hair on her forehead and focused on Mili. "My career is already very demanding and I am quite old to enter this profession."

"What does age have to do with solving cases? I know I can punch harder than most twenty-three-year-olds even today. Are you game for this?"

"And what exactly do you expect me to do, Ms Super Sleuth?" Gatha asked cheekily.

"Not much. Your badly-lit garage will serve as our office. You will help me with legal processes and research," replied Mili brushing off the kitty fur from her T-shirt.

"I am in," announced Gatha.

Gatha Trivedi, a cat-lover and successful criminal lawyer was Mili's rich neighbour. Their friendship grew stronger when Mili moved in to her current house a year back. Mili's parents had known Gatha's family for almost seven years.

Gatha's husband Naman Trivedi was her classmate at law school. In the last twenty years that they had been married, Gatha and Naman excelled in their careers. Their twin sons – Aarav and Bhairav had just stepped into teens and had inherited the minds of a lawyer – observant, judicious, and decisive.

Gatha's parents and parents-in-law were lawyers too. Her father Justice Rajveer Sharma was a respected judge in the highest law court of the country and mother Advocate Saloni Sharma handled civil cases. Gatha's parents-in-law were civil lawyers.

Gatha's brother-in-law Shravan Trivedi was the only non-lawyer in the family. He worked as Chief Operating Officer (COO) at Zarine Software. Shravan's ex-wife Bhumika was a lawyer too! Shravan shared a deep friendship with Gatha.

Anubhav Datye

Gatha and Mili were associated with Shakti, an NGO in Mumbai, which helped rehabilitate women in distress. This is where they met their third partner, Anubhav Datye, in June 2014.

Captain (Retd.) Anubhav Datye had served in the Ordinance Services of the Indian Army for five years. At twenty-eight, he decided to explore civilian life and started working as a private investigator. Footloose in the city, Anubhav had a tough time getting hold of a decent project that he could call a 'case'. After having solved twenty-one cases that involved reporting whereabouts of cheating spouses to their suspicious partners, Anubhav concluded that the human sort is naturally polygamous. He was tired of stalking people and secretly clicking inappropriate moments in shady motels. These cases usually ended in ugly fights and dirty allegations where even the detective was not spared! Besides, Anubhav hated playing the intermediary between couples and divorce lawyers.

All this while, Anubhav had been supporting few NGOs in Mumbai, Shakti being one of them. Anubhav met Mili and Gatha at Shakti during a discussion on rehabilitation of girls rescued from brothels. After the meeting, Anubhav shared some army stories and Mili saw streaks of a passionate investigator in him. His body language was relaxed, yet he was alert all the time. Standing at six feet, Anubhav's face was an inverted-triangle.

His crew-cut hair and intelligent eyes added character to his personality. Besides coming across as strong, fit, and confident, Anubhav was very particular about time.

"Army habits are difficult to forego, even if you have had a short tenure," reflected Mili. Her third partner was right in front of her. Instead of beating about the bush, Mili came straight to the point.

"Anubhav, are you keen on joining our detective agency?"

Gatha was startled at the sudden mention of 'our' agency even before the company had started operations. Besides, Anubhav was a stranger – what if he was lying about his army background! Gatha's face changed colour but she kept quiet.

Anubhav was not surprised!

"Yes, I will." His answer was short, crisp and immediate.

"Good then. See you at nine tomorrow."

"Hey, wait a second," Gatha found her voice finally. "What office are you guys talking about? I have to clean up the garage first. Let's not jump the gun right away!"

"Thank god, Gates. I thought you would say that the space is not available anymore. Leave the clean up to me. You have better and bigger goals to worry about," said Mili.

Saahil Fights for His Life

❦

At the hospital

8.30 a.m.
5 July 2014

"We cannot say anything before seventy-two hours," Dr Shah told a dismal looking Colonel Kerkar, Saahil's father.

"How did this happen?" Saahil's younger brother Amar asked. His thin face was visibly pale and his lips twitched now and again.

"I cannot confirm that. This is a police case. I am attending to Mr Kerkar at the request of ex-DCP Mili Ray," Dr Shah replied firmly.

"You mean *the* Mili Ray?" Amar asked, startled.

"Yes, she is the one who arranged for your brother to be sent here," replied the doctor.

"God bless her! How deep is the wound?" Colonel Kerkar asked, trying his best to stay unruffled.

"I am afraid, it does not look good. A sharp edged weapon was used, possibly a kitchen knife. There are multiple injuries on his left hand and wrist. His head and left side of the face is heavily swollen."

"Oh my God!" Suhasini Kerkar, Saahil's mother burst into tears.

"When can we enter the ICU, doctor? I want to see him," requested Amar.

"Sorry, not now. I do not want him to get an infection. The allergies don't look good," said Dr Shah. "Did Saahil consume anything he was allergic to last night?"

"He didn't eat with us, so we wouldn't know," Amar replied.

"Please check with the people he was with last night then," instructed Dr Shah.

"I will check with his colleagues. We were supposed to meet Saahil today," Amar added in a sullen voice.

"He doesn't live with you?" Dr Shah asked.

"We stay in Nasik. Only our children live here. Saahil stays at Versova. Amar and his family are about fifteen minutes away." Colonel Kerkar said.

"Now Papa and Aai are staying with me," Amar added. "Saahil was staying with us for the past few days. But last night, he was meeting his friends."

"You know who they are?" Dr Shah added.

"No idea at all."

"Is he allergic to any food item?"

"Yes, he is allergic to prawns. The very sight of them makes him sick," said Colonel Kerkar.

Dr Shah nodded and walked away. He was suspicious that Saahil had eaten prawns, perhaps a plate full of them!

Sub-Inspector Shirodkar was standing behind Dr Shah. Now he came forward to speak to Saahil's family.

"Who is Amar Kerkar here?"

"I am. I guess you called me earlier today, sir," Amar said looking at his visiting card in the Inspector's hand.

"Can you confirm if this is Saahil Kerkar's car?" Shirodkar asked Amar, pointing to a picture on his mobile phone.

Amar nodded.

"Our forensic team has scrutinized the car. There were others in the car, travelling with your brother last night. Do you know who he was with?"

"We have no idea at all," Amar said, while staring at his father.

"We didn't find any knife or blade inside the car or on the road. There is a possibility that Saahil tried to commit suicide. Was he upset about anything?"

Amar and Colonel Kerkar looked at each other, surprised!

"Saahil would never try to kill himself," Colonel Kerkar flared up.

Amar looked exasperated. The hospital smell was killing him anyway.

Shirodkar asked, "Did Saahil Kerkar use a mobile phone?"

"What does that mean?" Amar answered, irritated.

"We didn't find any phone in the car. Please give me his number," Shirodkar said mechanically.

"Saahil cannot do without his phone. I cannot believe someone stole his mobile despite the accident. Why didn't someone help him? The city is full of thieves and criminals," grumbled Amar as he wrote down Saahil's phone number for Inspector Shirodkar.

"Thanks. We will have one constable at all times for Mr Kerkar's security."

"But why?" asked Amar.

"I have instructions. We don't yet know if this was an accident. Did he leave any suicide note?"

"I think we have already told you that Saahil did not try to commit suicide," Amar said angrily.

"Everyone says that, sir. But we have to do our work. If you have any information, let me know. You can inform me at the police station later also," Shirodkar added unflinchingly.

After Shirodkar left, Colonel Kerkar asked Amar, "Can you contact Mili Ray and ask her to investigate?"

"I was also thinking about that, Papa," replied Amar. "I will get in touch with her before the police write this off as suicide."

The media coverage on Saahil's attack was huge.

IT Under Attack? Why was an innocent software engineer targeted? Who is behind this gruesome crime? If such an incident can happen in a so called 'safe' residential area, what does it say about the safety quotient of our mighty Mumbai?

Ayesha Mathur's news channel created further hype by disclosing Mili Ray's presence at the crime site. "Will this heinous act prompt the fiery Mili Ray to rejoin the police force?" she asked her viewers. "If you would like to see Mili Ray back in action, sms us now." The channel kept playing the same video, which showed Saahil's car from different angles and then zoomed in on Mili Ray's house. Sensational captions accompanied the video footage along with taglines for those hooked to social networking sites. #ITUnderAttack started trending on Twitter in no time.

At the police station

8.30 a.m.
5 July 2014
"Trehan, I want you on this case right now. This happened in the heart of the city. How shameful can that be?" Deputy Inspector General Virat Joshi yelled at ACP Purab Trehan.

"I will look into it right away, sir," replied Trehan, who had been newly appointed as the Assistant Commissioner of Police, Special Investigation Squad.

"I want action. You have forty-eight hours," Joshi banged the table in fury.

"Yes, sir," obeyed Trehan.

"I don't want any more attacks on innocent people. This guy is a harmless software engineer for god's sake!"

"Right sir."

"Dr Shah isn't very hopeful of Saahil Kerkar's recovery. So do not wait for his statement or anything. Start the investigation *now.*"

"Right sir!"

"Thanks".

Joshi moved towards the corridor and looked for a number on the way. He bumped into Inspector Thadani, who seemed to be in a hurry.

"Keep your eyes open, officer. We will be able to reduce crimes in the city then," he muttered. Joshi was angry at everything ever since Shirodkar had told him about the attack on Saahil Kerkar.

"Sorry, sir," Thadani responded. But he kept standing in the way.

"Where is Shirodkar? Has he taken the day off?" DIG Joshi asked sarcastically.

"No, sir. He is at the hospital, speaking to Saahil Kerkar's family."

"Hmm."

The DIG slightly tilted his head in acknowledgment. Thadani knew he had to leave now, but stood still.

Looking at a perplexed Thadani, the DIG commanded, "Out with it."

"Err....sir, the car was found near Madam Sir's house. I mean Ray madam's house," blurted out Thadani, hoping to get some brownie points from the police chief with this piece of information.

"You mean ex-DCP Mili Ray's house?"

"Yes sir."

"Does she know about this incident? If not, don't mention."

A hesitant Thadani admitted, "Madam only called the police station, sir. She was there, waiting for Shirodkar and left only after the ambulance arrived."

The DIG turned back angrily at Thadani. "Why the hell did you not mention it at the beginning?"

"Sorry, sir. I assumed you knew," Thadani lowered his head.

"Don't assume again. Anyway, she is an eyewitness for us. Send two police officers in civil clothes to the crime spot immediately and ask them to inquire with the people in the shopping malls, vendors, and residents around if they noticed anything suspicious this morning."

"Already done by Ray Madam Sir. Nobody saw anything."

The DIG was expecting this answer but still gave an angry look. Looking at his authoritative expression, Thadani added, "Sending a team right now, sir." He saluted and left.

Ex-DCP Mili Ray had been DIG Joshi's favourite officer. She had a unique knack of handling complicated cases and closing them in record time, sometimes in less than twelve hours.

Joshi needed to speak to his friend. As he dialled the number, he mulled over the findings from this case so far. Saahil Kerkar's wallet was intact, but the mobile phone was stolen. The doctor did not find any signs of combat from Saahil. Was he drugged so heavily that he did not feel the pain when his wrist was slit?

"Hi Vicky, Virat here. Needed some help."

"Can I call you back? I am at the jogging park."

"No, leave whatever you are doing and meet me at my office now," ordered Joshi.

"What happened?"

"Do you know Saahil Kerkar?"

"From my company?" asked Vikrant Sharma, CEO of Zarine Software. DIG Joshi and Vikrant Sharma had been schoolmates. Now they were family friends.

"Yes, there has been a murder attempt on him. As we talk, he may be breathing his last."

"What the $#@? I'll see you right away," Vikrant Sharma aka Vicky replied anxiously.

Brainstorming

Mili's home

9.00 a.m.
5 July 2014

"I inspected the car before the police arrived. Apart from his identity card, there was nothing. The culprit had a lot of time to clean up."

Anubhav proceeded towards the whiteboard with a marker. Then, he neatly laid out the facts. "Okay, there was a hanky, a set of CDs on the backseat, and a bottle of water in the car. In the dashboard, there were a few items. But Mili did not touch them. The car is less than a year old and it has travelled five hundred kilometres. The A/C was on and there was a pungent smell inside the car."

"There was no phone? No laptop?" Gatha was curious.

Mili did not disclose that she had the laptop.

"The doors of the car were not locked."

"May be that was done deliberately?" opined Anubhav.

Anubhav maintained his focus on the whiteboard. "There was no trace of mud or dirt on the floor of the car. It was rather too clean, given the weather. However, the attacker cleaned up the floor, but not the seats."

Mili jumped in, "The criminal wants us to find fingerprints."

"Or perhaps the assailant didn't have time for a complete clean-up,"added Gatha.

"How can you be so sure that Saahil was attacked? Why would his assailant leave without ensuring that Saahil was dead?"questioned Anubhav.

"May be this person did not realize that Saahil was alive? Besides, we cannot rule out the possibility of suicide," Gatha said.

"Yes, it may be a suicide attempt. But if not, then the attacker, who surely has a medical background knew that Saahil's heart was beating," Mili stated assertively.

Anubhav continued without a tinge of emotion, "I know Zarine Software. The company does not have basement parking. The parking area is in the open. So, Saahil would have to walk out of the office into the open area in order to get into the car. He could not have avoided contact with the rains. He did not have an umbrella or a raincoat. If we assume he was on his way home from office, at least the seats should have been wet."

"The air-conditioner was on. So...," Gatha started.

"I have seen the car tyres," Mili interrupted. "They were wet, as expected in the rains, but not dirty or muddy! If Saahil or whoever drove down to my neighbourhood from Zarine, which is around fifteen kilometres away, there would be mud on the tyres! Also, on the way, Saahil would have to cross the waterlogged by-lanes, one railway level crossing, as well as the sandy track off the lake. I can identify any car that enters my neighbourhood from that sand-smothered road. Saahil's car was not among them," Mili said confidently.

"Perhaps Saahil was visiting someone in our neighbourhood; probably the murderer drove him till this spot and left," Gatha added in an unexpectedly imperious tone.

"I walked almost a kilometre in the direction from which the car might have arrived. But there are no tyre marks on the road. Following the tyre imprints didn't help as the rain started again," Mili observed, ignoring Gatha.

Anubhav jumped, "Hey hang on. This means that the car must have taken the longer route through the jungles to your place. Saahil was with his attacker all the time. May be they even dined together – thus the allergies!"

"Even though the car hit the banyan tree, the windshield is not damaged – not even a scratch! The screeching noise did not come from Saahil's car." Mili stated, oblivious of Anubhav's comment. Then she carefully stubbed out her cigarette in the skull-shaped ashtray and stood up.

"Let's go to the crime site one more time."

"I have a question."

"Tell me Gatha," Mili said, finally paying attention to the others in the room.

"Why are we so bothered? Nobody has even asked us to work on this case."

"When we go to the hospital, Saahil Kerkar's family will ask us to investigate," Mili replied confidently.

"How do you know?" Anubhav asked.

"Let's go to the site, Anubhav," Gatha ordered.

The rains had stopped. The sun was bright and there was no hint of any storm! Municipality workers were back on the roads, cleaning the drains and ensuring a smooth getaway for the rain waters. The suburbs had started the cleanup soon enough to facilitate proper drainage. Mumbai showed great character once again.

However, neither Mili nor her team got any information from the bystanders, vegetable vendors, or shopkeepers. Nobody had seen anything.

At the Kwest office

5 July 2014

"The Internet is the greatest revolution that has blessed mankind," said Anubhav, as the trio returned from the crime site inspection.

"Mmmm…," agreed Mili taking a big bite of the apple that she picked up with the fork from the fruit basket on the table. While setting up the office, Mili had made it clear that she needed her daily dose of apples. Her associates also knew that they needed to keep the fruit basket well stocked at all times. Mili could do without her cigarettes, but a day without apples was unimaginable.

"I have discovered more about Saahil Kerkar over the net in the last couple of hours than his family would have known in months! His blog reads like a biography," said Anubhav.

"What is very interesting is his passion for the trees," added Mili. "Saahil was fond of studying trees and their unique leaves. The last research he was pursuing was on Methuselah, an age-old pine tree. What intrigued Saahil the most was that the site where this tree exists is a secret. You can call it an endangered tree that requires protection. Methuselah is over 4500 years old and supposedly the oldest known living tree and non-clonal organism in the world."

"You found all that in his blog?" asked Gatha. "I mean, if this was his research, like you said, then why would he put it on the net?"

Mili was silent.

Gatha continued. "Now the question is that did Saahil venture into the jungle near my home in search of any tree?"

"I wouldn't read much into the tree theory, Gates," observed Mili. "Saahil was a traveller at heart, his dream was to 'meet' the best pine tree in the world and play guitar underneath. You see… there was some kind of a spiritual connect that he sensed with his research. He was not a researcher; this was his passion."

"How do you know all that?" asked a rather perplexed Gatha!

"Look guys… now here's something I have to admit," Mili crossed her arms in defence.

"Hmm…I did smell something!" Gatha promptly responded.

"I have Saahil Kerkar's laptop. Don't scream now!"

Gatha and Anubhav shouted in chorus, *"Whatttttt?"*

"Nooo…no way! Let's immediately send it to the police!" continued Gatha.

"Relax Gates. I will hand it over to the police myself."

"Can we have a look too?" Anubhav asked curiously.

While pulling out Saahil's laptop, Mili had to be careful that connecting to the Internet did not connect her to the Zarine networks automatically. The last thing she wanted was for someone to see Saahil 'online' on the Zarine Software Messenger (ZSM). She signed out of ZSM and copied his mail file and chat transcripts.

Mili opened the Internet browser and surfed to the FriendMe website, the most addictive social networking site for youngsters. She did not need to hack into Saahil's account as he was already logged in. She quickly turned off the FriendMe chat option and sieved through his profile.

Social Networking

Saahil had 1,945 friends on his FriendMe account. His profile picture had been updated a couple of days back and he had already received over three hundred likes. The photo was a selfie clicked in a garden. Saahil looked dashing in his Hawaiian t-shirt and stone washed denim calf-length pants. He had a guitar with him. His smile was infectious. Who wouldn't want to befriend this charmer, Mili thought.

Mili clicked the 'Security Settings' option and found that Saahil's profile was partially open to visitors.

She surfed to her own FriendMe page through Saahil's profile. Shravan Trivedi, Gatha's brother-in-law and COO at Zarine, was listed as a common friend.

Suddenly Mili remembered why Saahil looked so familiar. When she found him in the morning, his face was swollen heavily. But now when Mili saw his FriendMe profile picture, she recognized Saahil.

The year was 2013. Mili was on the 8.30 a.m. Andheri local. An amusing couple occupied the seat in front of her: a charismatic young man and an attractive girl who wore an endearing smile. The girl's toe-ring had fallen on the train. The guy had discovered it and both of them could not stop laughing. There was naughtiness in their body language, a deep connect in their interaction, and a fulfilling happiness in their laughter. They sure are very much in love, Mili thought. Suddenly, the guy started singing. The girl was not surprised and looked at him approvingly. The passengers in the train did not seem to mind. Some of them even started humming the tune. His voice carried to Mili and she closed her eyes in silent admiration. Then Mili glanced at the girl. The girl could not take her eyes off her partner, who sang soulfully. She blushed each time someone appreciated him. Mili enjoyed observing the couple; they looked so happy together that their joy rubbed off on her too! On an impulse, she clicked a photo using her phone! Simple joys of life!

Mili recognized Saahil as the singer in the train. She did not have his photo anymore though.

While browsing Saahil's FriendMe account further, Mili started looking for the girl. She still remembered the twinkle in her eyes. Mili looked for the tagged pictures and most frequently contacted friends. But she could not find that girl. Mili's fingers were working super-fast as she browsed Saahil's photo albums. They were flooded with comments, mostly from women. But not a single comment from that familiar face! As Mili browsed through Saahil's albums uploaded in 2013, she noted that few of his friends had commented on every photo he had posted. Mili made a note of these names and opened Saahil's album titled 'Silhouette'.

"What a portfolio! I wonder why this man didn't take to modelling," commented Anubhav.

Mili gave him a sharp look. Gatha tapped Anubhav on the shoulder and put a finger on her lips, signalling him to keep quiet.

The maximum likes and comments on the Silhouette album were from two friends – Sheena Mehta and More-Rain-Ah. Sheena Mehta was a beauty – big blue eyes on a determined square face and a waistline that could well compete with Scarlett, the epic character from *Gone with the Wind*. Her comments on Saahil's pictures showed that she had an opinion on everything Saahil posted.

"A big fan," Anubhav whispered to Gatha.

Mili also found many comments from this person called More-Rain-Ah. There was no profile picture, and the name was grayed out. Mili tried to click on the blank picture, but the link was disabled. Mili quickly logged on to her own FriendMe account from her personal laptop and searched for More-Rain-Ah. There she was – the girl in the train with Saahil. Same eyes, naïve face, and an innate goodness about her personality!

More-Rain-Ah and Saahil had blocked each other on FriendMe. As a result, their posts and photos were not visible to each other. Mili found Saahil's comments on More-Rain-Ah's old photo albums and status updates. These were grayed out too, just the way her comments were grayed out on Saahil's profile. But why had they blocked each other?

More-Rain-Ah had only 220 friends on her list. Her FriendMe profile had a brief about the causes she endorsed. She had a page called 'Pet in Peace' where she discussed her vision of building a pet cemetery. She frequently interacted with two people – Varun Kulkarni and Divya Dave.

In her profile description, More-Rain-Ah had described herself as a pluviophile – a lover of the rains. Her choice of username explained that.

Finally, Mili discovered More-Rain-Ah's real name – Morena Dave.

Mili could not wait to meet Morena Dave. But before that, she had to return Saahil's laptop.

▼

"Hello!"

"Sir, Mili Ray here. Need to see you for ten minutes today. Possible?"

"Urgent?"

"Yes."

"What time?"

"In an hour?"

"Can you make it at noon, Ray? I am in the middle of something," DIG Joshi asked his friend to take a seat, while answering the call.

"Sure sir! I will see you at your office then."

"How's your new role going?"

"Good."

"I hear they are already flashing the Saahil Kerkar incident in the news."

"Right sir!"

"Okay, see you."

▼

Mili lit a cigarette.

"You go to Zarine Software, Anubhav. I need to see the DIG and hand over the laptop."

"Have you got everything you wanted?" asked Gatha.

"I know what this laptop has. Whether this information will help us, time will tell."

"Gatha, talk to your brother-in-law and see what he has to say about Saahil Kerkar."

"But Shravan wouldn't know!"

"Oh come on, Gatha. He is the COO at Zarine. On second thoughts, you also go to Zarine with Anubhav. Since we do not have the case yet, it makes sense a lawyer visits the premises. If anyone asks, just pretend that you are Saahil Kerkar's lawyer."

"What?" asked Gatha.

"Just in case," Mili winked. "In the evening, we will meet the Kerkars."

Morena's Friend Saahil

❦

Morena's house

9.15 a.m.
5 July 2014

"*Ah-choo!*" Morena delicately touched her running nose. The previous evening's downpour had left her all drenched and feverish. She wanted to call in sick but there was work pending on her German project. She made herself a second cup of tea while toying with the idea of working from home. She wanted to call her husband Varun but remembered that he was on the flight. She texted him: *I am working from home. Call me once you've landed!* Morena was surprised that the selfie she had clicked the previous night had not been delivered to Varun. She blamed it on the bad weather and hit 'retry'. Morena loved Delhi and decided to accompany Varun on his next visit to the capital.

For some reason, the newspapers had not arrived. Morena decided to catch up on some weather news and switched on the television.

"La la la...hun hun hun...." Morena kept smiling to herself while stirring the sugar in her cup. She was feeling happy and relieved.

The news anchor's voice played in the background.

'Is Mumbai increasingly growing unsafe for software engineers? With the brutal attack on Zarine Software employee Saahil Kerkar this morning, Mumbai is in shock. Was this a murder attempt? While Saahil Kerkar battles for his life, the country prays for his survival. With Rajvir Samarth, this is Chetna Parihar reporting for Current News.'

Morena immediately turned around. The Breaking News ticker read, *'Zarine Software employee Saahil Kerkar found in a pool of blood at Yarawada Road this morning! He has been hospitalized and is on life support.'*

Morena could not believe her eyes. She read it again. With trembling hands, she reached for her cell and dialled Saahil. She could not remember the last time she had called him.

"God god god, please please please..." she kept saying. Despite multiple attempts, Morena's call did not go through. She was greeted by a recorded message: 'This number is currently out of coverage area.'

Morena was numb with shock, fear, anguish, and disbelief. She forgot about her tea and got hold of a water bottle instead. She poured out a glass of water and found herself overcome with tears. She held the glass with trembling hands and let it reach her lips but had no desire to drink the water when an elfin drop touched her lips. Her grip loosened and she let the glass slip from her hands. She watched it pat her waist, roll down her right leg soaking her denim shorts and finally smash into pieces on the lemon-tiled floor.

Then, she did not know why, but Morena ran around the house, broke her favourite crystal vase, tore the bow-shaped ribbons from the curtains and threw the cushions on the floor. She rushed to the balcony, and yelled *"Saaahilll"*.

Tears welled up in her eyes. Saahil wanted a happening life. He wanted to find love. He wanted to play guitar under his favourite pine tree in Eastern Europe.

"I killed him; I killed Saahil. I am evil," Morena trembled with fear. "It was all going so well. Why did I ruin it? Why? Oh God, please save him!"

The phone rang. Morena did not bother to answer. It rang again, and again…and again.

After almost an hour, Morena looked at her phone. There were seventeen missed calls and she was in no mood to call back anyone. The last seven calls were from Varun. He had also left several messages. Reluctantly, Morena picked up her phone and dialled Varun.

"Where have you been, Ren? I reached office, and couldn't reach you. I am so worried. Why are you not taking my calls?"

"Hi, yes," Morena was crying over the phone.

"It's all right sweetheart. I am coming home in an hour. We will handle this together. It will be okay," comforted Varun.

Morena disconnected the phone without saying another word. What could be okay now? Saahil was on life support! Would he ever get back to life?

Varun was worried about Morena and prepared to leave for home immediately. People had been asking about the mysterious attack on the Zarine Software employee.

"Doesn't your wife work at Zarine? Did she know this guy?" asked the HR manager.

"No," retorted Varun.

The intercom rang. It was the boss. Varun sprinted to her cabin. "Yes Pooja, anything you need from me?"

"Not really. Was just inquisitive about this Zarine Software news! Morena works in the same office, right? Don't know why, but I feel I have met this guy. A charming fellow indeed!

I had bumped into Morena and her colleague at the Atria Mall sometime last year. Here, see Varun. Looks like this is the guy she introduced me to."

A hesitant Varun pretended to look intently at Saahil Kerkar's FriendMe profile on his boss's laptop. He dismissed her contention with as great a conviction he could. "No Pooja. You are mistaken. She was with some other colleague, not Saahil."

"I see," responded the shrewd elderly woman. She gave Varun a suspicious look angling her specs over her nose, with cringed eyebrows. Pooja did not miss the fact that Varun addressed the Zarine guy as 'Saahil'…not Saahil Kerkar! How many of us refer to an unknown person by the first name?

"I have to leave for home urgently, Pooja. Morena is not feeling well. I came to work straight from the airport today."

"All well with her? I hope it is good news and you come back with sweets tomorrow morning. I know some good gynaecologists. Let me know if you need contacts. As you know, I have a big family with fertile women across generations."

"Thanks. But it's not about that, Pooja," replied Varun, angry at her over-inquisitiveness. Pooja was the incorrigible boss and her team knew that what cannot be cured has to be endured. They avoided personal conversations with her to the extent possible!

"Oh my dear, then it must be a result of today's ghastly news! Poor child! What was the name of this young man now… yes, Saahil Kerkar?"

"I have to leave right now," Varun said sternly.

"Well yes. Just be accessible over the phone, dear Varun. You know how panicky our customers get when they cannot reach out to you. Being the Principal Architect is not an easy job. I do not want you to get into unnecessary legal entanglements," Pooja added.

Just then, there was a fire alarm! Employees started leaving their workstations.

Varun ran out of the cabin before Pooja Sathe could say any more. "Don't know how she finds the time to poke her nose everywhere," mumbled Varun as he walked past Tasha, his secretary. The fire drill alarm acted as his saviour.

"The elevator also had to stop working today! This is ridiculous!" fumed Varun. Due to the fire drill, Varun could not use any of the seven elevators in his office building. He had no option but to climb down all twenty-four floors. People were lazily strolling down the stairs, chatting with one another. Per practice, when a mock fire drill happened, all employees needed to vacate the building using the stairs. Varun wondered that if a fire really broke out at this time, would people have the luxury of these leisurely walks? As he overtook most of the people with a polite 'excuse me', he was disgusted. He felt a slight pain in his chest. This had happened earlier also, but he had postponed visiting a doctor, despite Morena's repeat reminders. He knew that tennis was his best medicine.

While rambling down the stairs, Varun kept worrying about Morena. Only last month, she had confided in him about how happy she was to have walked out on Saahil. She had been in a healthier mental state ever since.

Varun remembered the day he met Saahil for the first time. He was in Morena's office to pick her up. Saahil came out to meet him. While he put an arm round Morena and shook hands with Saahil, the latter had looked uncomfortable.

Varun was on the last flight of stairs now. How he wished he could fly like Superman! Weird thoughts clouded his mind in the eighteen minutes spent alighting the stairs. Finally, he was out of office.

"Taxiiii!"

Vikrant Sharma

✤

DIG Joshi's office

9.00 a.m.
5 July 2014

Vikrant Sharma, CEO of Zarine Software identified Saahil Kerkar from the photo DIG Virat Joshi had displayed on his table.

Vikrant pulled the chair in front of his friend Virat and sat down, in a state of utter disbelief. His first words to DIG Joshi were, "Saahil cannot commit suicide. He is my best man."

"So, are you saying it was a murder attempt?" asked DIG Joshi.

"No, no. It could have been an accident too! Who would want to kill Saahil? He was peace loving and full of life. How is he now? I must go to the hospital."

"He is on life support. I have a few questions for you. After that, you can go visit him."

"Go ahead," replied Vikrant. "I just hope he recovers and the media doesn't make a hue and cry about this. You know what I mean."

"Vicky, unfortunately, the news is already out. People are tweeting about it as we talk."

"What? Please keep Zarine Software out of it."

"I wish we could. But you know in the digital age, how difficult it is. People write about everything."

"So what's next? The police will start harassing my employees? I worked really hard to build this empire, Virat."

"I cannot keep the police off your office premises. I am sure you know that."

"What questions do you have for me?" Vikrant asked, baffled. "I must mention at the onset that even in the one-one session last week, Saahil was normal. He is a star performer at Zarine," Vikrant added.

"Any mention-worthy achievements you want to highlight?" the DIG asked.

"I haven't been so much in touch of late. But I remember the Singapore project – Kaaya; what a great performance it had been from Saahil and his team. For this project, Saahil and his colleague bagged the Best Collaboration Award in 2010-11. This is among Zarine Software's most prestigious awards. This year, I intend sending the same team to Frankfurt. But I haven't had the chance to sound it off to them as yet."

"I see! By the way, was there any trouble in office? Anything Saahil Kerkar was involved in?"

"Trouble? I am not aware of anything like that. Saahil was not that sort of a guy."

"Would you know if Saahil ate anything that resulted in allergic reactions?"

"No idea! Young people survive on junk food these days."

"Where does your office cafeteria food come from?"

"Oh… it is very hygienic. We have a trusted certified vendor. We have zero complaints about hygiene and cleanliness."

"Any information on Saahil you think could help this investigation? Even if you think it is trivial, please share," said the DIG.

"Honestly Virat, I see no reason why anyone would want to kill Saahil. I do not know all my employees personally. You know that is not possible for any CEO. I usually interact with the head of the departments, Finance, and Corporate Communications teams. My direct reports take care of the rest of the organization."

"Anything you say can help this case."

"Saahil is Senior Project Manager with the Quantum Imperial team. He loves software programming. Even though he is a PM, you give him a project and he will dig into the programming. He worked with me on a couple of crucial internal projects and I have always appreciated his intelligence and imagination. When you think you have reached a dead-end, Saahil will come up with a solution. A techie to the core, he has a crazy fighting spirit. He can never think of committing suicide!"

"A crisis manager there?"added DIG Joshi.

"Absolutely! He received the Best Performer Award two years in a row. When I picked him for a high-value assignment last year, the Board of Directors sanctioned his candidature instantly; Saahil was the unanimous choice. He is the king of pilot projects," said Vikrant.

"Anyone you suspect is particularly jealous of Saahil?" asked DIG.

"I don't think so. Saahil is also the president of our Cultural Club and a good singer. People love him," replied Vikrant.

"Am sure you have other bright employees in your company?"

"Yes, I know a couple of others. Morena Dave for instance, who has co-managed some projects with Saahil. Then there is Gopal, who is meticulous and technically brilliant."

"But Saahil Kerkar, you say, is an all-rounder."

"Yes."

"Hmm. Any enemies or professional rivals?"

"Nope. He mentors new people in the company. People look up to him."

"By the way, did you meet him yesterday?" asked DIG Joshi.

"Yes. In fact, I spoke to him too. Most of the employees wanted to leave early last evening due to the deteriorating weather. While I was talking to them, Saahil walked up to me."

"So he expressed concern about the weather?"

"No, he didn't seem to care. He just asked me if I would be in town next week, as he wanted me to take an induction session for the new people on his team. I had been postponing it eternally. So…"

"Didn't you find it strange that he wasn't worried like everyone else?"

"No, because Saahil is like that – indifferent and chilled out. In fact, now that you ask, I think he looked happy."

"Happy?" asked Joshi, surprised. He stopped spinning the paperweight in his hand abruptly and let it fall flat on his desk.

"Yes. Saahil thanked me and strolled down the corridor, smiling at his mobile."

"Sometimes I wonder why you gave up on your IPS ambition, Vicky. You could have given it a second shot at least. Even I wasn't lucky the first time!"

Vikrant Sharma smiled faintly and his crinkled eyebrows eased a bit after this remark from DIG Joshi.

After a pause, he said, "Saahil is a social networking buff. He is always on FriendMe and other sites. But I never had any problems because he is a top performer. The clients love him."

"Were you not worried about returning home last night, Vicky?"

"Unquestionably I was! And you know Nishita. She kept calling every half an hour!"

"That's natural. I do not blame your lovely wife. Ketaki has given up on me because I don't take her calls when I am on duty."

"But why?"

"What example will I be setting for the others?"

"But what if there is an emergency?"

"I can sniff it from the way my phone rings when she calls. Anyway, that is a different story altogether. I am surprised that you even considered going for a jog this morning. Didn't you return late last evening?"

"See Virat, you know that I have been a fitness freak all my life. Why would I skip my morning walk just because it rained last night?"

"I was just curious," replied DIG Joshi.

"Are you suspecting me?" Vikrant asked wryly.

"I am not saying anything Vicky. I have to ask you these questions since it concerns an employee from your organization. We don't even know if he will live."

"So this is an interrogation session, huh?"

"No, it is merely an enquiry."

"May I take your leave now? I wonder what the media must be up to now! My phone will ring all day today and people will tag me to ridiculous posts," Vikrant said.

"One last question. Where were you between 7 p.m. last evening and 6 a.m. this morning?'

"Wow, awesome! So my childhood friend thinks I slayed my employee. I couldn't ask for a better start to the day!" lashed out Vikrant.

"Please cooperate, Vicky!"

"Fine! I left office at around 5 p.m. and went home. I was home with my wife and kids last evening, watching TV. We had dinner by 9.30 p.m. and went to sleep. Per my routine, I went out for a jog this morning. I could not leave at my scheduled time, which is 6.30 a.m. due to the rains. I started at around 7.30 a.m. instead. I was on my way back home when you called and I ran to your office. You can see that!" Vikrant Sharma concluded, angrily.

Morena Goes Missing

❦

11.30 a.m.
5 July 2014

By the time Varun Kulkarni paid the cabbie, he was sweating heavily. When he reached his apartment at 11.30 a.m., nobody answered the door. Varun was beginning to lose patience.

"God, I hope she hasn't done anything stupid," he prayed. Varun rang the doorbell for a good ten minutes. No response. In his nervousness, he had forgotten about the duplicate keys in his pocket. With trembling hands, Varun somehow managed to place the key inside the key hole. He turned the front door knob slowly. Finally, he was inside his own home.

The rectangular drawing room that unfolded itself into a cosy balcony welcomed him. The door to the balcony was locked. Varun smelled trouble – Morena never closes that door. The balcony offers her a plentiful view of the garden overlooking their elegant three-bedroom apartment. In fact, the balcony was her favourite place in the whole house. Adjacent to Silver Oak Towers, the housing cooperative where Morena and Varun lived, was a jogger's park. The morning breeze was refreshing and Morena had bought lush green garden chairs to enjoy the greenery from the quaint veranda.

Varun was blank for a while and then tiptoed inside. He did not want to disturb Morena; perhaps she was sleeping. But the little he could see of the bedroom next to the kitchen indicated that Morena was not there. The stylish open kitchen made the already spacious drawing room look enormous. The colourful cushions that adorned the sofas lay still. How Varun detested these cushion covers! They were in bright pastel shades with unique block prints and kalamkari designs. Morena had bought them from Saahil's designer friend Aisha.

The fan and light in the drawing room had been left on. Surprisingly, the TV was also on and a music channel blared some song. Is she in her senses, he doubted? Surely, Saahil deserved more. Varun felt his headache worsening, as if someone was hitting nails on his head. Finally, he spotted Morena on the sofa facing the TV. At least he could see the back of her head! Varun closed his eyes for a moment and heaved a sigh of relief.

A coffee mug was placed on the teakwood polished glass centre table. The curtains did not show much movement except for the negligible swings prompted by the fan. The pristine ladder showcase beside the balcony decked with photo frames stood still. Morena's favourite delicate crystal vase that occupied a lion's share on the showcase was missing. Where did it go, wondered Varun, true to his observant nature. There was something eerie about the house today and it looked disturbingly unfamiliar.

Why had Morena not gone to the hospital? Something was just not right! Varun felt his throat getting dry again. He walked towards the sofa from behind and extended his hand to touch Morena's head. Suddenly she stood up and turned around.

"You! You gave me a start Varun!"

"Shouldn't I be saying that? I guess this is my house!"

"You can save the rudeness. But springing from nowhere like this – unannounced? That's spooky!" replied Rashi, Morena's childhood friend as she removed her soundproof headphones.

"I've been ringing the bell for over ten minutes. But you had these headphones on! Anyway, where's Ren?" Varun asked impatiently.

"I have no clue. Why are you so hyper?"

"How did you get inside then?"

"I had a meeting at Four Bungalows. It was cancelled, so I came down. Morena opened the door!"

"And?"

"And what Varun? Why are you behaving like an obsessive overprotective husband?"

"Where is she, Rashi? Where is Morena?" Varun shouted as he shook up Rashi.

"Hey relax!" Rashi replied, taking his hand. "She said she would be back in a bit. I thought she was going to the grocery shop downstairs. She does that often when I come. So…"

"Oh no! What kind of a friend are you, Rashi?" Varun said, pushing her hand away furiously.

"Will you tell me what happened?"

"How long has she been gone?"

"Not more than twenty minutes. What is wrong? Let me call her."

Rashi dialled Morena. "It's ringing. Just chill!"

"Oh yeah sure! It is ringing and I can hear it too. Damn. She's left the mobile in the bedroom!" said Varun.

Rashi was nervous. "Will you tell me what happened? Why are you back at this hour?"

"Somebody tried to kill Saahil Kerkar. I had called Morena. She could barely speak!"

"*Whatt?*" Rashi was shocked!

"I'll go down and see if I can find Ren anywhere. You stay here and wait for phone calls."

"Oh dear... I hope she does not do anything stupid."

"She may be on her way to the hospital. I hope so, I mean. I thought you were her best friend, Rashi!"

"She didn't tell me anything, Varun! Else, would I have let her go? She walked out casually. But I did think it was odd that she was wearing glares on a cloudy day!"

Varun looked at Rashi in disbelief. The tears must have taken a toll on Morena's eyes.

Rashi had a guilty look all over her face.

Varun ran downstairs and asked the security guard about Morena.

"But Madam didn't leave the building!"

"What are you saying?"

"I am sure, sir. 7A madam has not gone out of this gate. You can ask the security at the back gate. We all know when she enters or leaves the building. She always smiles and talks to us."

"Where is my Ms Congeniality now?" fumed Varun. He confirmed with the guard at the rear exit too. No trace of Morena.

Varun's head was spinning. He did not know the next step. He had lost his wife again...to depression this time. He dragged himself to the garden and sat down on a bench looking at the sunflowers smiling at him. The dampness in the air was increasing. Varun felt tired and defeated. He could hear workers fitting furniture on the ground floor apartment next to the garden. The cacophony of the sound aggravated his nasty headache. He closed his eyes. The pain was unbearable. Varun gasped for breath. The dampness, the noise, and the headache – all of it amalgamated into a cocktail of troubles.

Varun could not understand why a blast from the past started to haunt him at this moment. He recalled how Morena took care of people, how warmly she welcomed his friends and lent them a patient ear. Varun once told Morena about Maya, his colleague. Maya's husband used to beat her up. An IIT graduate, this man looked like the most peace-loving soul in the universe.

"In Afghanistan, nobody will care how much I beat you. You are lucky to have been born in India and you had better keep your mouth shut else I will dump you there," he would threaten her. This happened four to five times and then one day, Maya fled from her husband's home and went back to Darjeeling, her hometown.

Morena was angry when she heard Maya's plight. She gathered some friends and marched to Maya's house. Each of them carried a weapon – a bucket, a jug, a mop stick, cricket bats, etc. Angad, Maya's husband, opened the door and got the shock of his life. The friends beat him up disguised as bandits and Morena led them as Phoolan Devi, the bandit queen.

"I swear on the Taliban I shall kill you if you trouble Maya again," Morena warned. Angad was so scared that he left for Darjeeling the next day. After two weeks, Varun informed Morena that Angad had apologized to Maya before her entire family. But Maya had filed for divorce. Morena was happy that Maya had made her own decision.

It was over an hour now and there was no trace of Morena.

▼

The phone rang. Varun had lost sense of the time. He was still sitting on the garden bench.

"Hello."

"She is back," said Rashi, anxiety all over her voice.

Varun hurried back to his apartment.

Morena sat on the sofa like a piece of rock. Rashi was beside her.

"She had been to the hospital," Rashi whispered to Varun when Morena quietly walked towards her bedroom.

"They are not allowing anybody to meet Saahil."

Anubhav Visits
Zarine Software

❦

11.15 a.m.
5 July 2014

"The security guard knew their names?" Mili asked while driving towards DIG Joshi's office.

"No, he knew Saahil and his car. The receptionist identified Saahil's associates as Rounak Arora and Farzad Mistry. They are not in office yet. I got their photos from the Zarine Administration team. The security guard at the main gate downstairs recognized them from the pictures," said Anubhav.

"Okay, keep me posted once you speak to them," said Mili and disconnected the phone. She found it uncomfortable to speak on the hands-free. But then, there wasn't any other option while driving.

Anubhav liked the orange and white décor of the Zarine Software office. A huge model of the logo, ZS, stood tall as a magnificent backdrop to the front desk. The long glass desk, armed with multiple drawers, stretched on either side to form a semi-circle. Two young girls managed the reception area while attending to endless calls. They looked at the desktops in front of them every now and then and typed something vigorously. The desk was so long that Anubhav thought the girls needed a third helping hand. The reception was beautiful, shiny, and very cold. A member from the housekeeping team was constantly cleaning the glass doors and windows. Adjacent to the reception, on the left side, was the security room. Though there were already two security guards present at the reception area, Anubhav spotted at least three more of them inside that room. People entering the office had a card in their hand or one swung around their neck. Unless they swiped this employee access card, the door would not open.

"Does anyone know when these people come to office?" Gatha asked Anubhav, looking at her watch. It was already 11.30 a.m. "Can you check if Morena Dave is in?"

"Yes, I did. Work hours are flexible here. People can even walk in post lunch. Morena Dave is working from home today. Zarine provides that facility too."

"What else did the security person tell you?" Gatha asked.

"At the bus stop, these three men met Morena Dave, our FriendMe girl. She too climbed into Saahil's car," Anubhav added excitedly, expecting a surprised reaction from Gatha.

"Obviously!" said Gatha without any expression of astonishment. "The police found four sets of fingerprints. Remember?"

"But how would you know that the fourth person in the car was Morena Dave?" asked Anubhav with a bleak look.

"We have Rounak and Farzad in the car already. Rounak reports to Saahil Kerkar and Farzad is a close pal of Rounak's. Right?" asked Gatha.

"Yes, correct," Anubhav said attentively.

"The security guard said that 'Madam' was sitting beside Saahil. The two men were sitting behind. Rounak got down from the car and went behind. The lady sat in front. Why do you think that happened?" asked Gatha.

"I didn't think about that at all. But how did you know what the guard said? You overheard my conversation?" Anubhav was curious.

"I happened to hear you. I am sure you would agree that his voice was not particularly soft?"

Anubhav laughed.

"But how did you know it was Morena in the car?"

"I think I asked you a question about that!" said Gatha.

"Perhaps because Farzad and Rounak knew that Morena and Saahil were close to each other?" replied Anubhav.

"The most logical reason, considering the bad weather is that Morena would be the last to get off the car. If she tried to change her seat after the others were dropped, she would get drenched instantly," said Gatha.

"You've put a lot of thought into that," observed Anubhav.

"I haven't. I am sure even those three men did not. The weather condition was such that they all had presence of mind to make this arrangement, perhaps in a minute or two."

"But I still didn't get it how you knew the girl in the car was Morena Dave," said Anubhav, rather anxiously.

"I saw you showing your phone to the security guard asking for a confirmation on something. He enthusiastically nodded. I assumed you were showing him a photograph. Earlier today, I noticed that you saved a picture of Morena from her FriendMe account. Thus my conclusion that the girl in Saahil's car was Morena Dave," smiled Gatha.

"Excuse me, sir," the blue-eyed receptionist said suddenly. Anubhav walked up to her.

"I am so sorry to have kept you waiting. My colleague just informed that Rounak Arora is in the cafeteria."

Farzad Mistry

❧

DIG Joshi's office

11.30 a.m.
5 July 2014

"What the hell are you saying?" DIG Joshi was screaming at the top of his voice.

"His father reported a missing complaint at around two last night, sir. We found the body this morning."

"We are all going to lose our jobs!"

"Looks like a hit-and-run case, sir!"

"Oh shut up, Trehan! He was an employee of Zarine Software."

"Yes, sir."

"Saahil Kerkar is fighting for his life in the hospital. Now we have a second victim from Zarine Software."

"We have sent the body to the forensic team, sir. But it looks like an accident."

"What is the condition of the body?" asked DIG Joshi.

"It is in very bad shape, sir. The truck smashed him. There is almost nothing left of his face," Trehan said and lowered his head.

"Was his family able to identify him?" DIG asked. He could sense his blood pressure shooting up.

"His father recognized the body from the tattoo that covers almost three-fourths of his right arm. He also confirmed the clothes on the body," answered ACP Trehan.

"Why was he on the highway at 2 a.m.? Does anyone have a clue?"

"May I come in, sir?"

DIG Joshi consulted his watch. "This couldn't have been better timed. Come in, Ray."

Precisely at noon, Mili Ray walked into DIG Virat Joshi's office. Her entry in the middle of a heated discussion between police personnel was quite dramatic. The constables saluted her and she acknowledged them with the sunglasses in her hand. All eyes were on Mili whose enigmatic personality was perfectly complemented by her pristine white shirt and dark brown trousers.

"Looks like I interrupted your discussion. I'll wait outside," Mili said, breaking the silence.

"No. Stay," said DCP Joshi. "Ray, has Saahil Kerkar's family contacted you about this case?"

"Yes, sir. I just received a call from Amar Kerkar, Saahil's brother," replied Mili.

"Are you investigating then?"

"Yes, sir. The family unfortunately isn't expecting much from the police," Ray said, looking sharply at Shirodkar.

"Really?"

"Amar Kerkar asked me to intervene as he is afraid that the police might dismiss this as a case of suicide attempt," she concluded.

"Good. ACP Trehan is working on this case and he may consult you, if required."

"Right, sir," Mili replied immediately. Trehan looked at Mili indignantly.

"ACP Trehan, I expect you to cooperate with Detective Ray. She has deep experience in this field. Besides, we have a new angle now."

"Yes, sir," Trehan replied assertively.

"A new angle?" Mili was surprised.

"Another Zarine employee Farzad Mistry was found dead some time back."

"Whattt?" Mili could not believe her ears. "My associate Anubhav just informed me that Farzad Mistry was in the car with Saahil Kerkar last evening."

"Wow, this couldn't get better!" said the DIG sarcastically. "So, why did Farzad step out at that hour?"

"Farzad's father said that he got a phone call at around 11.00 p.m. and left home immediately. When he did not return for three hours and his phone was unavailable, his father lodged a missing complaint. The police found his body inside the bushes, by the highway near his home," Trehan informed them.

"Did he say where he was going or when he would be back?" asked Mili.

"No. He just said, *'Abhi aata hu'* and left," replied Trehan.

"What does his call record say?"

"His phone was also crushed. We found it near his body."

DIG Joshi interrupted.

"Ray, Trehan – I want this case solved in seventy-two hours flat. And *nobody* speaks to the media."

"Right, sir!" Mili and ACP Purab Trehan replied together.

"Sir, this is Saahil Kerkar's laptop," Mili said and handed it over to the DIG.

"How did you get that?" asked Trehan, visibly surprised.

"I found it in the car and wanted to hand it over personally," Mili replied, apologetically.

"Do not tamper with evidence, detective," Trehan retorted. "This is a serious offence."

"I agree. Leave it with Trehan," said DIG Joshi, easing the tension.

"Can I see the body, ACP?"

"Yes, in the evening. Dr Dighe's forensic team is investigating. We will get the post-mortem report tomorrow," replied Trehan.

"I will go visit Saahil Kerkar in the meantime."

"Do you want to speak to Farzad's family?" asked Trehan.

"Tomorrow. Today, they will not be in any condition to speak," Mili stated. "You have any update?"

"I met Farzad Mistry's wife," said ACP Trehan. "She did not utter a word. Tomorrow would be a better day, like you said."

Mili nodded.

Rounak Arora

Zarine Software

11.45 a.m.
5 July 2014

Rounak Arora was munching on hot chips with his coffee at 11.45 a.m., his first break since the morning.

"Someday, I will be there too, managing a team of software engineers at ZS," Rounak deliberated as he took another sip of the froth-filled cappuccino. Overworked and exhausted, Rounak cursed his manager silently for overloading him with work yet again!

Rounak was ambitious and his objective was simple – live life king size. He wanted to earn lavishly, go back to Chandigarh, and buy a farmhouse. There would be horses running around amidst the greenery of the bountiful land. Flowerbeds with exotic plants collected from all over the world would adorn the nursery at his luxurious abode. He also wanted a state-of-the-art swimming pool. Rosalind, his beautiful girlfriend of ten years, would do the landscape designs. He dreamed about sneaking a peek at her angelic expressions every time she went horse riding. Rounak was expecting a promotion in August and had planned for a November wedding.

Anubhav spotted Rounak at the cafeteria.

"Rounak Arora, software engineer with the Quantum Imperial team, right?" Anubhav asked, extending his hand.

"Lead software engineer. But you? New joinee?" Rounak shook Anubhav's hand unmindfully.

"Anubhav Datye, private detective from Kwest."

"H-how can I help you, sir?"

"Do you know Saahil Kerkar?"

"Yes, he is my colleague. Mm...my manager now," Rounak fumbled. "What happened?"

"Were you with him last evening?"

"Yes, he dropped me to the station. But why are you asking all this? He is not in office yet. Should I call him?"

"Saahil Kerkar is in the hospital. Don't you know?"

"*What*? What happened to Saahil bhai?" Rounak sounded panicky.

"We suspect that someone tried to murder him."

"Oh my god! No. I must inform the team."

"You can tell them later, after you answer my questions."

"But what can I say? I anyway have a client call in fifteen minutes. I have to attend that."

"Hmmm. If you prefer interrogation to inquiry, we will question you at the police station. Be there in one hour."

"I err... Well, no I did not mean that. I do not want to get into any trouble. I have nothing to do with this," said Rounak.

"If you are innocent, you have nothing to worry about."

"Let's get into a conference room," suggested Rounak and walked towards the one beside the cafeteria.

"Where were you on the 4th of July at 6 p.m.?"

"Probably in office, sir."

"When did you leave?"

"I cannot remember. I...I got a bus around 7.30 p.m. or so."

"But you just said that Saahil gave you a lift to the station?" Anubhav prodded, his sharp voice piercing through Rounak's ears.

"Yes... sssorry!"

"Okay, let me ask you again. What time did you leave office, Rounak? Hurry up; we don't have all day!" Anubhav banged the conference table with his fist. His gym trained wrists and no-nonsense expression frightened Rounak.

"Yes, I remember. Around 5.00 p.m. or it could have been 5.15 p.m.," Rounak replied.

"Who else was in the car apart from you and Saahil?"

"Farzad and Morena. Farzad is a really nice guy. He is innocent, just like me."

"You talk for yourself."

"R... right."

"Did all of you get off at the station?"

"No. Just me and Farzad."

"Where was Morena scheduled to get off?"

"I don't know."

"What time did you reach home on the 4th of July?"

"I was home by 9 p.m. I think. It took long because traffic was bad. I even missed two trains as they were overcrowded. You can ask Farzad."

Rounak did look unfit and obese to Anubhav. So it would not be surprising if he missed boarding a crowded train.

"What did you do after reaching home?" Anubhav asked.

"I had dinner and went to sleep. I was very tired."

"Who else stays with you?"

"I stay alone. But I often catch up with my neighbour Shankar after office. In fact, last evening we had dinner together."

"What did you eat?" Anubhav asked.

"W...what?"

"I asked, what did you eat?"

"Rice and chicken curry. The same cook works at Shankar's apartment and mine. She had not turned up so we had leftovers from the previous day."

"Give me Shankar's number."

Rounak wrote down the number on a piece of paper and handed it over to Anubhav.

"Did anyone see you enter home at the time you mentioned?"

"Yes, my security guard. I collected a packet sent through a courier service from him too."

Doesn't he have too many alibis, wondered Anubhav.

"Since how long have you known Saahil? Anyone you can think of who could have hurt him?'

"I've known him for three or four years, I guess. He does not have any enemies. He is friendly and gets along with everyone."

"How is he at work? Is he authoritative as a boss?"

Rounak appeared offended at the mention of the word 'boss'.

"Saahil is good at work. And well, he became my manager recently. I am anyway expecting a promotion soon," Rounak added sourly.

"I see," Anubhav responded, noting the resentment in Rounak's voice.

"Rounak, do you feel it would be difficult for your company to get Saahil's replacement?"

"Nobody is indispensable, sir. I may be a level below Saahil's but I am also five years younger. Besides, I am his senior at Zarine. I hand-holded him when he joined this team. I know all the work he does and can fill-in if the company needs me to."

"Saahil recently became your manager. So, technically he is two levels above now?"

Rounak's face turned red as he nodded. "Saahil is more experienced than me. That was the only reason he got recruited at a higher level."

"And what about his expertise?"

"He is good, I told you. But then, everyone at Zarine is."

"Did you feel bad when Saahil got promoted?" Anubhav asked, smelling jealousy in Rounak's answer.

"Why should I? I am happy for him. What are you trying to say? I tried to kill him because he got a promotion?"

"I am just asking a simple question, Rounak."

"I didn't feel great. Ever since he joined, I have not been promoted. The management is always like 'ask Saahil', 'call Saahil', 'check with Saahil'. It gets irritating after a while, when I am also working equally hard, you know. I am very fond of Saahil bhai. I did feel bad about the promotion, but I cannot even dream of harming him."

"Anything in particular you can tell me about Saahil that can help this case?"

"Not that I can think of at the moment."

"Anyone in office you suspect who would want to harm him?"

"Nope."

"Hmm. What do you think about Morena?"

"She is also a Project Manager, like Saahil," Rounak commented.

"No, I mean, would she want to harm Saahil?"

"I don't think so. She is a gentle, helpful girl."

"Did you notice anything suspicious when you were in the car with them?"

"No. They were both very quiet and looked uncomfortable in each other's company. Morena was reluctant to take the lift. But she finally agreed. Anyway, Saahil bhai wouldn't leave without her in such weather," said Rounak.

"And why is that?" asked Anubhav.

"Weather was so bad, sir! It would be inhuman not to offer her a lift."

"I meant, why were they uncomfortable?"

"Earlier, they used to be good friends. But now they do not talk to each other. He even stopped coming to this office."

"When did he start coming here again?"

"Since last month, I think. He has a bigger team to manage and most of us work from this building."

"When did they stop talking to each other?" asked Anubhav.

"I don't know. I don't think it's been too long though," replied Rounak.

"What caused the rift between Morena and Saahil?"

"I am not sure, but the promotion Saahil bhai got might be a reason."

"Morena didn't?"

"The budget was very tight last year. So only the cream of the lot got a promotion. Morena was offered an 'onsite' though."

"Where to?"

"Singapore. But she refused."

"Why?"

"No idea. Maybe because she had already been there earlier," said Rounak. After a pause, he said, "With Saahil."

"Ah! So who went finally?"

"I think they agreed to offshore support as they only wanted Morena."

"So, she is very good?"

"Yes, she is."

"Any love affair that you are hiding?" asked Anubhav with a raised eyebrow.

"Absolutely not!" Rounak added strongly.

"Okay. So you are saying that yesterday, on the 4th of July, Saahil and Morena first spoke to each other after a long time?"

"Yes, at least publicly."

"Hmmm, I see," said Anubhav. "We will call you again should we have any questions. Don't go out of station without informing the police."

"But why? I am not a criminal."

Anubhav did not respond but returned a disgusted look.

Rounak was worried now. Would they blame him? He needed to be alert. He had so many responsibilities to fulfil now that Saahil was not here. He had to convince Vicky Sharma that he is better, far better than Saahil. The post in the new office at King of Prussia, Pennsylvania allured Rounak. He had to bag that one, come what may.

"Sir sir," Rounak ran towards Anubhav who was heading towards the reception.

"Nidhi! Nidhi Sahoo. Ex-Zarine Employee. She may have motive to kill Saahil bhai."

Anubhav turned around. "Let's go back to your classroom, Rounak."

"Conference room, sir."

"Same thing."

Anubhav's phone rang.

"Yes Mili?"

"Are you done?"

"Not yet."

"Okay listen. Farzad Mistry is dead."

"Oh my god! How, when?"

"Will tell you once you are back. Keep an eye on this Rounak guy. He was with Saahil and Farzad last evening. Don't tell him about Farzad's death yet."

Meeting the Kerkars

❦

The property at Nasik

"The doctor has strict instructions – nobody can meet him. The allergies are bad…terrible, in fact. Somebody wanted Saahil to choke to death," said Mili. She poured herself a glass of water and parked herself on the sofa, waiting for an update from her team.

"Do you think Saahil Kerkar will survive this?" asked Anubhav.

"Dr Shah is not committing anything before seventy-two hours, which means we need to wait till the 8th of July at least," Mili said, emptying the glass in seconds. "What have you guys got for me?"

"We learned about a property in Saahil's name. Saahil inherited about two acres of land on the outskirts of Nasik, from Brigadier Rawat, his maternal grandfather. This is near the Sula vineyards," said Gatha.

"Wow! Quite a fortune!" exclaimed Anubhav.

"Yes, you can say that. I read a copy of the will on Saahil's laptop," said Mili.

"Ah! I intend attending the Sula Fest sometime," gushed Anubhav.

"We could do it next year," added Mili.

"By all means! I didn't know you are a wine person too!" Anubhav said, rather sheepishly.

"Not so much for the wine, more for the ambience! You can indulge in the wine."

Gatha cleared her throat and announced, "A portion of Saahil's land is still being used for farming."

"Saahil is a nature lover from what I read on his blog," said Anubhav.

"Correct," nodded Mili. "Perhaps that is why he was keen on farming too. However, even if part of the land was blocked for farming, almost one acre was remaining to be invested in real-estate."

"At the current market value, nothing less than four crores!" said Gatha.

"That's a lot of money for anyone, let alone an insurance agent like Amar Kerkar!" said Anubhav.

"Oh certainly!" exclaimed Gatha. "Brigadier Rawat's 'will' has a long section on this Nasik land. When I first read the will, I thought that the clauses related to claiming this property were very strange!"

"Meaning?" asked a confused Anubhav.

"Though I have read the copy, can you state them once again, Gates?" requested Mili.

"Sure, I will try my best to explain.

The first clause states that if Saahil dies a 'natural' death before he turns thirty-five, his wife and/or children will inherit this piece of land.

The second clause goes like this: If Saahil dies 'naturally' before turning thirty-five and is unmarried, childless, or divorced, his younger brother Amar will inherit fifty percent of the property and the remaining fifty percent would go to a trust.

The third clause states, if Saahil dies 'unnaturally' before his thirty-fifth birthday, the entire property will go to the identified trust, regardless of his marital status.

Fourthly, if Saahil is thirty-five and alive, he will continue to own the property. Until this time, nobody in the family, except Saahil's father, will have the right to change the 'will'. In case Colonel Kerkar dies before Saahil turns thirty-five, the 'will' shall remain as is," said Gatha.

"Finally, only Saahil will have the right to sell the property. However, if he does not sell the property before his thirty-fifth birthday or fails to nominate a successor, the entire property will be transferred to the identified trust after Saahil's death. Saahil will be the sole owner from his thirty-fifth birthday until his death, but not have any rights to sell the property."

"Saahil had not identified any successor nor had he sold the land. He was attacked just three days away from his thirty-fifth birthday!" Anubhav yelled.

"But do we know why there is a stress on the thirty-fifth birthday? I mean why not the twenty-fifth?" Mili asked.

"From what I have heard about the Brigadier, I mean Saahil's grandpa, he was fiercely decisive and his word was law. Once he had made up his mind to do something, nobody could change it. Perhaps, that is what happened with the will too," answered Gatha, shrugging her shoulders.

"Yeah, but strange, isn't it? Why did he assume that Saahil would not live till thirty-five?" Mili asked thoughtfully and walked towards her whiteboard. She listed down the clauses and sat down again, all the while staring at the whiteboard.

"Importantly, Brigadier made the 'will' when Saahil was only eighteen. Unfortunately, he died a year later," added Gatha.

"Which means, Amar Kerkar was very young at that time. Why did Brigadier identify Saahil to inherit this land? Why not a fair share to Amar? Do we have any reason to think that he loved his younger grandson any less?" queried Mili.

"Interesting," said Anubhav.

"Get me information on Saahil's past Anubhav – especially his childhood, and his relationship with his grandfather," instructed Mili.

Aubhav nodded vigorously.

"The money aspect doesn't end here," continued Gatha. "Saahil had a life insurance or rather a Term Insurance policy where if he died accidentally, his nominees or dependents would get an assured sum of one crore rupees. Saahil's beneficiaries in this case were his mother Mrs Suhasini Kerkar and his younger brother Amar. Each had a fifty percent stake per the insurance policy."

Mili was hesitant to think Suhasini Kerkar would be guilty. Whoever said, 'God cannot be everywhere, so he created mothers', said it well. But then, you cannot solve a case based on emotions.

"The term policy must have been done by his brother?" asked Mili.

"Yes, but the family has to prove that Saahil did not try to kill himself. They cannot claim anything if it is a case of suicide," said Gatha.

"But sanctioning the claims may be simpler for them since Amar knows the insurance business," said Anubhav.

"Is there a connection between Saahil's attack and Farzad's murder? Is someone targeting IT professionals? Get me Farzad Mistry's family history too. We should get a DNA test done if Dr Dighe's report also certifies his death was accidental," observed Mili.

"But Farzad's father has identified him, right?" asked Gatha.

"The body is in bad shape; rather it has no shape at all. With the new breed of clever criminals hovering around these days, one cannot be sure about anything unless there is concrete evidence," Mili stated suspiciously.

4 p.m.
5 July 2014

"Charity begins at home. Likewise, crime often has its genesis at home. Let's see what the Kerkars have to say," added Mili.

"Apart from Amar Kerkar, we can speak to everyone else now," said Anubhav.

"I have to tell you something about this man before we enter their house, Mili," Gatha said in a serious tone.

"Shoot."

"This morning, I noticed Amar Kerkar at the hospital café, with two unknown people, perhaps his friends. He got into a tiff with the soft-drinks vendor. Apparently, the guy got a drink that Amar hated. He screamed at the vendor and threatened to get him sacked! With his brother on deathbed, isn't it absurd that Amar was so obsessed with a drink?"

Mili gave Gatha a long look. "People often react strangely when in shock. I would give the benefit of doubt to the younger Kerkar there."

"The Kerkars were horrified by the police this morning. An officer told them that Saahil tried to commit suicide. The whole family unanimously objected," added Anubhav.

"Precisely the reason they decided to involve us in this case," said Mili.

"Saahil's mother told the police that Saahil used to say, 'Life is energy waiting to be unleashed'. To think he would attempt suicide was foolish," stated Anubhav.

"Very strong lady, this Suhasini Kerkar," added Gatha.

Anubhav rang the bell at Amar Kerkar's house.

Amar's wife Jyoti answered the door. Colonel Kerkar was standing behind her.

"This must be her eighth month," Gatha whispered to Mili.

"Please come in," Colonel Kerkar ushered them in.

"Sorry to bother you, sir. I can understand your state of mind. I got a call from Amar Kerkar this morning regarding this case," said Mili.

"You have my full cooperation. Do not worry about the money, Ms Ray. I don't know what the police will investigate, but I want justice for my son," said Colonel Kerkar.

Mili smiled. "We will take care. I know what it feels like and we are all praying for Saahil's good health."

"I would still want you to personally look into things," insisted Colonel Kerkar.

"I will," Mili assured. "Can you tell me what you were doing from 6 p.m. last evening to 6 a.m. this morning?"

"I was home. I went to play bridge with Mr Bhonsle at around 7.00. I returned at dinner time, at around 9.30 p.m."

"Mr Bhonsle?" asked Anubhav.

"He is our neighbour from the fourth floor, right above this flat. Whenever Suhasini and I visit Mumbai, we spend a lot of time with them. When the kids go to work, we chat up."

"Mr Bhonsle is retired?"

"Yes, he was with the Central Excise department. One year junior to me, he retired last year. This building is full of central government employees. We got possession of this flat almost twenty years back while I was still a young soldier," Colonel Kerkar said with a faint smile.

"So this flat is not Amar's?" Gatha could not resist asking.

"Now it is. I am happy with my home at Nasik. The children need this space in Mumbai more than we do. Saahil was always interested in migrating abroad. So I gave this flat to Amar."

"When did you last speak to Saahil?" asked Anubhav.

"Yesterday, that is the 4th of July in the morning at around 9.30 a.m. I asked him to skip office, as the weather was not conducive for travel, but he never listens. Instead, he said that he would be late."

Mili knew about Saahil's date plans but decided not to divulge.

Colonel Kerkar slowly removed his spectacles and wiped the moist glasses with a starched white handkerchief that reminded Mili of the table napkins used in army clubs. After tucking the sparkling hanky back in his left pocket, Colonel rubbed off his tears with his left hand while still holding the specs in his right. Mili noticed his broad wrist. That his biceps were gym-trained was obvious when the Colonel lifted his arms to push the spectacle-handles behind his ears.

"Did you work out today, sir?" Mili's question took Colonel Kerkar by surprise.

"I barely managed some free-hand exercises, detective. Why do you ask?"

"Sorry, just got sidetracked," Mili added promptly and caught Anubhav's eyes, who wore a *what-are-you-talking* expression.

Colonel's choice of clothing was classy. The pastel blue shirt had been ironed minutes before the Kwest team arrived – Mili just knew the steam-iron smell! The trousers were neatly pleated and looked as good as new. The Colonel's persona gave Mili the impression that Army discipline was still an integral part of his life.

"Do you know Farzad Mistry?" Gatha asked, trying to get Mili back on track.

"No, but I heard about him this morning. It is unfortunate."

"I agree, sir. By the way, we learned about the Nasik land that Saahil inherited. We were wondering why Brigadier Rawat might have kept such stiff clauses!" Mili said.

"Years ago, Saahil was severely infected with Hepatitis B and bedridden for months together. The Brigadier spent a lot of time with his grandson at that time and the two bonded very well. Saahil's recovery was nothing less than a miracle, and it might not have been possible without Brigadier Rawat. Everyone was in awe of him, but not Saahil. Grandpa was his best friend. The doctors had warned us that if the disease relapsed, even after ten or fifteen years, it could be fatal for Saahil. My father-in-law, I mean Brigadier Rawat was worried. Once he nominated Saahil for the Nasik land, Brigadier put in the rigid clauses because he didn't want anyone to take advantage of Saahil's ill health and snatch the property. Luckily, Saahil was completely cured and cent-per-cent healthy in a couple of years. However, Brigadier didn't live to see that day."

"Oh, I see! Any particular reason that he thought Saahil might not live until the age of thirty- five? I ask that because Saahil's thirty-fifth birthday is just a couple of days away!'

Colonel Kerkar returned a painful expression.

"Just the health bit that made Brigadier panic, I guess," Colonel Kerkar's voice broke as he forced himself to complete the sentence.

"I am really sorry, sir," Mili said.

After almost a minute's silence, Mili said, "Sir, I'd like to speak to Mrs Kerkar now."

"I'll get her here. Not sure if she will talk."

Halfway towards the bedroom, Colonel turned back and asked, "What if someone tries to harm my son again?"

"Please relax sir! I won't let anything happen to him," Mili managed to say.

Colonel Kerkar was getting restless. "Why do you want to talk to my wife? First go and arrest those killers."

Mili and Gatha exchanged quick glances. Anubhav put a reassuring arm around the Colonel's shoulder.

Five minutes later, the Colonel was back with his wife Suhasini Kerkar, who looked pale and sullen.

"Hello Mrs Kerkar. I am Mili Ray, private investigator with Kwest."

"Namaste!" greeted Suhasini Kerkar, folding her hands and slightly bowing her head. Her makeup-less beauty defied age and the salt-pepper hair added elegance to her personality.

"I can understand what you are going through, ma'am. But we need to ask a few questions."

"Okay."

"When did you speak to Saahil last?"

"Yesterday around 9 a.m."

"Did he say anything that you thought was strange?"

"No. He was planning a night out with friends at his flat and asked me not to tell his father, as Colonel does not like partying."

"Did he mention who was coming to the party?"

"No."

"Do you know any of his friends in Mumbai?"

"No, he has many Internet friends. I have seen him chatting with many on his laptop."

"Did he mention if the party was with friends he met over the Internet?"

"No."

"How often did Saahil go for these parties?" Mili asked.

"No fixed routine. He is a happy child. He plays the guitar and girls fall in love with him. But I know my son – he stays away from flings. He is a very good son, you know," she said and made eye contact with Mili for the first time.

Mili saw tears in Suhasini's kind, dreamy eyes. She took a deep breath and asked, "Do you know Farzad Mistry?"

"No."

"Do you know anyone from Saahil's office?"

"Yes, I met Morena. She came to our house in Nasik with her husband."

"Morena Dave? When?" Mili asked.

"Two years ago – 2012."

"I have one last question for you ma'am. Where were you on 4th evening and 5th morning?"

"At home, watching TV."

"Can anyone else confirm that?"

"The building people can, if you don't trust my family members. Jyoti and Amar were with the doctor. My granddaughter Muskaan was next door playing with Shikha, Mr Bedekar's daughter. Colonel went to play chess upstairs. I tried calling Saahil but the phone did not connect. Mrs Paranjpe came home in the evening asking for sugar, as usual. Today morning, I was at home only when Amar gave us the news."

Suhasini Kerkar said all this very matter-of-factly, much to the surprise of the Kwest team.

Next, Mili and team spoke to Jyoti, Amar Kerkar's wife, who was not keeping too well.

Mili meets Amar Kerkar

After a wait period of ten minutes, Amar was home with groceries and a remote-control car he had promised to his daughter Muskaan.

"Ms Ray, I do not wish to talk. I called you because that's what Dad wanted," specified Amar.

Amar looked a lot like his mother, thought Mili – the same oval face and dreamy eyes!

"Okay, just the basic questions. Where were you yesterday, 3.00 p.m. onwards?" asked Mili.

"I took my wife for a check-up. You can call Dr Sarita's clinic to confirm. Our appointment was at three, but due to the bad weather, by the time we reached, it was almost four 'o clock. The doctor was busy and we waited for around twenty minutes. The check-up lasted for another half an hour. Then we were on our way home. The rains had started, traffic was bad and we got home at 7.30 p.m. Then we went for dinner to my neighbour's place on the top floor. It was a birthday party. Jyoti, Muskaan, and I had dinner there."

"Whose birthday was it?" asked Anubhav.

"Sejal, Mr Patel's daughter."

"Did your daughter accompany you to the doctor's clinic?"

"No, she was with our next-door neighbour. We picked up Muskaan at 8.00 p.m."

"I understand that Saahil owns a lucrative piece of land at Nasik. If he does not make it, you will inherit the property. Is that correct?"

"This is ridiculous," retorted Amar. "I have a decent income which allows my family to lead a comfortable life. How dare you accuse me of something so horrible?"

"Look Amar, we have nothing against you or anyone else! When was the last time you visited Nasik or the land area?"

"I go to Nasik every month for client visits. I went there last on the 30th of June."

"That is four days before the attack on Saahil. Did you meet Saahil between the 30th of June and the 4th of July?"

"I met him on the 3rd and 4th. On the 3rd of July, he was staying with us. Bhai is very attached to Muskaan. He spends most weekends with us. This time he extended his stay since our parents are here," said Amar.

"Did you find anything strange or suspicious in his behaviour?" asked Mili.

"No. He was happy and talked a lot about his upcoming vacation plans."

"Where was he planning to go?"

"Bhai wanted to go to Eastern Europe. He was saving money for that."

"Was he not interested in the land at Nasik?"

"Not really! He told me that I could have all of the land. He just wanted the farm products to keep going to the orphanage he had adopted."

"Which orphanage?" asked Gatha.

"An NGO named Kishori in Nasik. They support education of girls whose parents cannot afford to send them to schools."

"Saahil does a lot of charity work?"

"Yes."

"Sorry, you were talking about the property."

"The will is complex and only my dad has the authority to amend it," Amar added sarcastically.

"Your grandfather's will?" Mili interrupted.

"Yes. Saahil laughed at all these clauses. He would say, 'I cannot live my life by a will.'"

Mili continued, "The most important clause being – if Saahil had an unnatural death, the property would go to a trust. Is that correct?"

Amar nodded awkwardly.

"One last question. Do you know Farzad Mistry?"askedMili.

"No. I am sorry to hear about him," said Amar.

"Who told you?" asked Gatha.

"The constable at the hospital," replied Amar.

"He was in the car with Saahil last evening," said Mili.

Amar did not say anything. After a while, Colonel Kerkar said, "Please pray that my son gets back his life. We will not be able to bear it if anything happens to him. Not again."

"Papa, nothing will happen to Saahil. Ms Ray, if you are done with the questioning, can you excuse us?" asked an irate Amar Kerkar.

"We will leave now. Take care of your wife, Amar. When is the baby due?"

"Next month."

ACP Trehan meets Sheena Mehta

4 p.m.
5 July 2014
Sheena Mehta, software engineer at Zarine, was working with Saahil on the same project. When Mili found hundreds of messages exchanged between Sheena and Saahil Kerkar on the FriendMe website, she requested ACP Trehan to probe. Accordingly, Sheena was summoned to the police station. She walked in with her husband Rishabh.

During the interrogation, Sheena maintained that she and Saahil were just friends.

"Every office has men like Saahil, who are perpetually pursuing gorgeous women. He may have been attracted to me, but I was never interested," claimed Sheena.

ACP Trehan was appalled! On the one hand, the lady calls herself Saahil's friend. In the same breath, she makes such a disgusting comment! Since he could not disclose the content of the messages that Mili had discovered from Saahil's FriendMe account, ACP decided to listen her out.

"Where were you between 6 p.m. on the 4th of July and 8 a.m. on the 5th of July?"

"I was working from home yesterday. So for this entire duration, I was at my residence."

"Can you prove it?"

"You can ask my domestic help and my husband. Rishabh came home at 9.30 p.m. and saw me home."

"Anyone you suspect?" asked Trehan.

"No, Inspector. Saahil was a harmless guy and there is no reason anyone would hurt him," Sheena replied.

"Anyone with whom he did not get along? In office or may be in his family?"

"How would I know?" Sheena asked, horrified.

"We have reason to believe that you and Saahil were more than 'just friends' Ms Mehta."

Sheena gulped as ACP Trehan finished his statement. Rishabh threw her a disgusted look.

"There must be a mistake here. Saahil and I interact a lot – but mostly about work," Sheena's face turned red.

"Your last month's phone bill – the one you submitted at Zarine for bill reimbursement – says you and Saahil exchanged about two-hundred sms-es in less than two weeks. For your current call records, I need to wait until tomorrow for my team to revert with details," Trehan said slowly, almost stressing on every second word as he spoke.

"I will wait outside," Rishabh fumed out of the interrogation room.

"You have to cooperate with us, Ms Mehta."

Sheena was on the verge of tears. She nodded.

"Saahil and I were seeing each other briefly. But post my marriage this May, we were trying to wrap up this affair. I never loved Saahil. I lied about our relationship because I was scared. I know nothing about who did this to Saahil. Please believe me," pleaded Sheena.

"Do you suspect anyone?"

"I know that Morena and Saahil were having kind of a cold war going on. They were not on talking terms. The last time they spoke, Morena had threatened to harm Saahil. He told me himself. She is such a troublemaker," disclosed Sheena.

"Any idea as to why they were fighting?" ACP Trehan asked, expecting more information from Sheena.

"Morena was jealous of me. She wanted Saahil. But he loved me. She could not tolerate that. I am not saying she killed him, but she did not have the best intentions for him. Saahil hated her."

"Do you have any proof?" asked Trehan.

"Women have strong intuition, sir. I simply know that Morena didn't like to see me and Saahil together," Sheena stated confidently.

"Do you know Farzad Mistry?"

"Please don't drag me into this, Inspector. I don't think I ever saw him in office," Sheena replied bluntly.

"But you work in the same office?" ACP Trehan asked, amazed.

"Zarine Software is a big organization and we have multiple offices. There are over 750 employees in Mumbai alone. We are so engrossed in our project that we do not even know the person sitting in the next cubicle! We only know our team; we work with them and hang out with them. There is hardly any time to socialize with the others. I had never heard of Farzad Mistry till this afternoon," Sheena said.

"Thanks, Ms Mehta. You may leave now. Do not go out of Mumbai without informing us. If needed, we will call you again."

After Sheena left, Trehan went through the horrifying pictures of Farzad Mistry's body. Maybe it *was* an accident, he thought. Why was Mili connecting the two mishaps? It could be a mere coincidence. And even if someone had tried to kill both the software engineers, it could not be Sheena, he said to himself. Or was a murderer really hiding behind that beautiful face?

Gatha Adds a New Suspect

❦

Kwest Office

8 p.m.
5 July 2014

"Sheena Mehta thinks Morena had reason to harm Saahil. I believe Rounak mentioned her too. So, let's meet Morena tomorrow," Mili announced as Gatha and Anubhav took their seats in the garage office.

"Shouldn't we meet up with Sheena first?" Gatha asked.

"Since Sheena already met ACP Trehan today, I don't think that's a good idea. But may be one of us can keep a check on her whereabouts over the next few days."

"Okay, I'll do it," Gatha responded.

"Good. ACP Trehan is taking care of her call records," added Mili.

"I just want to reiterate two things, for my understanding," said Gatha. "First, Sheena says Morena might be involved in Saahil's attack because she was jealous of his affair with Sheena. Secondly, per Rounak's statement, Morena was jealous because Saahil got a promotion and she didn't. Am I making any sense?"

"Absolutely Gatha! Both statements point us to a very jealous woman – Morena," Mili said with a laugh.

"What's so funny here?"

"Sorry, Gates, I am just trying to understand why everyone was pointing to the 'jealousy' angle. Could it be that Sheena was jealous of Morena and Saahil's friendship? Was Rounak jealous that Saahil got two promotions when he got none? Are these people telling us their stories keeping the gun on Morena's shoulder?" questioned Mili.

"Strangely, nobody has anything to share about Farzad!" said Anubhav.

"Oh, that reminds me, I met up with Shravan sometime back," Gatha said.

"Shravan Trivedi, COO of the most sought after IT firm in Mumbai – Zarine Software," said Mili and applauded.

"So are we going to hear the account from Mumbai's renowned criminal lawyer or from Shravan Trivedi's beloved sister-in-law?" asked Anubhav.

"If you guys are done pulling my leg, should I start?" Gatha replied, smiling.

"Please ma'am."

"For starters, Shravan doesn't believe that Morena Dave has anything to do with the attacks on Farzad and Saahil," said Gatha. "He has introduced a new suspect."

"If you are talking about Vikrant Sharma – then I'd say your brother-in-law surely has a detective's mind," Mili said, munching on an apple.

"You're right, Mili. Shravan spoke at length about his CEO today."

"Anything of interest to us?" asked Anubhav.

"You bet! As I understand, Vikrant Sharma is a self-made man. He single-handedly built Zarine Software from scratch and led the company to the zenith of success. His business insight is exemplary."

Mili chipped in. "Businessman of the Year...Best Entrepreneur...name any award and he has bagged it."

Gatha continued, "Shravan says that even though they have been working together for the last six years, he still cannot read Vikrant Sharma's mind."

Anubhav interrupted, "Let me synopsize his career graph for the benefit of all of us here."

"There goes the research expert. Shoot." Mili closed her eyes to visualize as Anubhav gave a profile update on Vikrant Sharma.

"Vikrant Sharma is one of the founding members of Zarine Software. He gave up a promising career with one of the topmost IT firms in the world to set up Zarine Software in 2007. The Zarine Group was already a well-known name in the auto industry. When they decided to venture into IT, Miara Zarine relied on her childhood friend Vikrant. With a background in Electronics Engineering from IIT and an MBA from IIM, Vikrant belonged to the crème-de-la-crème of academic professionals. He had been a topper all his life. Opportunities were galore when Vikrant opted for IT as his chosen field. Within twelve years, he had scaled great heights and was earning at least three times more than his contemporaries. At this time, to give up a job that paid so handsomely and dive into a start-up was a gamble. Vikrant took the plunge and joined the Zarine Group as CEO of their new company – Zarine Software. Of course, Miara made him an irresistible offer!" Anubhav paused to drink some water.

"Within seven years of its inception, Zarine Software emerged as a top player in the IT field. The assets Vikrant has accumulated are enough to let generations after him relax. Vikrant is married to Nishita Sharma. However, he is fascinated by beautiful women, I am told. He has had few female companions in the past, some of whom have been Zarine employees! The media loves him. Vikrant is an excellent communicator, a shrewd leader, and a photographer's delight. In a nutshell, he is the lifeline of Zarine Software."

Once Anubhav stopped, Gatha added, "He markets himself very well too. Modesty is not his middle name. Grapevine has it that Sheena Mehta and Vikrant Sharma had a fling. Shravan requested me not to quote him on this."

"Ah, that is news! I better update ACP Trehan," Mili said promptly.

Anubhav continued, "Vicky, as he likes to be addressed, is particular about hiring the 'right' people for the job. He says, 'Skills can be acquired. I hire people with the right attitude'. He still meets each new employee who joins his management team."

"The question is, where do Farzad, Saahil, or Morena fit in?" asked Mili.

"Vikrant has a Core Brainwave team comprising people proficient in their chosen field. He encourages them to innovate and pays them handsomely," answered Gatha.

"So Saahil and Morena were part of this Core Brainwave?" asked Anubhav.

"Right."

"Farzad?"

"No."

"We still don't have a single soul in Zarine with any motive to eliminate Farzad!" said Mili. "I wouldn't be surprised if he died the death planned for someone else!"

Gatha's enthusiastic voice overshadowed Mili's worried statement.

"What I am going to tell you now is confidential. We must keep it amongst us, else Shravan will be in trouble."

"Whoa! More secrets? Shoot."

"It would take one Saahil to end Vikrant Sharma's illustrious IT career," said Gatha.

"What does that mean?"

"Vikrant had a heinous secret. Unfortunately, Saahil learned about it and threatened to expose his CEO. Vikrant had offered him money but that agitated Saahil further," said Gatha.

"So?"

"So Vikrant apologized to Saahil and promised that whatever had happened wouldn't be repeated," Gatha said softly.

"Ah, so we have at least one person with a clear motive for murder," said Mili.

"I knowww! But what's the secret, Gatha?" asked Anubhav.

"Singapore," said Gatha and took a deep breath.

While Mili and Anubhav were keenly waiting for Gatha to share the secret, she asked for a loo break!

Mili got an excuse to light another cigarette.

Gatha was back soon. She started, "You see – Saahil was... rather Saahil is among the best technical minds at Zarine Software. In 2010, after months of relentless research, he completed his dream project – a unique software program which was no less than an invention for him – it was like his baby."

"What was this program about?" asked Anubhav.

"What I gather from Shravan, for an organization, this program was a first of sorts. Saahil named it The Personal Assistant or PA."

"PA?"

"Yes, because it functions like a memory planner, an assistant. It is targeted at senior managers and top management executives in organizations. If you have this program installed, it will give you a list of pending items to be completed, calls to be made, errands to be run, and so on."

"Any computer can do it these days. Even a Smartphone can. What's so special about this program?" asked Mili.

"Yes, right. Reminder options are available in most electronic devices we use today. They remind you about your pending tasks. Their action ends there. They do not actually perform the task for you. That's the difference."

"I don't get it," said Anubhav.

"Let's say Anubhav has five pending to-do items for today, two new meetings with clients at different locations, a dinner-date with his wife and… it also happens to be his mother's birthday! But Anubhav comes to office and gets a new assignment, which is so urgent that he prefers to delay his pending tasks for the time being, as they are not on his priority list. Result? They will be delayed further. Besides, the birthday cannot be postponed to the next day! So – here is what PA will do: The PA will read aloud your five pending action items. For example, *IT filing must be completed today. Else, pay hefty penalty.*

"So you will automatically fit that in your schedule. It will do the same with your other action items, after scanning their priority. Date is all-important in this application. It will not allow you to miss a date and will guide you to honour your commitments.

"It will call your mom in Denver, at a time when she is expected to be awake and at a time you are free! It will connect the call and tell you – *wish mother on her birthday now.* The next voice you hear would be that of your mom!

"PA even prepares you for your evening date. '*Clothes are not date-friendly*' or '*You have to leave in ten minutes to reach Worli Sea Face at 6 p.m.*' Such messages will keep coming to you so that you stay alert. The software is your Personal Assistant.

"PA travels with you anywhere you go. You do not have to hire a secretary. It will do your travel bookings and claim your reimbursement bills using a simple voice-based menu option on its user interface. By installing this software, an organization could save billions. Just imagine – nobody would ever miss a deadline. The application would also advise you on market conditions and provide tips on investments," stated Gatha.

"But does this mean too much data needs to be fed into the software?" asked Mili.

"No. Once you install it on your system, it programmes itself to know you. It learns all your data and selectively chooses the friends and family you should follow up with, based on your interactions with people," smiled Gatha.

"Hmmm, interesting," added Mili.

"Saahil and Morena were excited to travel to Singapore to install this software program at the client site," said Gatha.

"Saahil knew that the client could easily install it online, but since he was getting the opportunity to travel, he accepted it happily. But once he reached Singapore, he understood that things were not as simple as they looked. Client installation was delayed for days together. Saahil was asked to deliver the original program to the client and disable any 'copy' option. The only backup copy Saahil had kept with himself was mysteriously infested with bugs. Rebuilding it would take a long time and he reported that to Vikrant. But Vikrant asked him not to bother about rebuilding the program – just to deliver it."

"A genius too can be imperfect at times," said Vicky Sharma. "Close the project and come back."

"Sure Vicky," replied Saahil. "But anyone can write and close it as a simple program. What I had added was months of scientific research. It was my invention. I am feeling crazy that it is lost now. If we submit this to the client, I don't think they will ever come back to us!"

"Leave that to me," Vicky ended the conversation firmly making his point.

"Vikrant sold this program to the Singapore client for millions of dollars. Nobody got to know about Saahil Kerkar's contribution to this path-breaking program. The Singapore client bought the rights to sell, distribute, rebuild, and recreate it. It was Vikrant's personal gain, not Zarine's."

"How did Saahil find out?"

"Saahil understood what Vikrant had done only when he spoke to Shravan about the PA app. Shravan had no clue about this program. In fact, no one in Zarine did. Since Saahil and Morena were also working on two other critical deals at Singapore, Vikrant thought he could just slip this in without attracting attention. He had planned handsome incentives for Saahil and Morena to shut their mouths," said Gatha

"So they did nothing?" asked Anubhav.

"They needed to go to the police. But there was no evidence. Morena got some voice tapes from Vikrant's office secretly, but no concrete proof. They confronted Vikrant, but he denied that Saahil had created any such program! They had a heated discussion where Morena threatened to leak evidences. That is when Vikrant mellowed down. He promised them this would not be repeated."

"And they believed him?" asked Anubhav.

"Anyone would," Mili chipped in. "With a personality like Vicky Sharma's, it would be shocking if he couldn't sweet talk someone into trusting him."

"Exactly! And he proved that too. He gave Saahil and Morena full freedom to plan new projects. In 2011, he felicitated them for Innovation in Project Management. He more than made up for lost ground. He regained their faith," stated Gatha.

"Which means he had no reason to kill Saahil, right?" asked Anubhav.

"Wrong! Once he was certain his best employees were pacified, he would surely look at business expansion. But he would not like to feel threatened every time he bumped into Saahil or Morena. After all, he was the CEO," said Mili.

"But if this PA episode happened in 2010, why did Vikrant wait for four years to strike back?"asked Anubhav.

"In 2010, Zarine was barely three years old. Vikrant needed to retain top talent. Now, he has consolidated things. He could plan further without worrying about them," said Mili. "He also must have recruited plenty of talented new people."

"Yes, Vikrant was looking for new bait, Shravan told me. But in Saahil's presence, he was not able to progress at the pace he wanted to."

"Why was Shravan keeping quiet?"

"Shravan is being paid well for a job he loves. Besides, he has confessed that being in a family full of lawyers, he just does not have the orientation to fight for other people's rights. He is tired of seeing everyone at home do just that!" Gatha said dejectedly.

Part - 2
Saahil and Morena
(2010-13)

Friendships and More

❧

"**I** am very pleased to announce that two of our Core Brainwave team members will be travelling to Singapore for Quantam Imperial team's biggest project till date," Vikrant Sharma declared at Zarine Software's monthly town hall in Mumbai.

Rounak frowned the moment he heard 'Core Brainwave'. He had been let down once again!

"Saahil Kerkar and Morena Dave – we wish you good luck with this assignment," concluded Vikrant. A thunderous applause followed.

After the town hall, several employees walked up to Morena and Saahil's bay and personally congratulated them. Soon, congratulatory messages from Zarine's offices across the country flooded Morena and Saahil's mailboxes.

Rounak chose to stay away.

"This is an opportunity of a lifetime, Mornie," Saahil told Morena over coffee, that evening.

"I know what it means for you, Saahil. You have given your life in building this application. Once organizations start using it, Zarine will be considered a market leader, you know! And you – Saahil Kerkar – will be recognized as a new-age innovator. Wow!" Morena sure was excited.

Vikrant Sharma wanted his best employees on this project and Morena willingly participated as a software engineer, despite being a Project Manager herself. Saahil was leading the project and Morena was second in command in the five-member team.

"Feels like your own baby. The implementation should go off well," said Saahil.

"Vicky will take care. Once in a different country, security will not be on us anymore."

"Exactly what I am worried about, M. I am excited to travel and we will have great fun, I know. But think of this logically... does it make sense to finish three-fourths of the code here and to add the finishing touches in a foreign country?"

"I see your point. But may be expenses are high here and so Singapore?"

"Oh c'mon, Morena! I have been working like crazy on this project and wouldn't I know this much? This code can well be completed from my hometown Nasik, or even from Morena, your birth place," said Saahil.

Both of them burst out into laughter.

"Perhaps Vicky wants to show off? Client before self, or some other cheesy differentiator thingy he comes up with from time to time?" said Morena.

"Not a bad try, Mornie. But I doubt that. Remember what he told us yesterday: The client should not have an inkling that we are working on this code and we should use the client location *only* for implementation," added Saahil.

"But why on earth did he announce the project in the town hall today?" Morena asked, obviously surprised.

"He didn't mention the PA software anywhere. Did he? He just talked about QI's biggest project! You and I are already on that massive retail project, which also happens to be a Singapore assignment."

"Oh yes, that is a huge one too, Saahil! Good that we are thinking on similar lines. I just wanted to be sure you are equally worried," said Morena.

"You little devil!" said Saahil and pulled Morena's cheeks. "Thank you for keeping me grounded."

"Get ready for the 'no chewing gum city' now," smiled Morena.

They laughed again. In fact, they laughed at almost everything that day.

Singapore

August 2010

"Hahahahah, you are too funny Saahil," chortled Morena as she happily sipped her evening coffee.

Saahil continued his animated mimicry for some more time and then gave up.

"Okay, now done! Am not going to keep on imitating every second person we meet." Saahil chuckled.

"Let's complete the review document then," replied Morena as the train halted.

"We cannot do without mimicry on train rides, regardless of which country we are in," Saahil added as they walked towards their apartment on the busy Singapore street.

"Hey Saahil, you preserving the tickets I hope? Are you sure Zarine will reimburse our train journeys?" Morena asked, bewildered.

"Come on, Mornie! We have already saved Zarine's money by not staying in a hotel. Of course everything will be reimbursed," Saahil said confidently.

"I would have anyway opted for these service apartments, over those budget hotels!" Morena shot back while entering her beautifully furnished one-bedroom-flat on the eighteenth floor.

"Yeah me too," nodded Saahil. "I'll join you for dinner in sometime." His adjoining one-bedroom apartment was equally attractive and it overlooked the city of Singapore. The best part was that the local railway station was less than a minute's walk from the building.

Later that evening after dinner in Morena's apartment, Saahil started humming a romantic number. Morena was working on the review document, when suddenly she ran to the balcony and started crying.

"Hey, what's wrong?" Saahil walked up to her.

"I...I don't know. I have a feeling that Vicky is going to get us into serious trouble."

Saahil didn't utter a word. Instead, he gently hugged Morena. The moonlight kissed her hair as she clung on to him and cried. As Morena rested her head on his chest, his heart skipped a beat. He patted her head, trying to console her. Morena's forehead brushed against the stubble on his face. She smiled coyly.

Morena's phone rang. Slowly, she moved away from Saahil. His eyes travelled to the hollow of her neck – the suprasternal notch. She looked divine and for one weak moment, Saahil wanted time to stand still. The fragrance of Morena's body was all over him and he closed his eyes to seal the memory of the magical moment.

Morena returned a few minutes later, phone in hand.

"I am so sorry. I did not mean to... Err...I feel embarrassed."

"It's okay Mornie, it happens," Saahil said, aware of how superficial he sounded. Then he stared at her while she played with her hair, unable to make eye contact with him.

"By the way, who called?"

"Varun," Morena replied, finally stealing a glance.

"He wanted to know if all is well and if you have found a hot chic yet," she added.

"Haha! On that note, let's do coffee," Saahil suggested, bouncing back to his happy-go-lucky self.

"Yayy," Morena played along. "I have never had coffee at 3 a.m."

"Calculate India time and you won't freak out so much! I've had coffee at the weirdest hours one can think of," said Saahil. "You should thank me for giving you the opportunity to make coffee at this hour."

"What? Nooooo!" Morena laughed.

▼

The next morning, while Morena and Saahil were working on the PA software implementation at the client's office, an email popped up on their computer screens.

"Meeting invite from Vikrant Sharma at 3 p.m. Singapore time?"

"Yeah funny, isn't it? He never sets up direct meetings with us," Saahil said.

"Well, Dipasree must be on leave," said Morena, referring to her immediate supervisor.

"Dipsy has no leaves planned until end of the year!" replied Saahil.

At three, Saahil and Morena logged in to the conference call using Zarine's international toll-free number.

"Listen guys – you must hand over the PA software to Chiro Tahsima by tomorrow. Put it in a gift-box or something. I don't want any emails on this. If you have any questions, call my mobile."

"Sure Vicky. But tomorrow? I need some more time for backup," said Saahil.

"I will not tolerate any slippages, Saahil. Why do you need a backup? That's violation of the client contract. We will have nothing to do with the software once it is delivered. Am I clear?"

"I get it. But why are you so rude?" Saahil replied angrily. "You postponed the implementation date; we didn't."

"When we were leaving Mumbai," added Morena, in a polite yet firm tone, "you said that the code would be installed in Singapore, but the completion announcement would be made to the Board of Directors in India. We were supposed to deliver the replica to the client here and the original had to stay in our home server."

"Sorry guys! See, I am under pressure from the investors here. About the code, yes Morena dear, you are right. But we have had a change in plans. Vineet and Rubin – both our directors will be at Singapore next month and so I would like you to hand over the code to Chiro Tahsima."

Morena and Saahil decided not to argue further with the boss.

"Okay, sure," they replied together.

"Enjoy the city and make sure you visit the Botanical gardens there," signed off Vicky.

Saahil and Morena hardly slept that night.

"Why does boss want us to submit the original software to a Singaporean client?"

"Saahil, I guess there is more than meets the eye here. Let us do as he says, but we must keep a copy."

"Not possible, Mornie. The moment I copy it, there is a record. Every time someone copies this code, it creates a record."

"But you have designed it. Wouldn't you know a way out?"

"I am trying to figure out something. But given the time, I don't know how much I will be able to do."

"It's okay Saahil. You have done your best. We will investigate this once we get home."

"I am going to resign the moment I return to India," Saahil said on an impulse.

Morena promised, "If you quit, I'll resign the very next day. What will I do here without you?"

"Relax, M, I just got carried away. We'll deal with Vikrant Sharma… together."

Mumbai

March 2011

"How can you say that, Vicky?" Saahil shouted, forgetting for a moment that he was speaking to his employer, the CEO of Zarine Software.

"Calm down Saahil. It is just business," replied Vikrant Sharma, unaffected by Saahil's emotional outburst.

"I should have got a patent for my invention."

"What invention are you talking about, Saahil? My organization, my resources, my employees – you built something that I asked you to create. You used your expertise to earn your salary."

"This…this Ladybird app that J&J Singapore has just released, I created it," cried Saahil. "It is my research, my months of hard work. How could you just sell my creation…my PA software?"

"Take a seat Saahil," Vikrant said.

"I am quitting this organization," Saahil stated.

"Don't be silly. You are due for a promotion next month. Besides, I have already recommended a handsome raise for you!"

"Is my CEO trying to bribe me? Incredible, sir! I think I have got my social media topic for today."

For the first time, Vikrant Sharma looked baffled. Then he started: "When I joined the start-up you know as Zarine Software today, I was as angry and forthright as you are, Saahil. I do not have anything to hide from you – our company was in debt. Had I not sold PA, we wouldn't have been able to sustain the company, forget about going public in a couple of years. In other words, your invention saved us from bankruptcy, Saahil," Vicky said softly.

Saahil patiently listened.

"It was never my intention to deprive you. If you felt that way, I apologize, Saahil. This will never be repeated. You are the best member in my Core Brainwave. When you grow, the company grows too. I earnestly request you – stay with Zarine and let us take the company to the next level. You are an asset."

Saahil was indecisive. He didn't know whether to trust Vicky. He couldn't wait to leave the room and pour his heart out to Morena.

As if reading his mind, Vikrant said compassionately, "I owe my apologies to your colleague Morena too. I know she worked very hard on this project. I ask the two of you to trust me and keep doing your best. The future of Zarine is in your hands."

Saahil didn't flinch.

"Did I make any sense, Saahil? Is my secret safe with you?"

Saahil nodded. "I didn't know about the company's financial condition. I understand. But I hope that going forward, performers will be recognized and not threatened."

"Thank you, Saahil. You have my word."

As Saahil got up to leave, Vikrant said, "Please ask Morena to see me too."

Vikrant Sharma regretted sending Saahil and Morena to Singapore. The sympathy card had worked this time, but he would not tolerate an employee dictating terms to him!

Sheena Mehta

❦

Sheena Mehta joined Zarine as a software engineer in 2012. A software tester with ten years of experience in the IT industry, Zarine Software was Sheena's opportunity to get into software development. Morena was assigned as Sheena's mentor and soon the two became good friends.

For her first two projects, Morena was to be Sheena's project manager. Impressed with her performance, Morena recommended Sheena for a complex deal that Saahil was leading.

"You think I can handle this?" Sheena asked nervously.

"Absolutely! Besides, when Saahil is your project manager, you need not worry about anything. He has this uncanny ability to make the toughest of challenges look simple and interesting," Morena assured her.

Saahil meets Sheena

March 2012

"Sheena will be working from our location starting today. Finally, she is on your project," Morena gushed.

"Oh wow! I couldn't be happier," Saahil said, mimicking her voice.

"Shut up Saahil. She is a nice girl ya."

"Do you ever find fault with anyone Ms 'Righteous'?" Saahil teasingly asked.

Just then, someone sneezed behind him. Saahil turned around.

Saahil was bowled over by Sheena at the first glance.

"So fair!" he exclaimed to himself. Saahil could not take his eyes off Sheena. She was tall, slender, had big eyes, a tiny waist, and long athletic legs. She was stylish and had a smile to die for. She could give any model a run for her money, thought Saahil.

"Ah, so this is *the* Saahil Kerkar," Sheena smirked as she shook hands with Saahil.

"I am so glad you guys have finally met," said Morena.

"Oh yes, you are making that so obvious, Mornie," Saahil chuckled, trying to hide his excitement.

Fighting evil

June 2012

"Imagine what Nidhi must be going through right now. Somewhere, I feel bad, Saahil. Getting a job will be a big struggle for her," said Morena.

"Did you really want her to continue at Zarine and torture the newbies? It had to end somewhere, right? We were just facilitators," Saahil said, without an iota of guilt.

"Did you tell Rounak? He was close to Nidhi, I think," Morena said.

"Mornie, Mornie! Relax! Rounak and I have been returning home together for as long as I can remember; he has *never* mentioned Nidhi Sahoo," stated Saahil.

"That's strange! Anyway."

"You need a break, Morena! Tomorrow movie *pakka na*? Is Varun keen too?" asked Saahil.

"Oh yes, he is in," confirmed Morena.

"Cool! I will buy four tickets then. Dunno why I thought Varun was not into romantic comedies," said Saahil.

"I told him, I wouldn't go without him. You will have an arm candy for sure! So, he'd better tag along," stated Morena.

"Hey, I thought you would be happy to feast on Ashton Kutcher all by yourself. Also, had you dropped a wee bit of a hint, I could have skipped taking the girl along, Mornie. I didn't know you were so jealous of my dates?' winked Saahil.

Morena laughingly added, "I do not think we are getting back to work today Saahil."

"Hey, that reminds me, do you want to check with Sheena? Does she like romcoms?"

"Ah, I didn't think about that. You can ask Sheena if she wants to join us," Morena replied reluctantly.

"Next time maybe," Saahil said with a smile that Morena was not familiar with.

▼

"I just loved it," said Morena, and continued laughing as she walked out of the theatre.

Varun clasped her hand and whispered, "Shhh…you're too loud."

"That too without getting drunk!" Saahil poked in, when he overheard Varun.

Varun was irked at Saahil's unwelcome comment and wanted to say, "Mind your own business, you jerk." However, his cold eyes conveyed the message.

"Where do we head for dinner people?" Saahil asked, diverting everyone's attention.

"Let's try the new place I was telling you about this morning, Saahil. It's just round the corner," giggled Morena.

"I think that's great idea," said Ira, Saahil's friend. This was the first time she spoke since they left the movie hall.

The dinner session continued until late night. Varun had mellowed down by then. However, his tolerance level for Saahil was deteriorating day by day, especially after Morena and Saahil's Singapore trip.

Matters came to a head when dessert arrived. Varun was four drinks down. Ira, a teetotaller was waiting for her driver's call. Morena and Saahil were lost in a never-ending conversation. Suddenly, Saahil took Morena's hand and said, "You are the best thing that happened to me since I came to Mumbai!"

Then he told Varun, "Bro, you are a lucky man."

Varun gripped Morena's empty wineglass so tightly that it broke into pieces.

The Growing Distance

September 2013

"I am off to Geneva. Woohoo!" Morena announced as she entered office on a lovely September morning.

"So you finally bagged it, Missie. The coveted finicky-client project! Well done!" Saahil said, applauding her excitedly.

"What coveted? It came to me just because nobody else would've wanted to go anyway," Morena shrugged. "Finicky is the key here."

"Stop being modest, Mornie. Ask me. I would have gone if they selected me. But this project is different. It is an honour that the client selected you for this project."

"You are just making me feel good, Saahil. You just returned from the US last month. Maybe they wanted to give you a break," Morena said, smiling.

"That was a short one, come on. This is big," Saahil said.

"Okay, okay, thanks. I am taking Sheena along too. It will be a good experience for her," Morena added.

"What the…!" Saahil looked startled. "The client agreed?"

"Yes, they have appreciated her hard work. The last module she deployed helped them save a lot of money. So when I mentioned that I wanted to send her instead of me, they asked me to get her along," Morena replied.

"Has she even completed her probation period?" sighed Saahil.

"Yes, she is a confirmed employee now. She is over a year old at Zarine now, Saahil!" Morena replied, visibly shocked at Saahil's reaction.

"When are you leaving?" Saahil asked, pretending to ignore Morena's response.

"Next month."

"Wow! Mark the date, Mornie. You are all set to be the first messenger of peace from ZS to Geneva," Saahil said.

"Oh, you never get tired of pulling my leg, Saahil," Morena complained.

"How long will you be away?"

"Three weeks to four at the most."

"Long time," sighed Saahil and looked straight into Morena's eyes. She was caught unawares. Morena could not help looking back at him with the same pain in her eyes that she saw in his.

"No coffee today?" Gopal asked as he passed by Morena's desk.

"Yes, we are just on our way." Saahil answered and realized he and Morena had been staring at each other for an unusually long time.

"We'll talk every day. Time difference isn't much," Morena told Saahil on way to the cafeteria.

"Three-and-a-half hours," Saahil replied instantly.

Morena and Sheena left for Geneva in October 2013.

▼

"I am glad that the project was so successful. Congratulations!" Saahil wrote on Morena's chat window, the day before her flight back to Mumbai.

"I am very happy too. Sheena has made a mark for herself here. When we are back, she will get her first assignment as Project Lead. Isn't that amazing?" added Morena.

"Good for her. Okay, chat later. Getting into a meeting," Saahil cut the conversation abruptly.

"Sure, bye," Morena wrote.

This was the fifth day in a row Saahil had done this. He simply cut short the conversation after the customary "Hi, How are you?" Morena felt odd.

Saahil and Morena always chatted for hours over the office chat, regardless of the work pressure! But what was wrong with Saahil these days, thought Morena. Is Vikrant Sharma up to something again?

"Look what I got here! Sheena stated enthusiastically and hugged Morena from behind.

Morena somehow managed to minimize her chat window, stood up and turned around.

"I got an award: 'The Most Diligent Performer'. I am on cloud nine!" Sheena said, jumping in excitement.

"That's brilliant Sheena. Congratulations! Where's the treat tonight?" Morena said encouragingly.

"Treat back in Mumbai, Mornie. Today the Project Director has asked me out for dinner." Sheena was blushing.

"A date with Nico? Nico Balmer? Are you kidding me, Sheena?" asked Morena, startled.

"Oh, I am not joking. He did ask me out and I just could not refuse. He is too sweet. Do you want to join us?" Sheena asked nonchalantly.

"Let me just remind you that we are on a business trip and Nico Balmer is our client. He is not a Zarine employee. Meeting the client for a date may not be a good idea," Morena said firmly.

"Please don't worry, Mornie. Nik is a friend. Besides, I am not treating him. He will pay the bill. So there is no question of paying the client to get business," Sheena laughed wickedly.

Morena missed Saahil.

December 2013

It was over a month since the day Morena had returned from Geneva. Ever since, her interactions with Saahil had been unusually short and formal. Saahil kept very busy and barely found time to talk. Even after office, Morena did not have access to him – he was always unavailable. The chats, weekend movies and so on had abruptly stopped!

Morena opened her office chat and clicked on the 'chat history with Saahil Kerkar'. She read the messages exchanged with Saahil in November and December. The chat window looked like an overused template, without any customization of text.

The chats went like this:

Hi, good morning.
Hey, morning!
Coffee?
Let's go.

Morena opened her chat history with Saahil from January to September 2013.

"Yes, that's more like us," she said aloud, smiling at the lengthy conversations. "Was there anything we didn't talk about despite our hectic schedule?" She felt like compiling the chat transcripts – it would read like a book for sure!

Morena spotted a message where Saahil was even ready to share his Windows password with her last July.

Are you mad Saahil? I am not supposed to know your password.

Tanuj asked me to share the password with someone I trust and I thought of you.

Next, Morena browsed through her conversation with Saahil on his birthday in July 2013.

So how many people wished you today Saahil?

Oh many many! But some people are so useless. I have no connection with them but they continue to wish me every year. That bugs me.

You should thank your stars that people you don't care about, still call to wish you.

Forget the buggers. You know me, when I switch off, there is no looking back.

January 2014

Apart from the daily coffee break, Morena and Saahil hardly met. The weekend outings had stopped. Morena requested her Geneva client to postpone the daily meeting by half-an-hour to accommodate lunch with Saahil. But within a few days, Saahil had new excuses to avoid eating with her. On the days he ran out of excuses, he would be unimaginably quiet at the table. The coffee breaks were no different.

"You know what happened today, Saahil," Morena would say sometimes, trying to reawaken her friend in Saahil.

"Let's talk later. I have to finish something urgently," Saahil would reply.

Morena had been observing the change in Saahil for over three months now. He was drifting apart.

"What's wrong with you Saahil? Why don't you talk nowadays? Is Vicky up to something?" Morena asked one morning.

Saahil's phone rang.

"Hey Sheena, yes I'll be there right away," Saahil said excitedly.

"You going somewhere?" Morena asked after Saahil had hung up.

"Yes, talk to you later," Saahil said, in a rude tone that offended Morena instantly.

"Hey, I asked you something Saahil. Don't avoid me like this!"

"Oh please!" Saahil said, flaring up. "How many times will I tell you that everything is fine? I am *not* in love and Vicky has *not* misbehaved. Honestly, I think you need to put your mind to work, Morena! You've started asking stupid questions these days, almost like Gopal! Take this as feedback!"

Morena sat in the cafeteria, stunned. Saahil walked away.

21 February 2014

There was a mild fragrance in the air when Morena started for office. It had to be the freshness of the champa flowers in the garden adjacent to her house. She took a deep breath and walked towards the auto-rickshaw stand.

Morena reached office earlier than usual. Saahil entered about twenty minutes later.

At around 11 a.m., Morena received Saahil's customary ping. This at least, had not changed, she thought.

Coffee?

Let's go, she typed.

Friday was the only day in the week that employees could sport casual wear. Everyone looked happy and bright on Fridays. Morena wore a dark orange kurti, paired with her ice-washed blue-denim jeans. She brushed her shoulder-length hair backwards and tied a careless horsetail. Her dolphin-shaped silver earrings swayed playfully as she quickened her pace to catch up with Saahil.

"Looking good, Morena," said Rohan as he walked past them.

"Thanks," Morena responded and looked towards Saahil, who was busy reading something on his phone.

In the last three months, Saahil had barely noticed Morena. The same person, who would never miss an opportunity to compliment Morena's pastel-shade kurtis, was alarmingly quiet.

Saahil and Morena took the four-seater table at the end of the cafeteria. As usual, they ordered coffee and waited.

"Saahil, we need to talk."

"Later. I have to get back to work now," Saahil delivered his standard dialogue.

"No. I have to say this now." Morena replied, an unsure urgency lingering in her voice.

Saahil looked up from his phone. He kept it on the table and said, "Okay, tell me."

"Look, I have been observing this for over three months now. I even tried talking to you earlier. You know what I am saying," she paused, expecting a response.

Saahil kept staring at her, his eyes devoid of any emotion.

"Our friendship is suddenly so formal, don't you think? I mean, when was the last time we actually talked? We have not gone out for lunch in ages! I miss you, Saahil."

Saahil said, "It's nothing like that! Come on." He was aware of the unintentional, husky tenderness in his voice.

Morena tried to keep calm. "This formality coffee makes no sense to me anymore. This is our last coffee together."

"Are you serious?" Saahil asked.

Coffee in the office cafeteria has always been our thing... please tell me you don't agree Saahil, Morena found her inner voice shouting silently.

Saahil looked at Morena, his deep brown eyes diving into her dilated pupils searching for a reason. Then he fixed his gaze on the teardrop hanging from her left eye, threatening a free fall any moment. Morena could not hold it any longer and blinked even after a Herculean effort to stay steady!

Saahil looked away.

"If you feel uncomfortable, it is okay. I respect your decision. If you ever want to have coffee with me, let me know." Saahil did not even make a feeble attempt at contending Morena's statement.

It was all over.

At that poignant moment, coffee arrived.

Coffee, which had strengthened the bond between these two friends at Zarine Software, was suddenly intolerable. Even the coffee-wala's wicked smirk was not funny anymore.

From the next day, Saahil stopped operating out of the same work location as Morena. Zarine Software had three offices in Mumbai and offered enough flexibility to its employees in terms of work location and timings.

Part - 3
Mumbai, 2014

Nidhi Sahoo

❧

Police Station

10 a.m.
6 July 2014

"Farzad was my best friend," Rounak said ruefully. "How is Saahil bhai?"

"Saahil is on life support," ACP Trehan answered.

"Oh no!" Rounak looked weary and scared.

Trehan, who was relying on Rounak to unravel the Farzad mystery, observed the baby-faced, overweight man turn pale within seconds.

"Are you okay?" Trehan asked, offering Rounak the glass of water on his table.

Rounak did not say anything but his evasive eyes added to Trehan's intrigue.

Rounak drank some water and placed the glass back on the table with trembling hands. Trehan promptly instructed the constable eyeing Rounak's half-empty glass, to remove it. The constable swiftly wrapped a napkin around the glass before lifting it from the table. Once out of the Trehan's office, he walked to the adjoining room and placed the evidence in a plastic bag.

Anubhav, who had been waiting for the constable, immediately called Dr Dighe.

"Rounak Arora's fingerprints are ready," Anubhav informed.

"Great! Send them in please," Dr Dighe replied.

Back in Trehan's office, Mili asked, "You got off at the station along with Farzad, right?"

"I did. But we boarded different trains. He left before me," said Rounak, on the verge of tears.

"Do you know anybody who would want to hurt Farzad?"

"For god's sake, he was a harmless soul – a simple man who loved his family," Rounak pleaded.

"Farzad's wife told us that Morena had called him that night and that's why he left home. Do you know why?'

"How would she even have his number?" Rounak said, appalled. "I don't think Morena and Farzad ever interacted with each other. They work with different teams."

"But you were all travelling together last evening!" commanded ACP Trehan.

"Yes, but that is because Saahil offered us a lift."

"How was Saahil's relationship with Farzad?"

"They were just colleagues who knew each other because of me, their common friend."

"I see! Looks like you are the only one at Zarine with a motive to kill both Saahil and Farzad. Both were successful young men doing well in their careers. I smell jealousy here. The sooner you own up, Rounak, the easier it will be for you," Trehan said in an aggressive tone as he got up from his chair and walked towards Rounak.

Petrified, Rounak looked up at the imposing personality of the police officer, who though leaner than him, was visibly stronger. As Trehan adjusted his belt, Rounak peered at the pistol hanging from the ACP's waist and mumbled, "I swear on God...I didn't do anything."

Mili Ray walked in. Trehan whispered something in her ear and she nodded.

"Rounak, you told my colleague Anubhav yesterday that you suspect Nidhi Sahoo, an ex-employee of Zarine Software. Is that correct?"

"Yes, yes ma'am," Rounak said, nervously. "But she only knew Saahil – not Farzad."

"Why would she want to kill Saahil?"

"Nidhi Sahoo was sacked from Zarine Software. She blamed Saahil and Morena for her ouster," claimed Rounak.

"Calm down and tell us the story," Mili ordered, settling in the chair beside him.

"The year was 2012," Rounak began. "Citing major integrity issues, our Human Resources (HR) head asked Nidhi to leave ZS. Nidhi, an extremely self-centred and cunning woman had been climbing up the Zarine ladder at rocket speed, thanks to her influential superior Dr Ganpat Sriram. Following Ganpat's retirement, however, Nidhi was like a ship without an anchor. Her incompetence and malpractices were out in the open now, with nobody to cover for her."

"What was she working as?"

"She had some fancy designation – Program Manager. Nobody knew what program she was managing though."

"She was senior to Saahil?"

"Yes."

"Okay, go on," instructed Trehan.

"She wasn't popular among her colleagues. Nidhi would often skip office but her leave balance was always intact. Despite poor communication skills, she travelled abroad for client meets and trainings. Approvals from her boss guaranteed her seats in prestigious events too," Rounak added furiously.

"How does Saahil come into the picture?" Mili interrupted.

"Nidhi was infamous for manipulating people to get her work done, especially newcomers. Matters came to a head when Anisha and Jai, two new joiners were summoned by the Human Resources team following a major client escalation – they had messed up the pricing in a proposal. As a result, the client lost the deal, incurring huge losses. When Anisha and Jai tried to explain, Nidhi, the program manager for this deal convinced HR that the newcomers be shown the door! She submitted a report highlighting their poor performance and how despite her guidance and feedback, the 'brainless duds' had learned nothing. The two kids came crying to their seniors – Morena and Saahil."

"Interesting," said Trehan.

Rounak continued, "Saahil knew both Anisha and Jai were bright and hard-working. It was not difficult to understand that they were being blamed for Nidhi's non-performance. Morena agreed too. However, since Nidhi was always extra-sweet to Saahil and flirted with him at the slightest pretext, handling this issue was a challenge for him."

"Every second person in Zarine seems to have had a crush on Saahil. Funny, isn't it?" observed Mili.

"What happened next?"ACP Trehan asked impatiently, ignoring Mili.

"Everyone knew Nidhi was at fault, but due to lack of evidence, she always managed to get away. But not this time. Saahil and Morena collated all the information they had on Nidhi's slippages and went to the HR. The HR investigated further. CCTV camera footages proved to be very useful. The HR interacted with several other people, all of whom confirmed Nidhi's unethical work behaviour. In her statement, one manager said, *'I was waiting for someone to ask me about this horrible person. She leaks confidential information to Zarine's business rivals. She is a nuisance!'*"

"Nidhi knew that Saahil was behind this?" asked Mili.

"Yes," replied Rounak. "Nidhi was asked to leave the premises of Zarine within fifteen minutes. Her laptop, locker and other office belongings were seized and she was not allowed to access her email ID. This is Zarine's policy for people who are sacked for integrity issues. We don't want angry employees to tamper with the company assets or send hate mails."

"It's almost like getting arrested," added Trehan.

Rounak looked relieved for the first time, and prayed that the police would let him go.

"In Nidhi's termination note, the HR wrote: *'Your breach of trust and lack of professional integrity have led us to lose two of our most valued clients. This act is shameful and unpardonable. Your services are terminated with immediate effect.'* The HR head told Nidhi, *'Only at Saahil's request, we are not handing you over to the police!'* When Nidhi confronted Saahil and Morena, she had a security guard on either side escorting her out of the office premises. She stopped and angrily stated, *'I will not forget this. You will get back your due, Saahil Kerkar and Morena Dave!'*"

Nidhi kept hurling abuses at Saahil and Morena while storming out of the office.

"Where is this Nidhi now?"

"I heard she got a job in Nigeria. I do not know if she is back though."

"How were your terms with her?" Mili asked.

"We often bumped into each other at the office cafeteria. So we talked during lunch and tea breaks sometimes. But it was very formal, always."

"Thanks Rounak," Mili said. "You may leave now, but do not go out of station. You may need to come here again."

"I have not done anything!" Rounak said restlessly.

"Don't worry. If you notice anything suspicious, contact me immediately," said Trehan.

Kwest at Work

❦

"Rounak and Farzad got off at the railway station. Morena Dave continued onward with Saahil. It is likely that she was the last person Saahil met yesterday," Anubhav spoke in a daze.

"Did you get to speak to her at all?" Mili asked and lit a cigarette.

"No, she was not in the office today too."

"She is a vital lead. Can you get me her photo?"

"Sure. I got one from the Zarine HR records." Anubhav handed over Morena's photo to Mili.

"Anybody else you spoke to?" asked Mili.

"Yes, I briefly interacted with the CEO Vikrant Sharma. He did not divulge much – says he is in touch with DIG Joshi. All he said was that Saahil was among his best employees. He gave a clean chit to Morena. He never interacted with Farzad," said Anubhav.

"I also spoke to the receptionists, Saahil's manager Dipasree, and Morena's manager Tanuj. Women love Saahil...that is unanimous. He is very courteous, one of the women in the Security team told me," Gatha added.

"Good. Shravan Trivedi should be able to throw some light on Farzad, I hope."

"I have spoken to Shravan about Morena Dave," said Gatha. "But as I told you earlier Mili, Shravan says Morena is a warm person who excels at her job. She cannot be malicious."

"Why would she call Farzad Mistry the night he was killed then?" asked Mili.

Gatha was silent.

"Any luck on the call records?"

"The police have put the numbers on tracking. I have also asked for call records for 4 July and 5 July," replied Anubhav.

"Include Farzad's family also, if you haven't," instructed Mili.

"Done."

"Gatha, Anubhav, I want two things. One, display all the pictures we have in the office today – from both crime scenes. I need more close ups of Farzad and Saahil. Two, check call records of all names we have heard in this case so far. We need the motive," Mili concluded as the trio reached their garage office.

"Property and family feuds are common murder motives," added Gatha, speaking from experience. "But people will go to any extreme to get an alibi for themselves."

"Oh yes. But so far, Morena is the common link in both attacks. She was in the car when Farzad and Rounak got off at the station. Again, she was the one who allegedly called up Farzad."

"There you go, hopefully another lead," said Anubhav as 'ACP Trehan Calling' flashed on his mobile screen.

"Thanks! I wonder how it reached his garage!"

"They found Saahil's phone in his own garage then?" Mili said as Anubhav completed his conversation with Trehan.

"Yes, they did. But how did you know?" Anubhav looked astonished!

"Farzad's cell was smashed; we have the broken gadget as evidence. Only Saahil's phone was missing. You said 'garage', which made it easier to understand," said Mili, combing her shoulder-length curly hair with a boat-shaped hairclip.

"The newspapers are writing *anything*," said Gatha. "Did you read the headlines today?"

"Oh yes, they have killed Saahil before his death," lamented an irked Anubhav.

"Shravan has been very disturbed about the media hype," added Gatha, sympathizing with her brother-in-law.

"We have the pictures here," said Anubhav and turned the projector on. The garage suddenly looked like a movie theatre. The three of them looked at the close-up shots of Farzad's dead body.

"I learned that Farzad was a very good-looking man. The face is so badly damaged. Thank god the family was able to recognize him," said Gatha.

"As you suggested, the police will be looking at a DNA test, Mili," said Anubhav.

"Hmm. The police found the body in the bushes near the highway. After the truck hit him, someone pulled the body and dumped it there," said Mili.

"The police said that he was drunk," added Anubhav.

"The culprit must have taken advantage of his drowsiness and pushed him on the road," said Gatha.

"We cannot forget the call he received. Once we get the surveillance camera footage, it may throw some light on who called Farzad, or more importantly, who met Farzad. It is not necessary that the same person who called him had also met him."

"I think Rounak may have a hand in this," added Anubhav.

"But Rounak claims that Farzad was his best friend. Even if he planned an attack on Saahil, why would he harm Farzad? Do we have a snapshot of his family background?" asked Mili.

"Yes, Rounak belongs to a middle-class family. His father is retired and mother has serious health ailments. Every month, he spends a fortune on his mother's treatment, because insurance doesn't suffice."

"What ailment exactly?"

"One kidney is damaged and the other isn't in a good state. Chances of survival are bleak," said Anubhav.

"They stay with him in Mumbai?"

"No, they are in Chandigarh. His girlfriend Rosalind, a jewellery designer, lives in Mumbai."

"Childhood love?"

"Yes, they grew up together, in Chandigarh. Rosalind's family is pressurizing her to get married. Rounak missed the promotion at Zarine last year, and he is sour about it. He plans to get married later this year."

"Who got promoted instead of him?"

"Saahil. He also became Rounak's manager."

Post-Mortem

❦

Farzad Mistry's mysterious death made headlines.

On social networking sites, people were uploading pictures, engaging in protest campaigns, arranging prayer meetings, creating 'Justice for Farzad and Saahil' pages, and more.

At Zarine Software, employees were afraid to report to work. Zarine's top clients expressed concern about their ongoing projects, despite the CEO's assurance of timely delivery.

"A tough time ahead for us," Vikrant Sharma told Shravan Trivedi.

11.30 a.m.
6 July 2014
"This is ridiculous," said Cyril Mistry, Farzad's father.

"I can understand what you must be going through, Mr Mistry. I am just stating facts," replied Dr Dighe, trying his best to console a bereaved parent.

"He never touched alcohol in his life. How can you say he was drunk?"

"I found traces of a very strong sedative in his stomach. It was mixed with his drink."

"The driver said that Farzad jumped in front of his truck out of nowhere. It was so sudden that that by the time the driver pulled the brakes, Farzad was run over," added Inspector Thadani. "Besides, the road was wet and slippery."

"Why did the driver run away?" asked Cyril Mistry anxiously. "May be my son was alive. Couldn't he get him to a hospital?"

Inspector Thadani continued, "The driver fled, as is very common in hit-and-run cases."

"When Farzad left home at 11.00 p.m., he was sober. We all had dinner together after he returned from office," Cyril Mistry said coldly.

"I am really sorry, Mr Mistry," said Dr Dighe. He watched the old gentleman walk slowly towards the hospital exit.

"Excuse me, Dr Dighe." The doctor turned around and shook hands with Mili.

"I would like to see the body."

"Come with me," said Dr Dighe.

Once in the pungent smelling room, Mili tried to imagine how horrible Farzad's wife must have felt seeing her husband's lifeless body.

"From what I understand Dr Dighe, the drug that you found in Farzad's drink results in dizziness. Is that correct?" asked Mili.

"Yes, along with nausea and severe headache. Even if the person has not consumed alcohol, he will feel intoxicated. It is dangerous and can be fatal," Dr Dighe responded.

"We know that somebody sedated Saahil with an injection. Now we learn that Farzad was drugged too. But I do not think these drugs are available in the market," Mili stated bluntly, looking at Dr Dighe's report.

"Right! But somebody who has been a medical student, even if not a doctor, or comes from the medical background, can have access to these drugs," said Dr Dighe.

Mili listened to the doctor carefully.

"I believe we are going for the DNA sample, right doctor?" asked Mili.

"Yes," replied Dr Dighe. "Though the tattoo on his right arm and the clothes he was wearing helped Farzad's father identify him, we want to be hundred percent sure."

"Time of death?"

"Between11.30 p.m. and 1 a.m.," confirmed Dr Dighe.

"It fits in like a glove, Dr Dighe!"

"What?"

"Considering that the same person killed Farzad and attacked Saahil, your confirmation of the time of death helps! Saahil was attacked at around 4 a.m. Enough time for the murderer to kill Farzad and then attack Saahil on the other side of the city."

"How did the attacker know that Saahil would be available on the streets at that odd hour?" asked Dr Dighe.

"I am assuming that there are multiple of them. Maybe someone called Saahil also, just the way Farzad received a call. Or maybe Farzad was killed by mistake. What if he never was the target?" Mili concluded.

Farzad Mistry's call records

"Sir, apart from the call from the public booth, no other calls were made to Farzad Mistry post 6 p.m. on the 4th of July," Inspector Shirodkar informed ACP Trehan.

"How about before 6 p.m.?"

"He just got one call from his wife that lasted less than thirty seconds."

"I have checked call locations and records of everyone in his family. I have not yet found any motive for this murder."

"I think this is a straight case of hit-and-run. But because Saahil Kerkar was also attacked that night, detective Ray and her team are combining the two. It is just a coincidence that they both worked with Zarine Software," said Trehan.

"Yes, sir," Shirodkar added.

"Let me update our supreme commander," Trehan said sarcastically and dialled Mili's number.

"Yes ACP?" Mili asked in her trademark deep, intense voice.

"Morena didn't call Farzad on the 4th of July. At least, not from her mobile phone," informed ACP Purab Trehan.

"Anything suspicious on Farzad's call records?" Mili asked, munching on the unfinished piece of apple in her mouth.

"He had never spoken to Morena, not in the last three months at least, per the records. On the night of the 4th of July, the call he received was from a roadside paan shop. I will keep you posted," said Trehan.

"Good, thanks. Just find out if that area had a surveillance camera. If we can get a clip, it would help us speed up things," said Mili, and took another big bite from the apple.

"Yes, probably there is one. We found his body near the Horizon mall, which has a camera at the main gate," replied Trehan.

Saahil's phone records

"We have a parcel," Gatha declared as she received the courier.

"Some chocolates, I hope," Mili responded from her desk.

Gatha walked in with the call records, "ACP Trehan has sent these for you."

"He is fast, I must say. Let's go over these quickly."

"No major disconnect in Saahil's phone records for the last one month," deciphered Mili.

"Most calls were made home or to friends and colleagues. On the day of his attack, Saahil had made a customary call at home around 3.00 p.m. At 3.30 p.m., he had called Sheena Mehta and they spoke for 1.56 minutes. At 4.15 p.m., he had received a call from an unknown number. This was the last call received on his cell," said Anubhav.

"Yes, and that number was traced back to Neha, a twenty-four-year-old model from Lokhandwala, Andheri. She was nervous when the police called and even more so when they informed her about the attack on Saahil. Trehan met up with her this morning. She is clean," Mili said confidently.

"That's the first person you have not suspected on this case Mili," Gatha said in a surprised tone.

"Neha and Saahil were Internet friends. If they would meet on the 4th of July, it would have been their second 'in person' meeting. At the time of Saahil's attack, Neha was at a photo-shoot in Wadala. Trehan checked on her alibi. The art director has confirmed that she was stuck at the studio owing to the weather. Neha has requested the ACP to keep her out of this else her modelling career will be in jeopardy," Mili said.

"Between the 25th of June and the 3rd of July, Saahil exchanged the maximum number of calls and messages with Sheena Mehta. ACP Trehan met Sheena, and she has confessed about her affair with Saahil," said Gatha.

"Yes, we know that one," Mili said. "Next?"

Gatha continued, "Post 10.00 p.m., Saahil's cell was switched off. It was in the Andheri West Versova area for a brief while and then near Andheri on the Western Express Highway. That is the last location before the cell was switched off at around 10.15 p.m. When it was switched on at around 4.00 a.m., it was in Saahil's garage."

"Wait a minute," Mili stood up. "Why did Saahil switch the phone off? Low battery? But then, how was it switched on at 4.00 a.m.? Anubhav, make a note."

"What else have we got from Trehan?" Mili prompted Gatha to share more.

"Amar and Jyoti Kerkar were at the clinic, as they mentioned. Trehan confirmed with the doctor. Jyoti Kerkar's cell was switched off since 8.30 p.m. She blames it on her daughter Muskaan. Says the little one was fiddling with the phone and had unmindfully switched to the flight-mode. Jyoti realized that only the next morning," said Gatha.

"How about her husband?"

"Amar Kerkar's cell matches all the locations he claims to have visited," said Gatha.

"What about the parents?" asked Mili.

"Both Mr and Mrs Kerkar were at home on the evening of the 4th of July and the morning of the 5th of July, per the cell locations. Had they deliberately left the phones at home and ventured out, that would be a different story," said Gatha.

"Or maybe they went out, but left the phone at home. For them, perhaps it is not important to carry the phone everywhere. My mom never takes her phone to the market, despite a thousand reminders," said Anubhav.

"But they cannot surely plot their son's murder?" Gatha said.

"I am not ruling out the possibility," said Mili.

Morena Dave's call records were normal. She had called her mother and her husband on 4th of July. There were few unknown numbers, mostly spam calls from credit card and insurance companies.

"See this." Mili broke in.

"Morena and Saahil's locations have a perfect match from Zarine Software post 5 p.m. until 9.30 p.m. They were together definitely until about 10 p.m. when it is likely that Saahil dropped Morena home. They stopped at the Manor Jungles – almost for two-and-a-half hours. Then they moved to Versova. After that,

Morena's cell stays at Versova 10 p.m. onwards. Saahil moves to the highway and then his cell is switched off at 10.15 p.m. Next, his cell is on at 4.00 a.m. in his garage. Morena's cell is still active in Versova."

"What does that mean?" asked Gatha absorbedly.

"I am not sure if Morena was the last person to have met Saahil before his attack," Mili stated.

"She received a call from a Delhi number at 11 p.m."

"That one was from Varun Kulkarni, her husband. He was in Delhi for office work. The number is of the hotel where he was staying. They spoke for about two minutes," said Anubhav.

"Why would he call from the hotel landline?" Mili was curious. "How about his call records?"

"No gaps there. Varun Kulkarni was in Delhi from the 3rd of July to the 5th of July as he has claimed. His tickets and boarding passes have been verified. His mobile phone was in Delhi and switched off since the previous night," said Gatha.

"Varun Kulkarni's phone is switched off in Delhi. He switches it on only on 5th morning. Why was it off when he was travelling to the Delhi airport from his hotel?" Mili was thinking aloud. "Keep a tab on the husband. I want to see all his bank transaction records in the last three days. If he used his corporate credit cards in Delhi, I need the time he used them."

Gatha added, "I have them right here, along with Morena, Farzad, and Saahil's details. Apart from Saahil, none of them had any major expenses in the last two months. Saahil withdrew 90,000 on the 27th of May. Why would he need such a hefty amount in cash? I checked with the charities he supports – none of them received that big an amount from him. All his other donations are paid by check or through net banking."

"Was someone trying to blackmail him?" Mili asked, raising her eyebrows.

"Saahil liked meeting women. I guess it could be one of them! But wait, he was aspiring to be a professional singer...may be had to pay someone for his music album?" inferred Anubhav.

"The music company wouldn't ask for so much cash, unless it was an underhand dealing," Mili explained. "What else have we got on Morena?"

"For a moment, let's assume Morena is behind all this. At 11 p.m., Morena spoke to her husband. If she attacked Saahil Kerkar, she must have left her phone at home, say around 11 p.m. Then she travelled with Saahil to the spot where she planned to kill him. In between, she went to Thane to kill Farzad Mistry. Next, she came back to Saahil's garage, and switched on his cell phone at 4 a.m. Then she drove Saahil's car out of his garage and deposited him in front of Mili's house at 5 a.m. on the 5th of July. She dragged him to the driver's seat, before fleeing the scene. Wow! Doesn't this sound filmy?" Gatha asked.

"May be she had an accomplice?" Anubhav responded promptly.

"But what is her motive?" Mili asked.

"May be revenge? Saahil and Morena were not on talking terms. May be they were in a relationship and Saahil had walked out?" Gatha added.

"Possible," said Mili. "Saahil was keen on Sheena, not Morena, as I gather. So jealousy could be a motive."

"Could the husband have helped her attack Saahil?" asked Anubhav.

"Why would he? Varun Kulkarni could have killed Saahil for his own reasons. But why would he help his wife kill her lover?"

Mili lit another cigarette. "After this case, I will quit this damned smoking!"

Call details and financial transactions of other Zarine Software employees, including the CEO Vikrant Sharma and the

COO Shravan Trivedi were scrutinized as well. Nothing looked irregular.

Mili decided to activate her network of informers across the city.

Last homage to Farzad Mistry

Farzad's body was handed over to his family on the evening of the 6th of July. Mrs Shireen Mistry, Farzad's twenty-three-year-old wife stood at one corner of the drawing room hugging the pillar in front of her. People flocked to the Mistry home to pay their last respects. There were many Zarine Software employees including the top management: Vikrant Sharma, Shravan Trivedi, and Prerna Ruia. Farzad's colleagues Rounak, Gopal, Sheena, Apeksha, and the Opulus team members were also present. Gatha made her way to Farzad's house.

"I don't want the case pending in court for years, Ms Trivedi. I want justice for my son. I will pay you double your fees. Please take this as a personal request from me to investigate this case," Farzad's father pleaded to Gatha.

"We are on it, sir."

"My son was only twenty-five. He never harmed anyone. He left home in the dead of the night to help someone. Arrest that woman who called that night. She is the culprit. I want justice."

"I understand, sir. We are investigating."

"I heard that the Project Manager from the QI team, some Morena I think her name is. She is behind all this," Gatha overheard a female voice.

"Oh, who is she? I have never heard that name," a male voice asked, softly.

"Arey, she got that Best Mentor Award this year. Didn't I show you her picture in this month's ZS newsletter? She is a star performer."

Mili Ray Meets Morena Dave

✺

7 July 2014

"Please let me go inside just once," cried Suhasini Kerkar, as the security person outside the Intensive Care Unit vigorously shook his head for the third time.

Dr Akruti Krishnan, who had just walked out of the ICU firmly said, "You can meet your son at your own risk. Any infection is dangerous for him right now."

"Tomorrow is my Saahil's birthday," Suhasini mumbled, tears welling up in her eyes.

Colonel Kerkar put an arm around his wife and said, "If we have waited so long, let us wait for one more day."

Dr Krishnan, who was assisting Dr Shah with Saahil's case pointed out, "All I can say is that Saahil's reports are better than yesterday. So, we are being extra-cautious."

"It's okay, doctor. We will not go inside today," Colonel Kerkar said.

Meeting Morena

"Silver Oak Towers, Versova," said Anubhav, and pulled out an employee record form. "Here you go, Mili," he added and took the driver's seat. He beamed as he held the steering and inserted the key into the ignition point.

"You really like driving, don't you Anubhav?" Mili asked as she buckled up her seat belt.

"Who doesn't? You never give us the opportunity," he answered with a boyish charm. "I am switching on the A/C. Smoking is prohibited inside the car."

"Yes, yes, I shall oblige," Mili assured as she leafed through Morena Dave's employment record. "Morena was the last person to have met Saahil on the 4th of July. Technically, she was also the last person who spoke to Farzad on that fateful night."

"I still think she is clean," said Gatha.

"Did you tell her we would be visiting?" Mili asked, ignoring the comment.

"I called many times. Nobody answered," Gatha replied coldly.

At 5.00 p.m., Morena's doorbell rang. Varun answered the door.

"Yes?"

"Hi, I am Mili Ray, private detective with Kwest. We would like to meet Ms Morena Dave regarding the attack on Saahil Kerkar."

"We already spoke to the police this morning," Varun answered reluctantly.

"Ms Dave did not meet the police this morning," Mili stated curtly.

"She is not keeping well. Leave your number and I will call back when she is in a position to speak," Varun replied in a condescending tone.

"Sorry for the trouble, Mr Dave..."

"My name is Varun...Varun Kulkarni," interrupted Varun.

Then with an outraged look, he managed to utter "Goodbye detective" and almost slammed the door on Mili.

"Oops…not so fast Varun," Mili said, reflexively pushing the door back with her left hand. "Morena may be upset but one person is dead and the other is fighting for his life! You better cooperate."

Varun was taken aback by Mili's swiftness. He regularly worked on his biceps and had never expected a woman to thrust open the door with such force! Mili checked her impish smirk on time – she loved the bewildered look on his face. However, this was not the first time Mili was experiencing this fun moment. Whenever people saw a trailer of her acrobatics, they were zapped!

"How long will it take?" Varun asked, still baffled.

"Just a few questions and we will be done," Mili replied crisply.

Varun moved back from the door now, allowing Mili and her team to enter the stylish drawing room.

Mili looked around. She could sense that the couple earned handsomely and their taste in furniture was classy.

"Have a seat. She is not in any condition to talk. I hope you will respect the sensitivity of the situation."

Mili perched herself on the black-brown single sofa. The detailed woodwork was unique and complemented the soft cream cushion covers perfectly.

"Mr Kulkarni, I would like to have a quick chat with you before speaking to your wife."

"Sure."

"Was Morena friendly with Farzad Mistry?" asked Mili.

"We learned about his death yesterday. Morena is working with ZS since 2010, but she never mentioned Farzad Mistry."

"What about Saahil Kerkar?"

"They worked in the same team," said Varun. Needlessly, he removed the magazine lying on the couch and placed it on the centre table.

"The police are suspecting a murder attempt," said Mili, keenly observing Varun.

"Doesn't affect us," he said, trying to stay casual.

"Have you met Saahil Kerkar?" Mili asked the next question quickly, sensing Varun's discomfort.

"Yes."

"Do you suspect anyone who might have tried to kill him?"

"No idea."

"What about Farzad Mistry? Did you ever meet him?"

"This is nonsense! I just told you that I'd never heard of him before yesterday!"

"When did you last meet Saahil Kerkar?"

"I don't remember. I guess sometime last year. If you are done with interrogating me, I will get Morena."

"Where you were on the night of the 4th of July and morning of the 5th of July?"

As though reciting a well-rehearsed speech, Varun stated, "I was in Delhi from 3rd of July to the 5th of July. I returned yesterday morning. If you want air tickets and details of where I stayed in Delhi, I can share that as well."

"Yesterday, meaning 5th July? What time did you land?"

"Around 8.00 a.m., and I went to office straight from the airport," he replied, sharing more information than requested.

Gatha and Mili exchanged quick glances.

"Thanks! Anubhav, can you please collect the Mr Kulkarni's boarding passes?"

"Are you suspecting me? Do I look like a murderer? This is ridiculous!" lashed out Varun.

"Like I said, we are investigating a murder," Mili reiterated.

"I always take a morning flight on weekdays and go to office directly. This has been my regular routine. I frequently travel to Delhi and Bangalore," said Varun. "My boarding passes are in office. I usually keep them there for reimbursing official expenses."

"Anubhav, please collect the contact names of people in Delhi Mr Kulkarni interacted with last evening," added Mili.

"Sure."

"Can you get Ms Dave now?" Mili politely asked Varun. Gatha looked at Mili in amazement; she had never heard Mili speak so softly!

"Morena has not spoken to anyone for the last two days. I will try to get her here," said Varun and walked towards the balcony attached to the bedroom.

▼

After almost fifteen minutes, Varun re-entered the drawing room with Morena. He had given her a brief on Mili. But he was not sure she had paid any heed.

Mili recognized Morena the moment she saw her. Morena walked in slowly, head lowered. Varun helped her sit on the plump sofa facing Mili. For a minute, Mili was quiet. She remembered the girl she had met on the local train. The woman sitting in front of her was no match! That lively face versus this sullen look; those twinkling eyes against these dull ones locked behind tired, puffy eyelids; that endearing smile as opposed to this sombre, sickly expression!

Morena was wearing an off-white baggy top and a pair of beige pyjamas. She had a scarf around her neck, with which she rubbed her nose now and then.

"Ms Dave, I understand your state of mind. But I need to ask you a few questions."

Morena did not make any eye contact with Mili.

"Ms Dave, where were you on the 4th of July at 6.00 p.m.?"

"I already answered that," objected Varun.

Mili gave a sharp look at Varun and then whispered something in Anubhav's ear. Anubhav walked up to Varun and asked for the details of his Delhi hotel.

"But I cannot leave her alone."

"It's okay Mr Kulkarni," assured Anubhav.

Unwillingly, Varun trudged towards the wall cabinet in the guest bedroom. Anubhav tagged along.

"So, coming back to my question again Ms Dave, can you tell me where you were last night?"

Gatha remained a silent observer, trying her best to read Morena's body language.

Mili tried again. "Morena, I met you on the local train long long ago when you and Saahil Kerkar were sharing a hearty laugh over your lost toe-ring."

Morena responded with a startled look. She did not utter a word though.

Mili got up from her seat and took the empty seat next to Morena on the spacious sofa.

"I can understand what you are going through. But your colleague Farzad Mistry is dead. Saahil Kerkar is on life support. We do not want anyone else to be harmed now. Please cooperate," Mili said warily.

Morena nodded.

"Good. I want to know where you were on the 4th of July after 6.00 p.m.," inquired Mili.

A weak voice forcibly answered, "I was returning home from work."

"What time did you reach home?"

"Around 10.00 p.m."

"It was very dark and it was raining cats and dogs. How did you get home? Were you driving?"

"No."

"What time did you leave office?" Mili asked, stressing on each word as she spoke.

"Around 5.00 p.m.," said Morena.

"You left at 5.00 p.m. and got home at 10 p.m.? How were you travelling? The distance between your home and office would not be more than twelve kilometres," probed Mili.

"The streets were jammed. I got a lift. Traffic was slow and nothing was moving on the road. I reached home only at 10.00 p.m.," Morena said indifferently.

"May I know who was kind enough to offer you a lift on that wretched day?"

"No."

"Does your husband know?"

"No," Morena replied hesitantly.

"Am sure you called your husband for help?" asked Mili.

"No," she replied in monosyllables yet again.

"Did you call Farzad Mistry at 11 p.m. on the 4th of July?"

"Certainly *not!*" Morena shot back, furiously.

"Did Saahil Kerkar drop you home?"

No response.

"When did you speak to Saahil Kerkar last?" Mili popped the next question.

No answer.

"If you don't cooperate, Morena, I'm going to have to arrest you. I have evidence and witness to believe that you were the last person to have met Farzad Mistry and Saahil Kerkar. Let's not make this discussion difficult!" Mili warned.

"Please leave," Morena demanded.

"I'll ask you one last time. Who dropped you home on the 4th of July?"

No reaction. Sound of faint sniffle. Pause and again sniffle. And finally, a long pause. Mili lost patience now! She did not even wait for Morena to recollect herself.

"Rounak told us that you were in the car with him, Farzad, and Saahil on the 4th of July. Is that correct?"

Morena's pupils did not even tilt.

"Just give me a 'yes' or 'no'." Mili asked again. There was no response.

Mili's questions did not make any difference to Morena. She was cold, unfazed. Soon, her mild sniffles were overridden with a major deluge of tears! She cried, and cried her heart out.

Mili remembered Morena's employment form just in time. Drama was her passion and her spontaneous performances had earned her several awards. At Zarine, Morena had directed one-act plays and dance dramas.

"No more questions for today. But we will meet very soon – I promise you!" Mili said authoritatively before leaving Morena's residence.

▼

"You got the hotel details?"

"Yes, I checked with the hotel and with Varun's office. He was in Delhi and returned early morning on the 5th of July. Looks like he was telling the truth," said Anubhav.

"What did you gather about Varun Kulkarni from our first meeting?" Mili asked Anubhav and lit a cigarette.

"No cigarettes in the car, Mili," said Anubhav and switched off the ignition.

"Sorry! Ah…and why on earth did I climb up the car now? My bad! I need to go to Zarine Software. You guys carry on."

"Are you sure? We can drop you there," said Gatha.

"We should split up and work, in the interest of time," Mili replied, happily inhaling a long puff, standing on the pavement opposite Morena's house.

"Hmm, okay."

"Wait a second, people. Anubhav, you didn't tell me what you gathered about Varun."

"I was coming to that Mili. Varun has an impressive personality, is knowledgeable, and has candid views. However, he did not want to talk about Saahil-Morena's friendship. My guess is that he is either fiercely possessive of his wife and is guarding her reputation or..."

"Or what?" asked Mili, taking another drag.

"Or he is guarding a secret," added Anubhav.

"You mean a possible involvement in the murder?"

"Well...that cannot be ruled out. He would have wanted Saahil out of the way. Which husband would like another man so entangled in his wife's life?"

"I agree," said Gatha. "Morena did not recognize me today, which is good. I wouldn't have known how to react."

"You've met her before?" Mili asked, surprised.

"Yes, I met her once. Shravan had sent her to my office. They wanted me to conduct a session on Sexual Harassment at the Workplace – the Legal Implications."

"Whoa! Did you do it?"

"No, I recommended a colleague. I did not like the idea of going to my brother-in-law's office to interact with his employees."

"Good decision. I like it," winked Mili.

A Close Shave

§

7 July 2014

Morena stood by the window in her bedroom, lost in Saahil's thoughts. She did not want to go to the hospital again. They would not let her meet him, she knew. Morena noticed Mili and her teammates standing across the road. She saw a cigarette in Mili's hand. Morena hated people who smoked. She did not get a good feeling. She decided to step out of the house and get some fresh air.

"Should we wait till you get a cab?" asked Gatha.

"You guys carry on. I'll get one," Mili said.

"Okay, see you tomorrow then," said Anubhav.

Cigarette in hand, Mili started walking. The roads were darker than usual, the after-rain effect. There was no taxi on the main road. Mili decided to walk until the next crossing. She chose the by-lane as it promised a shorter route.

The road was empty. Mili heard loud footsteps behind her. She continued walking and as she turned right, she reached a dead-end. Mili frowned at the thought of walking back to the same street again. One should literally avoid short-cuts in life, she told herself.

Mili turned around and started walking back to where she was, five minutes back. She recognized the same footsteps behind her. It was the exact same pace, the same sound, and the same pair of shoes. Mili was alarmed but she did not stop, nor did she turn around. She did not want her follower to run away. She increased her speed and instantly texted Anubhav. *I am being followed.*

Suddenly someone hit the back of Mili's head with a rod, or perhaps a hockey stick. Mili managed to slip her phone in her skirt pocket. The moment she turned around, the whole world around her was black. Somehow, she clutched a branch of the tree in front of her. She was now standing right in front of Morena's house. Mili sensed a black shadow running away. Her vision was blurred. A taxi honked and halted in front of her.

"*Kidhar jaana hai madam?*" the driver asked.

"Yarawada Road," Mili spoke with great difficulty and jumped into the cab. She closed the door and struggled to keep her eyes open.

The cab driver started the meter – Rs. 21.00.

Mili barely managed to read it before she fainted.

"Stop the car," someone yelled from across the road.

The taxi driver panicked for a second and then pulled the brakes. The person on the street hopped in beside the driver.

"Stop or I shall kill you," the person had a hockey stick in hand.

"But…" feebly, the taxi driver tried to speak.

With great force, the passenger hit the driver's head with the stick.

▼

Mili woke up with a creepy feeling. She had no clue as to how she had reached this pungent-smelling room! Her head was reeling, as if she was on a high-speed merry-go-round ride. She was drowsy and the last memory she had was of boarding a cab outside Morena's house. She sensed acute pain on her nose. She gingerly touched it with trembling fingers and freaked out. Her straight long nose that often branded her as snobbish, felt round, hot, and badly bruised. A drop of tear trickled from the corner of her left eye down the swollen nose. Mili stood up, brushed her skirt, loosened the scarf, and tied her hair into a bun. The room had a damp, sweaty smell; there was nothing around – just a dim-lit bulb hanging from the ceiling.

As Mili started to walk, something obstructed her feet. She looked down and shrieked! An unconscious man lay on his chest on a heap of mud next to where she was standing. A steel rod was rolling on the floor beside him. From his grease-stained clothes, the stranger looked like a garage mechanic. Mili took a hurried step backward and looked for an exit door. She was quick to spot the pulled-down shutter. She experienced a shiver down her spine when she realized she had been locked inside an incongruous, empty garage with a messy man. Sweating profusely, she started searching for her mobile phone and purse. All she found was a piece of grimy torn cloth and a bottle of filthy water.

Vulnerable, Mili walked towards the man.

"Heavy hands for a frail physique," she observed as she tied his cold hands with her scarf. The mud made her hands sticky. The nauseating smell reminded her of her police days – most drug-peddling dens she had raided were characterized by a similar odour.

Suddenly, Mili remembered having been hit by a rod. Was it this one? She inspected the rod lying next to the man.

"Did this guy assault me?"

On an impulse, Mili picked up the rod and hit the man in anguish. The body did not move. She stopped, ran towards the locked shutter and knocked vigorously.

Thump Thump Thump.

She screamed, "Hello – *koi hai?* Anyone there?"

There was no response.

Mili was gasping for breath. She came back near the man who was still lying there like a rock. Mili needed to talk. She had to figure a way out of this dungeon before her attackers returned! She decided to untie the man's hands. Next, with all her might, she rolled his body over so that she could see his face. He was covered in blood. The mud had absorbed most of the blood by now. The man was dead. Mili felt eerie. Why am I discovering bodies every other day, she wondered.

She reached for the man's shirt pocket and found a crumpled piece of paper. A bunch of keys dropped on the floor as she unfolded the paper. She made her best effort to read the incorrigible handwriting: 'Girl black dress.' She looked at the man's face again. It was the cab driver.

Mili got a headache. Who killed this taxi driver? Was this a warning for Mili to step back from this case? What was the meaning of 'Girl black dress'? Mili was sure that the person following her was a man. Did the cabbie write the note or did someone else slip it in his pocket to mislead her? How was this connected to Farzad's murder?

Mili looked closely at the cab driver. He had saved her life. Mili closed her eyes and tried to remember how the cabbie had entered the scene. Hit by a rod, she had been trying to keep her balance by holding on to a tree in front of Morena's house. That is where the cabbie saw her and offered a lift.

Mili felt horrible that this man was killed in her presence.

Using the keys that she got from the driver's pocket, Mili opened the garage shutter. She found his driving license. His name was Nirmal Kanitkar. He was only twenty-one years old.

She glanced at her watch. It was 11.00 p.m.

The 7th of July had become a memorable day.

Part - 4
Family Matters

The Kerkars

❦

2009

"Can you please keep that window open? It's suffocating!"

"But Papa, the traffic is disturbing. My guitar will never get tuned."

"If the traffic in Nasik is bothering you, how will you survive in Mumbai?"

"Oh come on Pa. I have lived in Pune already. There is nothing so daunting about Mumbai! It is my dream city. Besides, not everyone gets a job at Zarine Software!"

"What software software all day, Saahil? You must focus on your music. Don't forget – I sacrificed my modelling career in my prime only for you. Don't mess up," added Suhasini Kerkar.

"Arrey Aai, why do you have to repeat the same sob story all the time? I cannot take responsibility for what happened before I was born! I love the IT space! And of course, I cannot live without music." Saahil tried to convince his mother.

"Why not get another job in Pune? It is anyway a better place to stay than the rowdy Mumbai!"

"Please Papa! Six years in Pune – I am done! Now it is time to give Mumbai a chance. You people are treating me like a kid!

I am thirty, for God's sake! Why not convince your younger son to leave Mumbai?"

Decisive and spirited, Saahil Kerkar looked forward to a new, eventful innings in Mumbai.

"I don't understand why you and Amar are not staying together! In our time, we were a dozen siblings living under the same roof. There was no concept of 'cousins' – we were one big family. And look now – Amar is your own flesh and blood," lamented Colonel Kerkar, Saahil's father.

Saahil, who had already done up his studio apartment in Mumbai eyed his father sceptically.

"There's hardly any space in Mumbai, Pa. Besides, soon they will be a three-member team," Saahil laughed. "I have no intention of piling on! And yes, our taste in furniture doesn't match!"

"What will I do with this stubborn fellow," Suhasini mumbled as she headed for the kitchen. "He is taking his study table along this time too!"

Saahil was possessive about his study table and he believed that that little artwork of wood defined him. He had designed it himself and when the carpenter delivered it, Saahil had secretly patted himself. He would fold the table and carry it along wherever he travelled. The table helped him think, write new poems, create new tunes on his synthesizer or serve as a resting place for his overworked guitar. Saahil was proud that his study table gave him undivided attention whenever he needed it. There was no question of not taking his prized possession to Mumbai!

Saahil's younger brother Amar Kerkar was quite a contrast to Saahil. While Saahil enjoyed his carefree life, Amar was more planned and business-minded. He was always looking at ways to increase his income. Amar married early because he wanted his college-going kids to idolize their young, entrepreneurial father.

At twenty-five, he had a decent business – the export of leather bags. He also worked as a part-time insurance agent.

Amar's wife Jyoti was a beautician.

"I know...*I know* Jyoti! Stop repeating yourself."

"What can I do? You had promised to finance me, Amar. Now you say that land will not be yours. Is this some kind of a joke? My business plan, budgets, headcount planning – everything has been done! What do I do without the money?"

"It is not my property and you know that! Papa wants to be a Good Samaritan and Saahil bhai doesn't care."

"If he doesn't care, you can have it! That is what you had told me. Remember?"

"Yes, I did. But that is not working now. Do you get it?"

"Very well then! Better arrange for my delivery at some corporation hospital. Aah," Jyoti feebly replied as the life growing within her suddenly kicked.

"Relax Jyoti! Do not insult me. I do not have to sell a land to get your delivery done! It is our baby and I will give both of you the best. Just sit here for a while. I'll get you some water."

"Aah... Amaaarrrr...wait," squealed Jyoti. "Aaahh... ohhh... I...I guess the water bag has broken. I need to go to the hospital *now*!"

"*Whattt?*...Don't panic okay? I...I am getting the ambulance...I ...I mean, am getting the caarr. Gokul Nursing Home it is."

"But it's expensive Amar!"

"You need not worry about that! Look at you! Bookings have been done. It is just a matter of adjusting the dates, I will handle it. God!! Why am I even telling you all this?"

"I have no idea," Jyoti quivered. "What about the property then, Amar?"

"Will you stop it now? I will talk to Papa again and re-read Dadu's will. Happy? This is not the time!"

"Aah...my baby... ah... can't take it anymore, Amar."

"Hang on." Amar rushed to get the car out while Jyoti waited at the main door.

New arrival

Saahil and his parents reached Mumbai a day after Jyoti and Amar Kerkar welcomed their first born into the world.

"Ooaaah," the bonny newborn greeted Saahil uncle as he entered Jyoti's cabin inside the maternity ward.

"Such an angel," beamed Saahil. "I am going to call her Muskaan."

"Me too," seconded Suhasini, Saahil's mother.

Suhasini Kerkar was reminded of her youth when she saw little Muskaan in Jyoti's arms. The baby's arrival almost coincided with Jyoti's decision to start her own beauty parlour. Jyoti was not keeping well and probably her business plans would be stalled for a while.

Suhasini remembered the day etched in her memory – the day that changed her life forever.

She quietly left the maternity ward and walked towards the garden adjacent to the hospital. On an impulse, Suhasini called up her childhood friend Shobhaa.

"Hello! It's a baby girl," Suhasini informed her, smiling heartily.

"Great, Suhasi. Congratulations!"

"Thanks Shobhaa. I suddenly remembered my modelling days. Couldn't control my emotions – had to call you!"

"Don't think so much, Suhasi. Be happy… you are a granny now."

"I was going to sign the contract with Stellar Fashion House that day, as their fresh new face."

"*Kai zala?* Think of the positive side – you got such life-changing news that day!"

"I had cried so much! I was not ready!"

"But it was happy news, Suhasi. Wasn't it?"

"It was the saddest day of my life Shobhaa. You know that! I lost the contract. I was not supposed to get pregnant. I could have enjoyed motherhood a year later. Why at that point? Why?"

"Come on now. Hasn't life been happy for you? Look at your children – so successful and caring. What more does a mother want?"

"I wasn't a mother then, Shobhaa. I was just a girl who had bagged the biggest opportunity of her life. It slipped from my hands in seconds."

"This is not the time to look back, Suhasi! You still receive modelling and acting offers – why can't you consider facing the camera again?"

"I was barely twenty-one then. I am not interested now, Shobhaa."

"Bury the past, Suhasi. I know you have been through a lot in life. You must look forward."

"I will not let Jyoti compromise her dreams. I will ensure she gets what she wants."

"You sound like a kid," laughed Shobhaa.

"Honestly Shobhaa... I feel so angry when I look at Saahil sometimes. I had even wished him dead once. May be that's why God took away my....." Suhasini couldn't control herself. She burst out crying.

"I knew this was coming! You have to get over this, Suhasi. What is destined will happen. You have to be strong," Shobhaa replied with a lump in her throat.

"I can't forget it, Shobhaa. And Saahil is a constant reminder," Suhasini said, wiping her tears with the long pallu of her sari.

After a pause, Shobhaa said, "Tell me about your grand-daughter."

"Oh, she is an angel!" Finally, Suhasini was smiling again.

▼

Colonel (Retired) Vinayak Damodar Kerkar was ecstatic at the birth of his first grandchild. For a person used to proudly sharing stories from his army days, this was a new subject and he just could not stop raving about Muskaan.

"I am going to send her to the best school in India."

"Papa, where is the money?" added Amar. "The land is anyway not going to be sold!"

"Shut up, Amar! How shameless you are! At least today do not talk about the property."

Forthright and idealistic, Colonel Kerkar had always put country before self.

"Had at least one of them joined the Indian Army, he would be leading a disciplined life today!" he complained while sipping a quiet evening tea at the hospital cafeteria.

"Did I ever stop them?" Suhasini retorted.

"No, but you pestered Saahil to try modelling, and then singing!"

"Would you have fallen for me thirty-five years ago had I not been crowned the May Ball Queen?"

Colonel would get all starry-eyed every time Suhasini said this.

Daughter of Brigadier Rawat, Suhasini, fondly known as Suhasi, was a real beauty. Colonel Kerkar (then Lieutenant) was instantly bowled over by her elegance. Soon they fell in love and tied the knot within a year. Their love story was quite a hit in the 1970s.

Each time Colonel Kerkar looked at Amar, he regretted not having spent enough time with him. The family had travelled across different cities in India, never settling down anywhere for more than three to four years. The only exception was the 1990s, when they spent a good seven years in Nasik.

After retirement, Colonel and his wife decided to make the ancestral home at Nasik their permanent residence.

The Nasik property

Whenever the topic of the Nasik property came up, Saahil would ignore it.

"Please Papa, don't start it now."

"But Saahil, if we don't talk about it now, you might lose money!"

"I really don't care, Papa. I do not even have the time to think about it now. If you need the money, please sell it. I will sign wherever needed."

"How dare you speak to your father like that, Saahil?" Suhasini screamed. "Apologize right now!"

Colonel Kerkar's face turned red instantly. He did not want to speak to Saahil after that.

The day after Muskaan's birth was when they had the last conversation about the Nasik land in the Kerkar household. Incidentally, that was also the last proper father-son conversation between Saahil and Colonel Kerkar.

"I am sorry, Papa."

Colonel left the room. He felt humiliated by his son.

Later, Colonel confided in his wife. "He will have to pay for it one day. When I served my country, I made many sacrifices for my family. But my sons do not have the maturity to understand or even respect that! Is money more important than relationships? We must secure whatever is left of our future, Suhas. Our sons won't even care!"

"I'm sure it is not like that Vinayak. They love us."

The Daves

❧

Little girlie chubby cheeks
Come to Mama and plant a kiss
Precious angel grow up soon
Be happy-go-lucky and reach for the moon

These lines had been penned by Morena Dave's mother to describe a beautiful picture of three-year-old Morena. In that picture, Morena's curly locks had gone haywire but she had a divine smile on her face. She was wearing a tiny red frock and held a little pup in her arms. They were both equally dirty with mud on their hands and faces. This picture was Morena's mom, Minakshi Dave's favourite.

The elder of two siblings, Morena loved animals, especially dogs. She dreamed of building a pet burial ground one day.

2008

"Is it critical?" Minakshi Dave asked her husband before switching off the night lamp.

"It is a police case now," Dr Jaywant Dave replied, anxiety robbing him of a good night's sleep.

"Relax!" assured Minakshi. "Get some sleep now."

Minakshi was accustomed to the highs and lows in Dr Dave's life – the price one pays for being married to a doctor. Among the topmost heart specialists in the country, Dr Dave lived with his family in Pune, Maharashtra. He was also a visiting faculty at one of the premier medical research institutes in the city.

Apart from providing steadiness in his life, Minakshi Dave worked at an NGO. Both her daughters Morena and Divya had inherited her calm and compassionate nature.

Divya, who was four years younger and more self-conscious than Morena, aspired to be a doctor, like her dad. By the time she was twelve, Divya knew more about medicines than most adults with a non-medical background did. She had learnt the art of giving injections painlessly, simply by observing her father. Early in life, she knew she wanted to be an oncologist.

When Varun Kulkarni met Morena Dave

Varun was introduced to Morena at a common friend's party in 2009. He was in Pune at that time for a short-term assignment. He liked Morena instantly and sensed that she reciprocated the feeling. After chancing upon each other a few more times here and there, they exchanged phone numbers. Soon, they became friends.

Morena and Varun realized that they needed to live in the same city in order to spend more time with each other. Marriage seemed a viable option.

They tied the knot in January 2010 and the following month, Morena joined Zarine Software in Mumbai.

Morena loved pampering Varun, buying him his choicest books and treating him at his favourite restaurants. More than anything, Morena loved fulfilling Varun's childlike wishes.

One day Varun wanted to go skating in a children's skating area. Obviously, the authorities would not allow him. Morena confidently entered the venue, hand-in-hand with her husband. Varun had his skates on. Morena suddenly flung her purse with great force so that it landed in the middle of the rink.

"Oh my god...Someone fetch my purse, please."

At that hour, the rink was empty and only the cleaners were around. Nobody could get into the main rink without skates.

"Varun, please help me get my purse," Morena demanded.

"Here I go," and whoosh, Varun was on the skating ground.

"Oh sir, this is against the rules here. Please get off immediately," the security guard shouted.

"The gentleman is only helping me get my purse back. What is the problem?" asked Morena.

"Madam, this zone is only for kids. The floor will get damaged if adults skate here."

"Well, you see this is an emergency. Besides, do you have it in writing anywhere that adults should not step on the skating rink? I don't see it anywhere," said Morena.

"It is not written. But everyone knows the rules."

Morena kept the security person engaged in mindless conversations while Varun continued to skate freely.

Once back, Varun was smiling ear to ear.

"Let's go."

The security guard asked them to see the manager. They left the manager's office in the next five minutes, thanks to Morena's people skills.

"Hats off to you! You made it happen, Morena!" cheered Varun.

The next day, the skating arena had a big board displayed at the counter:

'Only for children between 6-16 years. Trespassers will be fined Rs 500/.'

The scent of Mumbai

There was a certain scent about Mumbai, which made Morena feel as though she belonged there. However, the best part was that her parents were just three hours away!

When Morena joined Zarine Software, Rounak was the first person she befriended. Slowly she mingled with the others too.

Morena chanced upon Saahil at the office cafeteria when he was playing the guitar. She loved his voice instantly.

Later that day over lunch, Rounak introduced Morena and Saahil.

Over the next few weeks, Mumbai became dearer to Morena, thanks to Saahil. They just couldn't stop talking to each other!

Morena had found her first friend in Mumbai – Saahil Kerkar.

Part - 5
The Finale
Mumbai, July 2014

Friend or Foe

Mili Ray's home

9.00 a.m.
8 July 2014

Mili was still recuperating from the previous night's ghastly strike. Her head was badly swollen and the headache was killing her. Two cups of strong cappuccino and three cigarettes had not helped. She didn't even have any strength to bite into a juicy apple, her favourite remedy for any ailment.

Gatha was by her side like a motherly friend, applying ice bags on her head. Though seething with anger, she sported a pretentious smile and avoided speaking.

However, Anubhav was furiously pacing up and down the room. Only if Mili's sms had been delivered to him the previous evening!

"What?" Mili snorted, looking quizzically at Anubhav.

"I am going to rip him apart, I swear," Anubhav said, pursing his lips.

The weather was pleasant. The mild drizzle in the morning had been followed by an abundance of fresh air that filled Mili's room. However, that did nothing to cool down Anubhav and Gatha's boiling temper.

"Forget about my injury," Mili said sternly, calling out to her associates. "The painful truth is that we have a second murder now!"

Mili pointed to her mobile phone on the chair opposite her bed. Gatha reached for the ringing phone and handed it to Mili who looked desperate to answer the call.

"Thank you, Dr Shah! I will be there in half an hour." Mili disconnected the phone and sprang up from her bed.

She sounded boisterous when she announced, "Guys, we need to go to the hospital right now. Saahil Kerkar has made it!"

"Whoa! Now all our problems will end," said Gatha, rather seriously.

"Or begin," said Mili.

"Mili – you need to rest. Gatha and I shall go to the hospital."

"Are you kidding me?" Mili said, limping towards her wardrobe.

"Saahil Kerkar has gained consciousness. He will *speak* to the police. I am on the right track and someone does not like it. I did sense that someone was stalking me."

"Okay fine," Gatha said in a pacifying tone almost immediately, sensing the dormant anger in Mili's voice.

"This Zarine connection in these murders is very interesting. Don't you think?" Mili stated as she noticed the newspaper headlines staring at her.

"Two employees are attacked on the same day. One of them – Farzad Mistry, dies; the other – Saahil Kerkar, miraculously springs back to life after three days. Both of them were travelling together on the night of their attack. Now, a third person – Nirmal Kanitkar is probably attacked in front of Morena Dave's house, another Zarine employee!"

"You are a common factor in two of these attacks too Mili," Anubhav added, sounding oddly accurate.

"You found Saahil inside the car. Again, you chanced upon the dead body of Nirmal. Some coward attacked you, even though you have no connection with Zarine Software," reflected Anubhav.

Mili nodded her affirmation.

"Let us go meet Saahil Kerkar now. It is his birthday today."

▼

Saahil had been moved from the ICU to the Recovery Unit and was allowed minimal visitors, only when approved by the police. His single-bed room was spacious and comfortable. The window by his bedside overlooked the sea and if left open, transported the music of the sea waves back into the room, making the ambience tranquil. However, Saahil had kept the window closed and covered it with the dark-blue hospital curtains.

When Mili and her team reached the hospital, ACP Trehan was waiting outside Saahil's room.

"Saahil is meeting his family," he said before Anubhav could knock on the door.

"Is Dr Shah inside too?" Mili asked.

"Yes. By the way, did you notice the crowd at the reception?" Trehan whispered.

"Yup, I spotted Vikrant Sharma, Shravan Trivedi, Rounak, and Sheena along with a few others, who are probably Zarine Software employees."

"I saw Cyril Mistry too, Farzad's father. Feel really sorry for him," Gatha added, softly.

"Yes, he has been sitting at that corner for quite some time," responded Trehan.

"I don't understand why the media is here though," Mili said, gritting her teeth in frustration.

"We won't allow them to meet Saahil," Trehan confirmed.

Morena Dave and Varun Kulkarni were conspicuous by their absence.

Mili meets Saahil

10.15 a.m.
8 July 2014

"You can speak to him now," Dr Shah told Mili and ACP Trehan as he stepped out of Saahil's room.

Amar Kerkar waved at Mili as he headed towards the corridor with his father.

"Did he share anything with you, doctor?" asked Mili, once the family members went out of sight.

"He does not remember eating the prawns! He cannot stand the sight of prawns, let alone eating them. Saahil has no clue as to how or when his wrist was slit," Dr Shah replied.

"Thanks doctor," said Mili and tapped on Saahil's door.

Saahil was speaking to his mother Suhasini, who had pulled her chair right beside Saahil's bed. She was gently petting Saahil's forehead when Mili and Trehan entered.

"Okay Aai, I will talk to you later," Saahil said moving her hand slowly as he noticed Trehan and Mili walk towards him.

"Happy birthday, Saahil! How are you feeling today?" Mili greeted Saahil and realized that his infectious smile had rubbed on her. His face was not swollen any longer. Mild blemishes were playing truant with his cheeks and nose, but they failed to impair the freshness of his overall physical appearance. There was a kindness in his eyes and a mischief in his smile, despite his ill health.

"Thank you ma'am," said Saahil, trying to sit up on his bed. "You saved my life and I will be ever grateful to you. I…I cannot believe that I am meeting you in person. I am a huge fan," Saahil confessed, the smile not leaving his unreasonably attractive face for even a moment.

A tad embarrassed, Mili smiled, "Meet ACP Purab Trehan. He is leading this case."

Trehan threw a quick, startled glance at Mili before refocusing on Saahil. She had never said 'Purab' before. It was strangely soothing to his ears.

"Many happy returns of the day, Saahil! We are very sorry about your colleague, Farzad," said Trehan.

Mili gave a piercing look to Trehan. His face turned red.

"Farzad? What happened to him?" Saahil asked impatiently. "Tell me what happened to him. Is he okay?"

The damage had been done. Mili regretted not having briefed Trehan before meeting Saahil. She had not intended to bombard Saahil with an overdose of information.

Mili took a deep breath and said, "We lost him, Saahil."

"What are you saying? He…he…I dropped him at the station," Saahil held his head with both hands. "Where is Rounak? Is he okay? I dropped them together."

"Rounak is fine. He is waiting downstairs, along with your other colleagues. But we will talk about that later. First, we want to hear you out," Mili said, keeping her hand over Saahil's.

"I didn't think I would bring this up. But now I have to. I have to get justice for Farzad's family," said Saahil, his voice choking.

"Detective, please leave," said Suhasini, who had been quietly standing by the window so long.

"You are right, Mrs Kerkar! We will talk later Saahil," Mili stated, looking at Saahil's disturbed demeanour.

"I want to give my statement right now. What do you want to know?" Saahil asked.

"What happened on the evening of the 4th of July?"

Mili was dying for a smoke. But this was not the time.

The Last Meeting

❦

The fateful evening of 4th July 2014

At office, Morena had an eerie feeling all day that Saahil wanted to speak to her. She looked at him through the corner of her eye quite a few times and the last time she cast a glance, their eyes met. In that split second, Morena felt a knot in her stomach. She looked away immediately and realized that Saahil had been staring at her with pensive eyes. She dared not look back for she was afraid she would cry. He would not like it. He hated it when she got emotional and that made her miserable.

The rains were boisterous and their intensity increased as the clouds roared. The Zarine Corporate Communications team made an announcement about the precarious weather conditions. Most people were leaving office.

At around 5.00 p.m., Morena decided that it was the most opportune moment to leave. However, she noticed Saahil leaving office. His voice carried to her.

"Anyone interested in a lift? I can accommodate three people comfortably."

Morena turned a deaf ear and pretended to focus on her laptop. Her heart was beating fast. What is taking him so long to leave? she thought, irritated.

As he was out of the QI team facility, Morena packed her bag at rocket speed.

While leaving office, Morena bumped into Saahil again, outside the washroom. She consciously avoided looking at him this time and hurriedly started towards the elevator. She could hear her thumping heartbeat and dreaded making eye contact with Saahil Kerkar again.

▼

At around 5.15 p.m., Morena was stranded at the bus stop outside office. Despite multiple efforts, she had not been able to convince any auto-rickshaw or taxi to drive her home. The rains had entangled the city in the worst way possible. The buses looked like enraged beehives – she did not intend to board one. She overheard other people around expressing concern over the cancelled trains. With an anxiety-smitten face, Morena decided to give herself ten more minutes at the bus stand.

Suddenly, like a Bollywood movie, Saahil came along in his olive-green SUV and stopped in front of the bus stop. He had two others accompanying him – Rounak Arora and an unknown colleague. Morena looked away. Saahil pulled down the window.

"Hey, can I drop you somewhere?" Saahil said nervously, clearing his throat.

"No thanks, I...I will manage," Morena struggled with her speech.

"Err...you will not get anything here today. I shall drop you home," Saahil forced himself to say.

There was no way he was leaving her alone in this weather. He did not care if their friendship had gone to the dogs.

Rounak quickly got off the car and opened the front door for Morena to hop in beside Saahil.

"Please, Morena, let's not waste any more time. We all have to go home. Our families are worried. You know Saahil bhai will not leave without you. So please come with us," pleaded Rounak.

"Oh, am sorry. Thanks." Morena got into the car reluctantly.

Once she was seated, Rounak said, "By the way, this is Farzad."

Morena turned her face and glanced at the handsome man seated beside Rounak.

She smiled.

"I know you – Morena, right?"

Morena smiled at Farzad again and then turned around to wear her seatbelt.

One fleeting look at Saahil and she recollected their last conversation over the phone. It had been so humiliating! She hated herself for taking a lift from him.

Saahil was in a very gauche situation too. To ease his nerves, he started fiddling with the radio. The FM channel that was playing was paused. The sound of the hard-hitting rains almost pierced through the car roof. It was scary!

To resume the music, Saahil hastily pressed the CD/USB mode instead of FM. Before he could change it back, the music started playing.

'*Today was a fairytale*
Today was a fairytale, you were the prince
I used to be a damsel in distress
You took me by the hand, and you picked me up at six
Today was a fairytale, today was a fairytale…'

Morena swallowed and then cleared her throat. Saahil was embarrassed and tried avoiding any distraction. This was Morena's favourite soundtrack and earlier, whenever Saahil would drop her home, Morena would play that CD in his car. Didn't matter even if they were listening to the same song every day!

"The turn from the next right, Saahil bhai. Yes, that is it. I will get down here. Thanks." Saahil and Morena gave half-smiles as Rounak got off.

"I'll join Rounak. You wouldn't need to take a detour, Saahil," said Farzad.

"You sure?" Saahil asked.

"Absolutely," Farzad replied as he stepped out of the car. "Thanks buddy. See you around."

After a while, Morena turned back for a quick glimpse of the empty seats. She did not like the feeling. Without uttering a word, she tried to unlock the door. It was raining heavily and Saahil had just picked up speed. Morena's movement took him by surprise.

"Hey wait, don't do that!"

"Stop the car, I need to get off."

"Don't be mad! It's raining like crazy."

On an impulse, Saahil gripped Morena's wrist with his left hand. Shocked, Morena turned towards him. Braving the rains and low visibility, Saahil continued driving with one hand. Morena tried her best to free herself. Saahil's grasp became tighter now. Morena's hand started hurting and she squealed. Soon, Saahil felt a warm teardrop on his hand. A tree fell on the road right in front of his car and blocked the road. Saahil managed to pull the brakes on time!

Saahil had no clue which route to take now. Besides, he felt helpless when Morena cried.

With great difficulty, Saahil took a 'U' turn and entered the adjacent by-lane. There was thick traffic all around and the by-lane was perhaps the shortest route to the highway. The road was pitch dark and waterlogged. As the car meandered through the pothole-filled road, Morena kept crying, adding to the intensity of the rains. The ground clearance of Saahil's car was good, so the water had still not got into the car.

Saahil could not take it anymore. In the middle of the water-filled, black road, he abruptly pulled the brakes. Morena, who had removed her seat belt already, was pushed forward due to the unforeseen jolt and to balance herself, she involuntarily clutched Saahil's shirt.

When she tried to collect herself, Saahil pulled her closer. He clasped her palms and put her head on his shoulder. Morena did not resist.

Saahil wiped off the tears from her cheek and kissed her forehead. He did not know why he was doing this when he hated her! Morena snuggled closer.

Saahil stroked her hair gently and patted her head. Then he came back to what he loved doing the most – pulling her cheeks. Her pink cheeks grew red and she blushed. He loved her chubby cheeks and today he suddenly realized how tender Morena was. Morena put her hands round his neck and hugged him. They looked at each other and relived glimpses of their good old times.

At last, Saahil broke the silence, "Would you sing two lines for me?"

"*Lag ja galey…*" Morena sang soulfully. Saahil secretly switched on the 'record' mode on his cell, closed his eyes, and lent a patient ear to the soothing melody of her voice. He missed his guitar!

"Your turn now," Morena said after she completed her song.

"My pleasure ma'am," added Saahil and started singing the romantic Hemant Kumar number "*Na tum hamey jaano…*"

Saahil's voice was intoxicating. Once the poignant rendition was over, they realized it was time to go home. The rains had subsided. This was the best time to leave.

As they buckled up, Morena wondered if she would ever be able to erase the bitter memories. Saahil's ego, his humiliating words, and his uncouth behaviour for months – they pricked her to no end.

He would have to pay for it. She just knew it.

Saahil's Statement

10.30 a.m.
8 July 2014

With Dr Shah's permission, ACP Trehan and Mili Ray got ready to record Saahil's statement. A psychologist and Dr Shah were the only other people present in Saahil's room. Saahil's family waited outside along with Anubhav and Gatha. Amar decided to take his parents to the hospital cafeteria.

Back in the room, Saahil requested Trehan, who was leaning on the windowsill, to pull the curtains.

"I can't bear the sunlight."

Mili was amused. It was a gloomy day and the sun had hardly peeped into Saahil's room.

Saahil looked disturbed ever since he had learned about Farzad.

Mili reiterated, "What happened on the 4th of July, Saahil? Tell us everything you remember."

Saahil who was half-sitting on the hospital bed with his legs stretched over the blanket, unmindfully combed a hand through his hair and said, "Yes, I will have to tell you now."

All eyes were fixed on Saahil.

"The 4th of July – of course, I remember. I didn't have much work and thought of leaving office early. But the rain spoiled all my plans. I decided to head home anyway, at around 5.00 p.m. I had my car so I offered to drop Rounak and Farzad to the railway station." Saahil paused for a moment.

"We know," chipped in Mili. "Then?"

"It was raining heavily, very heavily in fact. I somehow managed to drive out of office. Farzad noticed Morena, our colleague, waiting at the bus stand opposite the Zarine building. So we asked her to join us. Traffic was terrible. I dropped the boys at the station. Since Morena and I live close by, I decided to drop her home. We were stuck in traffic for almost three hours, or more. My legs were aching badly.

"After a while, Morena's phone rang and she asked me to stop the car. She got down."

"Which place was this and why did she get off?" Trehan asked, puzzled.

"She said someone was going to pick her up from the Right Food restaurant near the highway. I didn't ask for details. I dropped her there," Saahil said, almost letting the words run out of his mouth, all at once.

"I continued driving towards home. I was too tired by then. After more than half-an-hour, as I was crossing a bus stop near my house, I met Morena again."

"*What?*" Mili asked, exasperated.

"Yes, I was shocked too," Saahil replied coolly. "I pulled over and she hopped in. I felt weird and so didn't ask her anything."

"Didn't she tell you how she reached there?" asked Trehan.

"Nope. She looked nervous though. She was dressed differently too," added Saahil.

"Differently?"

"She was wearing a black gown, I think; could be dark blue too. I freaked out!"

"Didn't you ask her about the dress change?"

"No, I just wanted to go home."

"What time was this, when you offered her a lift for the second time?" Mili asked.

"It was 10.00 p.m. My watch beeped as I usually set a reminder to watch my favourite TV show."

"Why was Morena standing at the bus stop when she could have walked home?"

"I did not ask her that. I was dying to go home. I had even cancelled my date! My mind was not working," Saahil replied.

"Yes, we know about Neha."

"Is...is she okay?"

"Neha is fine," replied ACP Trehan. "Please continue."

"Morena asked me for Farzad's number. She wanted him on her team for the next project. I shared his number. Then she wanted his address. I was startled!"

"Did you share his address too?"

"I only had a vague idea about where he lived. So I couldn't help her with that!" Saahil clearly stated.

"Did she call him from her cell?" ACP Trehan asked.

"No, she was facing some issue with her phone," replied Saahil. "She wrote down his number on a piece of paper."

"Do you know which project she was considering him for? As I understand, Farzad's skill-set is very different from what you and Morena do. Right?" asked Mili.

"Yes, but I do not know the details of her project," Saahil stated.

"And then?"

"Morena was generally asking me about Farzad. Then she suddenly asked me if Farzad liked partying! I thought that was weird," said Saahil, and reached for his glass of water.

"Why weird? Didn't Farzad like to hang out with friends?" Mili probed.

"It was weird because Morena was asking that question," responded Saahil. "Besides, I don't know Farzad very well. Rounak is his best friend. According to Rounak, Farzad wasn't into socializing. He is...I mean...he was a teetotaller."

"Did you share that with Morena?" Mili asked Saahil.

"No."

"I see. What happened next?"

"I continued driving at snail's pace due to the slow moving traffic. Morena wasn't talking anymore."

"So this time you were planning to drop her home, right?"

"Yes, but that did not happen," Saahil said in a fierce tone. "I felt a sting on my arm...I think it was a syringe. I looked at Morena, aghast. She scratched my face with her overgrown, pointed finger-nails, Saahil blurted out and covered his face for a second.

Dr Shah looked at the screen beside Saahil. His blood pressure was fluctuating.

"You can stop if you want, Saahil," the doctor said.

"I am fine doctor. I have to get this out of my system. It has been killing me."

"She was wearing dark blue nail paint," Saahil continued excitedly. "I will never forget those nails; it was as if a wild cat had pounced upon me, the sharp claws distorting my face!"

Mili remembered that nail paint. During her visit to Morena's house, Mili just couldn't miss the devilish nail polish each time Morena sneezed into her handkerchief.

"I lost control of the steering," said Saahil. "I don't know what happened after that. I must have fainted. When I woke up, I found myself here, at this hospital."

"So you had not attempted suicide that night, I assume," Mili asked Saahil, throwing a side-glance at ACP Trehan.

"Of course not!" Saahil protested vehemently. "*Never!*"

"Do you remember what you had eaten that night, Saahil?" Trehan asked sheepishly, trying to avoid further embarrassment.

"I did not have time for dinner that night. If you are asking me about the prawns, I hadn't eaten them. I am allergic."

"Do you always carry anti-allergy pills?"

"Huh! No, why would I?"

"Hmm. Anything else you want to share?" inquired ACP Trehan.

"I wouldn't have given Morena's name. She used to be a friend. But when you told me about Farzad, I decided to state the truth – no matter how painful it is."

"So are you saying that Morena injected the drug on your arm, force-fed you with prawns, and then slit your wrist?" asked ACP Trehan.

"I am only saying that she pierced a needle on my arm. What took place after that I am not aware of."

"What do you think could be her motive to attack you or kill Farzad?" Mili queried anxiously.

"I don't know. It is shocking that she would do this to Farzad because they barely knew each other," added Saahil. "She had a thing for good-looking men and Farzad was reasonably handsome. I don't know if that helps."

"It does. Any information is useful," said Mili. "Why do you think she attacked you?"

"No clue. We used to be good friends once upon a time. Then one fine day, she decided to stop talking to me. I didn't know she was so moody, till that day."

"Why did she do that?" Mili asked.

"She felt that our friendship was becoming formal. Perhaps, she was bored," Saahil said curtly.

"And when exactly did you guys stop talking to each other?"

"Well, she ended the friendship in February this year, on 21st February to be precise. I never contacted her after that. She apologized last month and wanted to be friends again. I was not interested. Friendship cannot depend upon someone's whims," Saahil retorted.

"But friends can have misunderstandings. That is normal," said Mili.

"I do not need such friends who measure conversations and have such silly expectations from me!"

"What does that mean?" asked Trehan.

"Just because we did not talk for a while, she ended the friendship. That is just unacceptable. I am better off minus such troublemakers in my life," Saahil said ruthlessly.

"I understand. Thank you for your cooperation, Saahil. Please take care and get well soon," said Mili and shook hands with him.

"Thank you ma'am. It is an honour meeting you. I already feel better." Saahil smiled.

"We will get back to you if needed," added ACP Trehan.

As soon as Mili and Trehan came out of Saahil's room, the journalists mobbed them. Mili whispered to Trehan not to reveal anything about Saahil's statement. Trehan complied.

As they walked past the media personnel, Mili heard familiar footsteps behind her.

Thump. And then thump thump. And then thump again. The pace, the timing of the foot landing on the ground – she knew the sound well. Despite being surrounded by so many people, Mili couldn't be wrong about the sound of these footsteps. Yes, it was the same person – her stalker on the 7th of July.

Mili turned around immediately, her eyes burning in anger. All she could see was a bunch of reporters. If she took a step towards them, they would take three, microphones in tow.

There was no way she could swim through the crowd. Perhaps, her attacker had fled, or was standing camouflaged among the multitude of cameras.

"We have to take Morena into custody immediately," Mili told Trehan once they were out of the hospital.

Morena's home

12.30 p.m.
8 July 2014

Mili did not waste a single minute after recording Saahil's statement. Along with ACP Trehan and Gatha, she went to Morena Dave's house at around 12.30 p.m.

Varun answered the door.

"Mr Varun Kulkarni, your wife Morena Dave is under arrest for the murder of Farzad Mistry and the murder attempt on Saahil Kerkar. She is also the prime suspect for the murder of Nirmal Kanitkar," ACP Trehan stated.

"What are you saying? Who is Nirmal Kanitkar now?" Varun protested.

"Nirmal is the taxi driver who was attacked in front of your house last evening. He died later," replied ACP Trehan.

"Which criminal would commit a murder in front of his own house, Inspector?" chided Varun.

"Saahil Kerkar has identified Morena Dave as his attacker," said Mili. "Call her now."

"He is a liar," Varun said, furiously.

"Morena was the last person to meet Saahil Kerkar and Farzad Mistry on the night of 4th July. She has to come with us right now."

"Priya, can you please listen to what detective Ray is saying?" Varun turned around and called someone.

"Hi, I am Priya Shergill, Morena's lawyer. Do you have an arrest warrant, Inspector?" Priya asked ACP Trehan. "A private detective who has been a cop cannot assume that she still has the authority to arrest someone," she added, sharply looking at Mili.

"Hello Priya!"

"Gatha? You are representing Saahil Kerkar?" Priya Shergill asked.

"Err...yes. We will come back with the papers," Gatha responded, rather surprised to see her colleague Priya at Morena's house.

"Wait, wait!" Morena came running to the door. "How is Saahil? Is he able to speak? Can I meet him?" she asked, looking intently at Mili. She looked ill.

Mili grabbed this opportunity to step in and ask, "Morena, did Saahil drop you home on 4th July?"

"Yes," Morena said without any strain on her face.

"Are you sure he dropped you *home*?"

"Saahil dropped me home. He never left me alone... *never!*"

Mili said, "We found your fingerprints on the steering. Saahil's phone has a song recorded in your voice at 8.15 p.m. How long were you two together on the evening of 4th July?"

Morena did not say anything.

"Did you ask Saahil for Farzad's number?"

"No, why should I? Why do you keep asking me about this Farzad?" Morena shouted back.

"Your friend Saahil Kerkar has given us his official police statement today morning. He says, you tried to kill him," ACP Trehan stated, blankly.

"My client will not take any questions at this moment," Morena's lawyer Priya interrupted.

"No wait, I want to hear this. Saahil said I tried to kill him?" Morena asked, disbelief written all over her face.

"He also said that you might have been involved in Farzad Mistry's murder."

"Saahil said that?" Morena asked, horrified.

"That horrible man," Varun screamed. "He always wanted to harm my wife. He is a liar."

"No wait, Varun. Saahil is right. You can arrest me," Morena said calmly. "But I did not kill Farzad."

"So you admit that you attacked Saahil on the night of the 4th of July?"asked Mili.

"My client is not in any mental condition to speak. Please leave, otherwise I will have to file a harassment case against you."

"Fair enough! I will soon be back with the arrest warrant," ACP Trehan said.

"I will have the anticipatory bail papers ready by then," Priya Shergill contended.

After ACP Trehan, Mili, and Gatha left, Varun sat down on the sofa, feeling dejected.

"Is there anything else you want to share with me, Morena?" Priya asked.

"No Priya. I need some time by myself. Thank you for your help."

"Sure, take care. I shall leave then," Priya added.

"Varun, you should also leave for office. You're already late."

"I will call Rashi. I don't want you to stay alone."

"I will be fine."

Mili's adventure

1.00 p.m.
8 July 2014
Once out of Morena's building, Mili had something going on in her head.

"You guys carry on. I will join you in some time."

"Not this time!" said Gatha. "I am not leaving without you!"

Mili caught ACP Trehan's impromptu smirk at Gatha's spontaneous comment.

"ACP Trehan is with me," she said sarcastically. "You guys carry on!"

Gatha and Anubhav stared at Mili for a while and then left.

"What's the plan detective?" Trehan asked, laughing.

"Shhhh!" Mili said, with a finger on her lips, as she noticed Priya Shergill leaving Morena's house.

Then she turned to Trehan and said, "Can you follow up on the call records for me? I need some time alone now."

"I thought as much." Trehan left almost immediately.

Mili took the elevator and as she reached the seventh floor, she stepped out and tiptoed towards Morena's apartment. She remembered that Varun was home. She jumped back into the elevator and climbed to the terrace. Then she walked towards the emergency exit and walked down to Morena's floor. The main door was flung open. Mili swiftly ran to the refuge area opposite Morena's apartment. A dance class was in progress. Mili watched the kids rehearse while snooping at Morena's balcony. An empty hammock was swinging negligibly, trying to match the tempo of the flimsy breeze.

After a while, Mili resurfaced from her hideout. The main door of Morena's apartment was closed now. Mili softly planted her ear on the door. Brisk footsteps were making way towards the door. Mili sprinted back to the refuge area in the nick of time.

She heard the door unlock. Click.

"Give me a call and if need be, I can come down tomorrow," a female voice said. Soon after, the door was closed. Thud.

Mili returned to the front of Morena's flat and then ran down the stairs.

When she reached the ground floor, Mili saw a woman wearing a deep-blue South Indian silk sari walking towards a car.

"Excuse me," Mili called out.

The woman turned around.

"My God! Miliii... really?" the woman screamed.

Mili forgot what she wanted to say. She looked at the woman standing in front of her, astonished! Then she ran towards the woman and they hugged.

Death Beckons

❦

4.00 p.m.
8 July 2014

Morena was sitting in her favourite corner, gazing out of the balcony into the open greens. She reminisced how she and Saahil would go for evening walks after office only to talk to each other about nothing important.

"Friends should never get separated by a pole. Let's walk on the same side," Morena would say if they had to pass by a pole or lamppost during these leisurely walks. Saahil would happily oblige.

Morena was absorbed in her thoughts when reality dawned upon her. Saahil was sending her to jail.

As Morena cupped her chin with both hands and looked at the gulmohar tree, she sensed a furore. The crows and pigeons were restlessly flying around from one branch to another. Morena got the feeling that they were asking for help. She kept inspecting the tree as closely as she could, until she found the branch that had triggered the uproar. A crow sitting on that branch was fluttering its left wing impatiently. Through the grills of her balcony, Morena tried widening her eyes the maximum she could and kept her head still. The crow's wing was stuck in a node of the tree. The wing was forced open and the little creature was unable to free itself from this trap. Morena wanted to help, knowing very well that she would not be able to climb up that tree! And, even if she did, why would the crow allow her to get close?

Morena felt claustrophobic. She could relate to the pain the crow was experiencing. Her plight was no better!

"Should I call the People Rescuers?" she thought.

Within minutes, the frantic twittering of the birds stopped, pigeons were back to where they fit best in Mumbai – balconies of residential homes. The crows were no longer hovering around the branch of that tree. Morena was curious to find out about the rescue operation. The branch where the trapped crow was perched was empty. On the adjacent branch, she spotted two crows. One of them was scratching his left wing and the other was rubbing her nose against the partner's injured wing. Morena easily identified the braveheart. She felt lighter. Morena hated to see animals in pain.

The determination with which the crow had freed himself with encouragement from friends was exemplary. Giving up had not been an option! Morena had never imagined that Saahil would give up on her.

The cuckoo clock in Morena's drawing room announced that it was 6.00 p.m. Morena loved the beauty that she had picked up from Geneva. She had presented another exact same cuckoo clock to Saahil. It used to adorn the bright blue wall of his studio apartment. At least last year it did. Morena had not been to Saahil's house this year.

Ting Tong.

Morena peeped out of the balcony to look at the clock again. How could Varun return so soon, when he had left after twelve? Or was the detective back with her arrest warrant?

Morena was panicky. The doorbell rang again.

Morena realized she had to answer the door.

The bell rang for the third time. A bit longer this time.

Morena dragged herself to the main door. She prayed that it was someone else.

The doorbell rang again.

Morena wiped her tears and made a frail attempt not to look devastated as she approached the door. She took her own time to answer, hoping against hope that the visitor would get tired of waiting and leave.

Disgusted, Morena finally opened the door, a good two minutes after the last ring.

"Yes?" Morena unwillingly asked the person standing in front of her, dressed in black.

"Just thought I would come around and meet you," smiled the visitor adding, "Did I disturb you?"

Finally, Morena was able to see the face of her visitor. She stared in awe, unable to speak.

"So how's work going? You not joining office soon, Morena?"

Morena had lost her voice; she just could not take her eyes off the visitor.

"I know, Mornie, you are upset about Saahil. But you ought to be stronger. Life has to go on. Okay?"

Morena hated the visitor addressing her as Mornie. But she didn't protest.

"Look what I got for you. This will make you feel better."

The visitor handed a book to Morena. "I know just how much you love reading!"

Morena loved the smell of books, especially that of old books and notebooks created from handmade paper. A smile made its way from the corner of her lips and lit up her face.

"Ah, how lovely you look when you smile. I don't want you to get into your depressive mode again. Just feel the magic," insisted the guest and held the book open for Morena.

Morena balanced the book evenly on her palms. It was titled *The Book of Happiness*. The author was M.S. Wise. She had not heard that name before. The writing style was Victorian; the paper handmade. It looked like one of those fancy fairytale storybooks. Morena felt that the book had been tailor-made for her.

Taking advantage of the distracted Morena, the visitor stepped inside the house.

Morena felt hypnotized by the smell of the book. It was so calming. She felt sleepy. She slowly spread her left palm over the pages, closed her eyes, took a deep breath and drew her face closer to the book. She had forgotten that there was a stranger in the house.

"Closer, Mornie. Enjoy yourself till I go fetch myself some water," the visitor said and ambled towards the kitchen.

By this time, Morena had her face dug into the book. She was fascinated by its fragrance. The visitor was back from the kitchen with two glasses of water.

With a smile, the intruder handed over a glass to Morena.

"Oh thank you," Morena said and sipped the water. She flipped through the pages of the book, and then drank some more water. The visitor sat down beside Morena, closely observing her every move.

"It is strange but every time I am looking at you, I can see a reflection of myself. It is as if I am speaking to my conscience," Morena told the visitor, mesmerized by the scented book. "Are you a fairy or something?"

"Yes, I am your conscience, sweetheart. Redemption is the key. It will relieve you from all suffering," came the convoluted response.

Morena wore a puzzled look. Suddenly, she felt nauseated and her vision got blurry. Just then, she smelled a familiar fragrance. Then, it was gone. Morena knew she had to keep her eyes open. She failed to understand why the detective had not reached!

Morena's guest was nowhere in sight.

Morena managed to crawl towards the centre table and grab a newspaper. She got hold of the pen on the table, scribbled something with trembling hands and collapsed on the floor.

The visitor reappeared from the kitchen now, with a sharp-edged knife in hand. Morena's eyebrows cringed; she battled her eyelashes several times in disbelief to what she was seeing.

She pointed to the culprit and managed to say *"You?"*

"Goodbye, my dear!"

Morena could not see anything anymore. Her world turned hazy.

"But why?" Morena weakly murmured.

"The punishment for murder is death. That's why," came the answer.

"M-murder? Meee?" Morena struggled to keep her eyes open.

"Yes bitch. You crooked mind."

"I don't know wh...what youuu're ttaalking..."

Morena lost consciousness.

"Enigmatic, ain't I?" giggled the visitor after ensuring that the odourless, colourless sedative that had been mixed in Morena's glass of water had done its bit.

For the next five minutes, this person walked around the place where Morena lay, cleaning up fingerprints. Next, the culprit slowly crawled beside Morena. With the knife procured from the kitchen, the person started slitting Morena's wrists. As the job was halfway through, Morena's feeble hand moved a little. With shaking hands, the killer tried to slit Morena's wrist for a second time.

However, nervousness took over and the person was unable to tamper with Morena's wrist again. The knife dropped on the floor and the visitor stood before Morena, numb. There was blood, all over the floor. It was time to run. While hastily trying to flee, the killer's eyes travelled to a tear that had bulged out of Morena's right eye on to her cheek. For a brief moment, the person felt an inexplicable sadness.

Ting Tong!

The murderer froze. Who could it be? The alternate route of escape was not possible in broad daylight. It meant fleeing through the dry area behind the toilet. Climbing down the pipe at this hour would be suicidal.

Ting Tong!

The bell rang again. The culprit's heart missed a beat! Someone was trying to open the door, turning the knob vigorously.

The visitor tiptoed to verify that the door was locked from inside.

"Thank god!" But what is the way out now?

Worried, the culprit made a quick call.

The doorbell rang again. Morena's phone started blinking too! The culprit had put Morena's phone on silent mode before starting the operation.

Ting Tong!

The culprit took a deep breath, grabbed the flower vase from the drawing room and walked towards the door.

Suddenly a song started playing:

'*Heal the world, make it a better place...*'

Then a female voice said,

"Hello...oh hi! Yes okay. Is it? Had no idea. Good then. Sure, sure. I'll do that. In fact, I'll go right away. You're such a sweetheart! Wine never harms anyone. Ya, okay. Bye."

The call ended. It was almost 6.30 p.m. The murderer's ears were stuck on the door. The noises that followed were sufficient proof that the visitor was leaving.

"Phew..."

The culprit walked into the kitchen, washed the knife and kept it next to Morena.

Before leaving, the culprit walked up to Morena. There was one split second of repentance.

7.00 p.m.
8 July 2014

The carpet was swamped with blood and Morena's hand was still bleeding. Blood started seeping from under the door of her apartment.

Mrs Silvy Dubey, Morena's next-door neighbour, noticed the blood stream, as she stepped out of the elevator to head towards her apartment. Petrified, she ran to the security guard.

After ringing Morena's doorbell and knocking on the door several times, the security guard reported the matter to the building secretary.

The secretary rushed to Morena's apartment with the duplicate keys of the flat.

The door was opened. The neighbours screamed as they saw Morena lying on the floor, with blood all around.

"Oh my God!" cried Mrs Dubey. "Morena has committed suicide."

Mrs Dubey called Varun. She asked her daughter to call for an ambulance.

The ambulance reached before Varun.

Morena was rushed to the hospital.

The police was informed too.

Six-Sixty-Six

Morena's house

8.00 p.m.
8 July 2014

"Had we managed the arrest warrant on time, this could have been averted," regretted Trehan.

"It could have happened inside the cell also ACP," Mili said defiantly.

"Do you mean that this was a suicide attempt?" Trehan asked, surprised.

"I doubt that. But let our findings do the talking. I should have taken a cue from my stalker this morning."

"You were stalked again?" screamed Gatha. "Why didn't you tell us?"

"It was all too sudden. But I sure know those footsteps by heart. It was a danger alarm."

"What's 666?" Anubhav asked, and handed over the newspaper to Mili.

"The number is considered inauspicious. Referred to as the devil's number, people can get superstitious about it," replied Mili.

"The way we have an unlucky 13, we have a devilish 666. That's the obvious first answer that would come to anyone's mind," Gatha added.

As the forensic experts inspected every corner of Morena's house, Trehan's phone rang.

"Okay, thanks Inspector," Trehan said before disconnecting the phone.

"Inspector Thadani is at the hospital. He says Morena and Saahil's wrists were slit the same way, perhaps by the same person."

"How is Morena doing?"

"Not good."

"Perhaps solving the mystery behind this number that Morena left for us will lead us to her attacker."

"Six-hundred-and-sixty-six. How do we know Morena scribbled this? It could have been Varun or someone else too," Anubhav said, absorbedly.

"Apart from the four of us, who else was here this morning? Morena, Varun, Morena's lawyer and another lady, apart from the two housekeepers. It could be anyone," Mili agreed with Anubhav.

"Both the housekeepers left when Varun was in the house," confirmed Anubhav. "Besides, they don't have duplicate keys to the house."

"Whoever wrote this, we have one confirmation that it was written today," ACP Trehan chipped in, pointing to the date of the newspaper – 8 July 2014.

"I am sending this to the handwriting analysis experts," Mili announced.

"One minute Mili," Gatha added. "You said that one more lady was present here this morning. Who?"

"Morena's psychologist, Dr Snigdha Sengupta. She happens to be a close friend."

"Oh! So Morena was already seeing a shrink?" ACP Trehan asked, puzzled.

"Yes. She has been visiting Snigdha for almost four months now," Mili answered.

"From the time she and Saahil were having issues?" asked Anubhav.

Mili nodded.

"Let's not get sidetracked people. Coming back to the number, what if it means nothing?"

"You might be right, ACP. But we cannot take a chance."

"Agreed! I am activating my team; they will look up all possible numbers and codes."

"Good! Don't let go of any cars, buses, bikes, phones, credit cards, addresses, bank accounts with 666 which may have a connection with Morena, Farzad, Saahil or the people in their lives."

"Right."

"Did anyone touch things around here?" Mili asked for the third time.

"I don't know why you keep asking this. According to the neighbours, none of them touched anything. They were waiting for the police. We entered this apartment along with you," replied Trehan.

▼

Varun was crestfallen when Mrs Dubey called him. He felt breathless for a while. Finally, when he reached, he was numb with fear. A crowd had gathered and the police was not allowing anyone inside the apartment. He meandered his way through and found ACP Trehan.

"The site is under inspection, Mr Kulkarni. I am sorry but you cannot enter the house."

"Where is Morena?" Varun lost his patience.

"She is at the hospital."

"If anything happens to my wife, I will kill you, detective. I swear," he lashed out.

Mili was tight-lipped. She wanted to walk over to Varun to talk but Gatha stopped her.

"Not now Mili; let him come back to his senses."

Mili was thankful that Gatha was around. Varun rushed to the hospital.

"Have you informed her parents?" asked Mili.

"They are on their way from Pune," Trehan promptly responded.

The forensic team took a long time to complete their investigation.

"Dr Dighe, when can I get the details?"

"In less than twenty-four hours."

"This is urgent. Make it fast."

"You can come to my office later tonight, Ms Ray. I should be able to give you some information."

"That would help, doctor."

At the hospital, Varun was not allowed to go near Morena. He just wanted to hug her once. She was unconscious, looked pale and wounded. Varun felt helpless.

He remembered how Morena would go out of the way to fulfil his childlike demands, whether it was skating inside a children's skating rink or embarrassing people who pee on the streets. Then, suddenly he mustered the courage to run to his wife and hug her for one fleeting moment. The police came running after him. He did not care if they sent him to jail.

He hated Saahil Kerkar. "I should have completed what I started," he groaned.

Kwest brainstorm

"Team, let us do a quick 4th July recap," Mili announced as the trio gathered at the Kwest office later that night.

"Saahil, Morena, Rounak, and Farzad – all left office at around 5.00 p.m. on the 4th of July."

As she spoke, Mili drew something like a circle-spoke diagram on the whiteboard. Then she started sticking photos of people involved in the case inside each circle. However, in the central circle, which was surrounded by the other circles, she stuck two photos, instead of one – those of Saahil and Farzad.

"Saahil dropped Rounak and Farzad at the station at around 6.00 p.m. Then he was off to drop Morena," observed Mili. She jotted down the time and the names of the destinations too.

"Rounak reaches home at around 9.00 p.m. Farzad reaches about half an hour later, almost at 9.30. Both stay at home. Farzad leaves home at 11.00 p.m. when he gets a call from Morena," continued Anubhav.

"Hang on – Morena doesn't call from her cell phone. So where was she at eleven at night?"

"The public booth was traced back to Farzad's neighbourhood," added Gatha.

"The funny thing is – why did Morena make it so obvious to Saahil that she wanted to contact Farzad? I mean, if she wanted to kill Farzad, I would expect her to be better planned," Mili said.

"Besides, how did she manage to get Farzad's address that night? Saahil couldn't help and neither had she contacted Rounak. She would obviously not connect with her office at that hour! How did she get the address then?" asked Anubhav.

"Maybe she lied to Saahil. She already knew Farzad's address," Mili stated, taking a puff from the lit cigarette she had balanced on the skull-shaped ashtray.

Gatha said, "Per Morena's call records, she was at home at 10.00 p.m. – the same time when Saahil's watch beeps – reminder for his TV serial. According to Saahil's statement, Morena was in his car at this time, this being the second time he offered her a lift."

"Yes, but Saahil also said that Morena told him that her phone was not working and so she noted Farzad's number on a piece of paper," replied Mili.

"So, she left her phone at home when she went out for the second time," said Anubhav.

"But how did she answer her husband's call post 10.00 p.m. with the phone location showing as her home?" Gatha shot back.

"Don't forget she is an IT professional, Gates," said Mili. If Morena had planned to murder Saahil, she must have chalked out a foolproof strategy. She might have pre-recorded a message for Varun, we do not know! That would work as a perfect alibi."

"What if Saahil is being blackmailed to trap Morena?" said Gatha. "I have seen many such cases in my career."

"Let us get our facts right first," Mili said instantly. "We will try permutation-combinations later."

"Fine! If Saahil was sedated at 10.00 p.m., how did Morena reach Farzad's neighbourhood by 11.00 p.m.? It is not a short distance after all. She didn't even have a car?" Gatha said, sternly.

"Point!" said Mili. "Saahil drops Morena on the highway at around 9.30 p.m. This is where Morena's accomplice comes into picture. Let us assume Morena met her partner in crime on the highway at 9.30 p.m. This second person was mapped to Saahil. He or she followed Saahil continuously till Morena was able to keep her phone at home and come out again," said Mili.

"But my dear, at 9.30 p.m., Saahil had dropped Morena on the highway, near Right Food," Gatha said persistently. "From there, Saahil took half an hour to reach the bus stop where he spotted Morena for the second time. So how could Morena, who supposedly didn't have a car, go home, drop her mobile, and then meet Saahil at 10.00 p.m. again? Is she a superhero?"

"Perhaps Morena did not go home at all! Her accomplice dropped the phone at her residence. Morena just kept a tab on Saahil," said Mili.

"And in all this confusion, Morena found time to slip into a black dress too, Mili? Who is trying permutation combinations now?" Gatha said sarcastically.

Mili did not laugh. Instead, while slowly enjoying the last drag of the evil cigarette, she said, "If Morena really accomplished all that and then travelled a long distance to kill Farzad, we have a shrewd criminal in the making."

"According to our call records, Morena was at home at 10.00 p.m., and Saahil at the bus stop," Anubhav recapped.

Anubhav continues, "Morena drugs Saahil at around 10.15 p.m. and he loses consciousness. Dr Shah has confirmed that Saahil was injected with the sedative between 10 p.m. and 11.30 p.m."

"Do we have a list of mobile numbers that were on that route from Morena's house to Farzad's that night?" asked Gatha.

"It's not a foolproof list. Due to the bad weather, networks were jammed for a considerable period of time," said Anubhav. "ACP Trehan doesn't consider this list useful."

"Saahil was fond of singing. After his attempted murder, we recovered an audio file from his phone. What did we find? A song rendered by Morena, in her own voice. But in his statement, Saahil did not mention this," remembered Mili.

"Also, isn't it too fantastic that Morena sedated Saahil, then fed him the allergic prawns, slit his veins, and then within an hour she met Farzad and killed him," Gatha said, stunned.

"Come on Gatha, she was not alone! Besides, reports show that Saahil consumed prawns much later, possibly after Farzad's murder!"

"Maybe the assailants were using Saahil's car all this while. Once we get the surveillance camera footage, we can confirm whether Morena actually met Farzad that night," Anubhav said, sensing the tension between Gatha and Mili.

"So you are saying that Saahil was inside his car, unconscious, when Farzad was killed?" asked Gatha.

"I am not ruling out that possibility," Mili shot back.

"According to Dr Shah, Saahil consumed the prawns at least four to five hours after being sedated. Apart from Saahil's family, only Morena knew that he was allergic to prawns," she added, observing Gatha's tendency to defend Morena.

"I think Morena and her accomplice force-fed Saahil once he gained consciousness," said Anubhav.

"Wait a minute! If Saahil was being force-fed, would he not try to resist?" asked Gatha.

"Saahil had not eaten his dinner that evening. When the action of the sedative was gone but the drowsiness remained, he was hungry. So he gorged on whatever he was being fed," replied Mili.

"That is not convincing enough," said Gatha.

"If you have a better approach to share, we are all ears. But you cannot defend the main suspect just because you know her, Gatha! That is outright criminal," Mili stated candidly.

"I am only speaking from facts, as a lawyer should. I am not assuming anything, as you are," Gatha replied sharply. "Anyway, let's hear you out."

"Thanks. Appreciated," said Mili. "Next, the assailants ensure a photo finish. They drive to my place, hit the banyan tree, shift Saahil to the driver's seat, and walk away, unperturbed."

"Maybe they had a car parked somewhere nearby," said Anubhav.

"Absolutely! Even if Morena did not commit the crime, anyone who did more or less followed this pattern," said Mili. "Dr Shah mentioned that the injection used to sedate Saahil was mild and might have kept him unconsciousness for about twenty minutes. This means that even if he was injected at 10.15 p.m., he gained consciousness latest by 10.45 p.m."

"Around this time, Farzad was being attacked. If Saahil was inside the car and in his senses, why did he not notice Farzad's murder?" Gatha was curious.

"There can be so many possibilities Gatha! I am appalled that you asked this question! They must have used a different car. Why would they drive a tipsy Saahil to Farzad's location?" Mili fumed.

"What if we find out that Morena was drugged too?" asked Gatha, equally annoyed.

"Okay, once and for all – I want to make this crystal clear. If we are emotionally attached to an idea or a person that is part of this case, we cannot think objectively. Gatha, if you want to take a break till we get details on Morena, please do so," Mili said aggressively.

Gatha got up to leave.

"Guys, please please don't lose your cool," Anubhav pleaded. "This is our first case together. We have to stick together. If the culprits can collaborate to commit a crime, can't we stay united to get hold of them?"

"I am sorry if I overreacted, Gates," Mili apologized.

Gatha nodded and sat down. Anubhav shrugged his shoulders.

"What I do not understand is that why did the assailants do so many things to Saahil? Feed the prawns, slit the wrist, and drug him? If they wanted this to look like suicide, they could have simply drugged him and slit his wrists," said Anubhav.

"Excellent point, Anubhav!" said Mili.

"Don't get me wrong, Mili. But probably the assailants wanted all the evidence to point towards Morena," Gatha said firmly.

"I agree with Gatha on this," smiled Anubhav.

"Me too," said Mili. "What is more intriguing is that after all this, they even banged the car against a tree? Did they really think the police would consider this as an accident?"

"Let us focus on Morena. Assuming she did all this, what is her motive?" asked Gatha.

"We have multiple sources confirming that Morena and Farzad had no connection with each other," said Anubhav. "Even if she were the last person to have met Farzad, I don't see any motive."

Mili contended, "But Morena had motive to kill Saahil. Revenge and jealousy are strong motives. Maybe Farzad knew Morena's secret. Maybe…in some way, he had learned about Morena's plan to kill Saahil."

"Net net – Saahil's murder was planned, even though it failed. Farzad's murder was accommodated at the last minute," said Gatha.

"Bang on!" jumped Anubhav in agreement.

"Morena's father is a surgeon. Her younger sister is an oncologist. Procuring the drugs would be easier for her, than anyone else at Zarine Software at least. Maybe the culprit knew that the police would suspect Morena due to her medical background," added Mili.

Gatha was taken aback by this statement. She thought Mili did not like Morena.

Trying to be neutral, she said, "Maybe Morena knows how to give injections to people. She is a doctor's daughter after all!"

"I do not buy that logic, Gates. Can we expect a pilot's children to know how to fly planes?" asked Mili.

"The taxi driver was attacked in front of Morena's house. Maybe that was done deliberately too!" added Anubhav.

"Similarly, when we look at what happened to Morena today, there are two scenarios," said Mili.

"One – Morena hurt herself to get away with Saahil's murder attempt," said Gatha.

"Two – someone actually tried to kill Morena," added Anubhav.

"That reminds me – I gotta go meet Dr Dighe now. He should have some reports ready," Mili said and got up to leave.

"We'll go too!"

"No Gates, I need you guys in the office. Trehan may send in some stuff."

The Loss

Rashi Singhi's house

Late Night
8 July 2014

Dr Dighe declared Morena dead at around 11.00 p.m. Nobody was allowed to see the body until the post-mortem was completed.

After meeting Dr Dighe, Mili left for Morena's close friend Rashi Singhi's residence. The police were still not allowing people to enter Morena and Varun's Versova apartment. So Morena's parents had decided to spend the night at Rashi's house.

Apart from Morena's parents and Varun, a few close friends had also gathered at Rashi's cosy row-house that night.

"Morena did not commit suicide, detective," those were Rashi's first words to Mili as she entered.

Mili remembered just in time that the Kwest team had missed sticking Rashi's photo on the circle-spoke diagram. Did Rashi have an affair with Varun? Or was she attracted to Morena? She had motive, for sure. But Farzad? That was a complete gray zone.

Morena's parents were exceptionally quiet, as if they were not present in the room.

Varun had no clue what 666 was! Nobody in the family knew.

"Morena did not kill herself," Rashi repeated.

"Morena was going through a bad patch and she was willing to take help. I did not give her anti-depressants. Therapy was working fine with her," added Dr Snigdha Sengupta, Morena's psychologist.

"Hmm."

"When I met her earlier this evening, Morena had no suicidal tendencies. If she tried to kill herself, someone must have instigated her," Dr Sengupta said. "I have already told you that Mili."

"Right Snigdha," Mili nodded.

For Mili, knowing that Snigdha was Morena's psychologist was like a bumper prize!

Suddenly Varun screamed, "My wife is not in this world today for this wicked detective."

Mili in a maze

The number 666 continued to allure Mili like a conundrum that ignores logic.

Was it 999, Mili wondered?

She looked at her Smartphone and touched the calling screen. The number 6 had three alphabets written next to it –MNO. Three times 6 would be MNO MNO MNO. It meant nothing! Nothing had clicked so far.

On the 9th of July, the news was creating havoc – TV, newspapers, and the social media only had one news – Zarine Software.

"What is Mili Ray's role in this case?" reported Ayesha Mathur. "Why did Farzad Mistry's family need a private detective? Have the common people lost faith in the police?"

"She is disgusting," grumbled Mili.

This was the fourth day since Farzad's death, and Mili had no leads in this case.

The two days – the 4th of July and the 8th of July were labelled as black days in the history of ZS.

"Are IT professionals not safe in their own homes?" reported another news channel, reacting to Morena's mysterious death.

Chat shows had topics on colleague-rivalry, violence at the workplace, and more. Besides, people resorted to social media to lash out at the police! People were on the streets for peace marches, demanding justice for Farzad Mistry, Nirmal Kanitkar, and Morena Dave. Topics like #JusticeforFarzadMorena were trending.

A popular TV channel created teasers overnight, for their new story – 'The twin murder that rocked ZS'. They planned to air it on their popular 'True Crime Story' program.

"I should meet the director of this show! How can they air this story when we have no inkling as to who is behind these attacks? Why do the media people complicate things?" Mili yelled over the phone.

"Relax detective," said ACP Trehan. "I am sure this is not the first time you are facing such reactions!"

Trehan was right, Mili thought. "I shouldn't get worked up."

DIG Joshi was under great pressure from the Home Ministry.

The Human Resource and Corporate Communication teams at Zarine Software had a tough time handling the situation. Employees were instructed not to interact with the media. If anybody had to answer police queries, a member from the Legal or Corporate Communication teams was to accompany them.

But importantly, employees were scared to report to work.

"Could I be the next target?" was the thought in their minds.

Mili had checked car numbers, phone numbers, employee

IDs, bike numbers, even debit/credit card numbers of all key suspects as well as those of Saahil, Farzad, and Morena.

She had visited the decoding expert too. However, there was no secret code attached to the number 666. Mili was going round and round in a maze, unable to figure a way out.

Was this pointing to a monetary transaction? It could not be the time on a watch – that would read as 7:06 instead.

Add 666 and you get 18, multiply and you get 216. Perhaps number of a bus or a certain route to someone's home! Nothing seemed to work.

Mili was frustrated.

Saahil reacts

9 July 2014

When Mili met Saahil Kerkar on the 9th of July, she asked him about 666 too. As expected, he was clueless.

Saahil expressed grief when Mili informed him about Morena's death.

"Amar told me last night. I feel extremely bad now, Ms Ray. She was a friend. Did she know that I had named her?" Saahil asked, wrinkles crowding his forehead.

"Yes, she did. We are investigating if this was an abetment of suicide," Mili said.

"I have seen that emotional girl, Ms Ray. She was an extremist. If she had realized it was her fault, I am sure she tried to kill herself," Saahil stated, ruefully.

"What mistake?" Mili asked.

"Killing Farzad and attacking me," said Saahil, giving Mili a startled look.

"But we have no proof that she killed Farzad," Mili replied. "She didn't have a motive."

"Farzad was a good-looking man, ma'am. Perhaps Morena tried her luck and he refused," Saahil said sternly.

"Would a girl like Morena kill for that? This is an accusation. Are you sure? Did Morena say anything to you? Nobody has spoken about her character so far!" It was Mili's turn to be shocked.

"She tried to get close to me also. I told her that I don't date married women!" Saahil revealed.

"When are you getting discharged, Saahil?" asked Mili.

"I think tomorrow, unless the doctors have other plans. I have so much work pending. I feel terrible when I think about Farzad," Saahil said.

"Did Farzad's father come to see you?"

"Yes, he did. But he didn't say a word. Morena got her punishment. That is his only solace. I could read that on his face."

"When did he visit you?"

"During the visiting hours last evening."

1.00 p.m.
9 July 2014

"There is no time for introspection, ACP," said DIG Joshi. "Your seventy-two hours are over."

"I need seventy-two more hours, sir. There have been two murders and one murder attempt. Multiple people are involved," ACP Trehan replied.

"Where are the leads, Trehan? You have not arrested a single soul until now. What help has detective Ray extended? Nothing, no results."

"Please trust me, sir. Three days at the most. You will have the culprit right here," Mili said.

DIG Joshi firmly said, "If you cannot solve this in three days, ACP, I will have to give it to someone else. And detective Ray, you would not need to assist Trehan anymore."

4.00 p.m.
9 July 2014

The 9th of July was a busy day for Mili. She and Dr Dighe had to complete a lot of work, without anyone else's knowledge.

In the evening, Mili reviewed her suspects list again. If Varun or Sheena were guilty, what could the motive be? Or was it Rounak and his desire to climb up the corporate ladder? But what would he gain from killing Farzad? Vikrant Sharma's involvement could not be ruled out. Saahil's family members would have a motive from the property angle. But would they have any motive to kill Morena or Farzad? Morena has two surgeons in her family – her father and her younger sister. So logically, she had the easiest access to anaesthetic drugs. But what was her motive? Morena's friend Rashi has motive too, assuming the 'affair' angle.

No motive to kill Farzad had surfaced yet.

Was there someone who wanted to destroy Zarine Software?

Dr Dighe's report

"There may be a pattern in Farzad and Morena's attacks, DCP Ray," Dr Dighe said. "Sorry, I try not to call you DCP. But…"

"It's okay Dr Dighe," Mili smiled. "So, was Morena drugged too?" she asked, remembering Gatha's insight the night before.

"See, it is very difficult to find traces of these kind of sedatives. Besides, there are no signs of resistance in Morena's body, if we assume that someone had attacked her."

"So did Morena try to commit suicide?" askedMili.

"No, she didn't. The way her wrists have been slit show that it was not her doing."

"I thought so too," said Mili. "Then what about the sedative?"

"Technology has evolved to an extent that we are able to detect these invisible drugs from a victim's body nowadays," said Dr Dighe.

"Maybe the culprits don't know that yet?" said Mili.

"Possible. The same drug was used to sedate Farzad and Morena. Farzad was offered odourless alcohol. I learn that he was a teetotaller. So perhaps, he mistook his drink for apple juice! The drug was mixed in his drink. It made him drowsy. To people around him, he would look like a man who was heavily under the influence of alcohol. He had no balance over his body and so it was easy to push him in front of a racing truck."

Mili listened intently without interrupting Dr Dighe as he spoke.

"In Morena's case, the same drug was used. But it was mixed with water, instead of alcohol. Once Morena drank the water, she must have had a headache, along with sweating and uneasiness. Finally, she would have blacked out. Something similar to a heat stroke, you can say. Since she was unconscious, it was easy for her attacker to slit her wrist. I must also tell you that this drug results in temporary amnesia," said Dr Dighe. "A survivor can wake up after two to three days or even weeks and remember nothing!"

"It was a flawless plan, doctor. This is like those date-rape drugs, I guess."

"Yes, you are right. It is similar to that," Dr Dighe answered. "This drug can only be available to someone who is connected to chemical labs or hospitals."

The Search Continues

❦

Forensics revealed that the person who slashed Morena's wrist knew she was left-handed. Apart from Morena's family, Saahil, and Rashi, nobody knew this little piece of vital information.

"Yes, you could call her a southpaw," confirmed Varun. "However, if she was typing on the computer, she was right-handed. You know what I mean, right?"

"Yes," Mili sighed. She wondered who could have the motive to attack Morena.

Mili closed her eyes. Morena had attacked Saahil. But maybe when her accomplice killed Farzad, she threatened to go to the police? Perhaps that is why she was attacked? As the questions got knottier, Mili lost sleep.

"What am I missing?"

Kwest office

7.00 p.m.
9 July 2014
"What did Farzad's father say when you broke the news?" Gatha asked Mili.

"I have not told him anything yet. The family is in a state of shock. I just met Shireen, Farzad's wife, sometime back," Mili replied.

"I can understand what she must be going through," said Gatha.

"She told me what a doting husband Farzad was and how he was always there for his family. Where is Anubhav?"

"ACP Trehan found Morena's diary. Anubhav has gone to look into that."

"Hope he has some news for us," sighed Mili. "Though I am sure today's discussion with Shireen will give a whole new perspective to this case."

"Whoa! What did she say? Did she have any idea why Morena called Farzad that night?"

"She does not know who Morena is and never heard her name before that night," said Mili.

"One thing is for sure. We need to delve into people's history sometimes. The past often has stories that come back to haunt the present. Can you ask Anubhav to get me a history of the Dave and Kerkar family when he is back?"

"Sure. He was collating some new information on that this morning."

Morena's diary

"In this age of IT, people still write diaries? I am impressed," exclaimed Anubhav.

Anubhav leafed through Morena's diary in detail. He divided the contents into three parts:

- Letters written to Saahil
- Important dates
- Notes on fragrances

While looking through the letters, Anubhav got mesmerized by Morena's handwriting. All twenty-two letters, written in a conversational tone, were addressed to Saahil. Some were short and some went up to three pages. The letters expressed Morena's fondness for Saahil, love for Varun, and passion for her job.

As far as important dates were concerned, Morena had listed down birthdays of some 250 people! Who lists birthdays in a diary in this digital age, Anubhav wondered. He pierced through every date trying his best to find a connection with '666'.

"Got anything?" Trehan asked, amused at Anubhav's changing facial expressions.

"Nope," Anubhav frowned.

Finally, Anubhav focused on the notes that Morena had made on fragrances.

"See this," Anubhav called out to Trehan. "During her school days, Morena was moved by the flavour of tea. The love for tea grew over the years, and she was especially fascinated by Darjeeling tea."

"Good," said Trehan. "On that note, mind if I get a cup of tea while you finish with the diary?"

"By all means," Anubhav smiled.

As Anubhav leafed through the other pages, he discovered Morena's love for the fragrance of books. Visiting second-hand bookstalls and classic bookstores was her passion – not so much for the love of reading, as for the fragrance of books. She had admitted in her notes that the smell of books transported her to a different world.

Next, Anubhav was introduced to Morena's affair with perfumes. She loved scents and did not mind spending a fortune if a particular fragrance caught her fancy.

The diary listed exotic perfumes – names that Anubhav had never heard of and ones that Morena had won at auctions. There was the mention of a perfume or *aatar* that was centuries old – apparently a favourite of the Late Mughal Emperor Bahadur Shah.

Anubhav rubbed his eyes in disbelief. He was discovering a whole new angle to Morena's personality.

As Anubhav read on, he found elaborate descriptions of scents – and the formula of *Rosé*, a perfume created by Dr Jaswant Dave, Morena's father.

Morena wrote at length about other perfumes too, along with scented candles and cards, erasers, incense sticks, aromatic oils and more.

There was a page titled 'Mistress of Fragrances'. The first paragraph read:

I am blessed. Else, how is it possible that even with eyes closed, I can detect the fragrance of any perfume, its brand, make, manufacturer, and year of release! Nobody taught me to love fragrances – oh I can smell hot chocolate now!

Anubhav could smell mystery the more he dug his head into the scented diary.

Aroma of freshly brewed coffee, tea, chocolates – no matter how mild, Morena knew them; she loved researching about them.

Suddenly Anubhav was distracted by a smell – of piping hot roadside tea, served in half-filled transparent glasses, and famous as 'cutting chai' in Mumbai.

He turned around to find ACP Trehan.

"Here – one for you!"

"Thanks!" said Anubhav. "You will be surprised to know what I found today!"

"The answer to 666?" Trehan looked excited.

"No man," Anubhav replied dejected. "You should know that just as a gundog can sniff out a criminal, Morena had the ability to identify different kinds of fragrances. Ah...see this, sandalwood." He flipped on to the next page and found a wooden bookmark with the sandalwood smell.

"Let's leave now, Anubhav," Trehan said, patting his companion.

"I gotta call Mili, she will appreciate my finding," Anubhav retorted.

In Flushed Fragrances

❧

9.00 a.m.
10 July 2014

"What? So much for one packet! God sure does want me to give up on my only vice!" bickered Mili as she paid the vendor for a pack of cigarettes with an improved MRP.

She frowned for a fleeting moment and walked away. The city could do with some rains, she reflected. After the maddening downpour on the 4th of July, there was hardly any monsoon-ish rain. Just like the murderer, the rain had also disappeared.

Mili entered office, took a stroll down the extended open area that she had marked as 'smoking zone', and was about to light a cigarette when an unpleasant smell distracted her – the kind one gets if smoking a bidi. Mili hated the smell and wondered who had been smoking a bidi in the office. She did not find anyone around.

Back in the office, Mili recalled that the carpenter had been given keys to work on the new workstations with wooden lockers, as suggested by Gatha. A bidi stub lay on the floor – someone had finished it in a hurry and had not bothered to dispose it off in the dustbin. Mili could imagine the half-lit bidi lying there, its flame glowing for a while before wearing out, causing the obnoxious smoke to fill the room.

The smoke vanished after a while; its repugnant smell did not. Mili visualized the carpenter Vishnu working on the space with the unlit bidi stuck behind one ear and a pencil tagged to the other. She angrily started for the cupboards looking for some room fresheners and banged open all the windows in the garage-office.

"Thank god we decided to retain fans in the office." The smell of the bidi sure gave her a buzz and Mili knew that this headache would not leave her in a hurry.

Smell can be so characteristic of some people.

Finally, as Mili lit her cigarette, she had some random smelly thoughts. She recalled Professor Banerjee's Economics class in college. The entire department could smell him (rather his socks) when he entered the 3.00 p.m. class. How much they wished that his sessions were shifted to the morning! The explanation of the demand curve would do a tangent and dive past students as most of them were focused on his 'ewww socks'. Mili and her group had even sent detergent powder sachets to the staff room addressed to Professor Banerjee. But until Mili moved to second year and Professor Banerjee retired, there was no respite from the incorrigible odour of his unwashed socks!

"Yuck," said Mili and laughed out loud.

Her mind then travelled to other smell memories - The new post-graduate department building was being painted. Memories of the PG building always brought back a fond memory of the smell of fresh paint.

But yes, the best of scents was the aftershave and cologne her first boyfriend used. Ah…sheer magic. It might have been Old Spice or something else. It did not matter! It made him so deliciously desirable. Not just Mili, half the college would be drooling over him, almost like those deodorant advertisements.

That was quite a source of tension (for her) and attention (for him) back in college!

Mili brushed aside the strand of hair from over her eyes and fondly recalled the brief romantic spell in college. Back then, love made her world go round. The aftershave was magical. Mili could almost get a whiff of the intoxicating scent as she thought about it. If he were around today wearing the same cologne or aftershave, she would identify him with her eyes closed.

Smell indeed defines personalities.

"Oh my god!" shrieked Mili and threw her half-lit cigarette in the ashtray. "Why hadn't I thought about this earlier?"

"What…what did you tell me last night, Anubhav? Repeat, repeat," Mili demanded, almost pouncing upon Anubhav when he entered the office.

"Whoa! What happened?"

"Morena's diary has all our answers…well not all. But a starting point," Mili sounded thrilled.

Gatha gazed at Mili.

"Okay look, Morena was fond of fragrances, right? Her home is full of scented things! Her perfume collection has fragrances collected from all over the world."

"Yes…I was fascinated," said Anubhav. "She had stocked up the most expensive aatar, a rare concentrated perfume. Only 10 ml is sufficient to last for years. In ancient times, royal families would take pride in the aatar they possessed. The style would be to open the lid, and toss the tiny bottle upside down covering its mouth with the index finger. Then the drop of perfume that would land on the index finger had to be applied behind each earlobe. If the aatar were applied on garments, the fragrance would linger for months, even after multiple washes. Some princes, in order to woo their wives and mistresses, would almost soak their attires in aatar. Morena's aatar collection was a gift from her dad who shares her love for fragrances."

Mili added, "The incense sticks Morena uses in her puja room are classic. Her bathroom boasts of a great collection of bathing gels, potpourri of fragrant petals and soaps. Have you observed her balcony? It is a mini-garden, overflowing with fragrant flowers."

"Will you come to the point now?" Gatha asked.

"Quick memory trips are such a saviour, Gates," said Mili, almost trembling in excitement. "Morena is a techie. Yet she makes all her notes in a personal diary. Why?"

"Many people maintain diaries till date. It may be rare but hasn't become obsolete yet," suggested Anubhav.

"No, Morena is different. She writes the diary because of her love for fragrances – her notebooks are made of scented paper. She also uses an ink pen to write her diary because she loves the smell of the ink when she refills the pen," explained Mili.

Anubhav added, "Well, she also made a note about herself. Her body fragrance was great and she never needed a deodorant."

"Hair too," said Mili. "Saahil was inadvertently drawn to the fragrance of her freshly-washed hair."

"She maintained a diary because of her love for fragrances?" asked Gatha.

"Yes, by all means," replied Mili. "The number 666 must have some connection with a fragrance."

Morena's love for the 'smell of books' was amazing too! Mili had read somewhere that people like smelling old books because of Lignin, a polymer. When it is used to create paper and then stored for years together, it produces a nice smell. The older the book, the nicer the smell.

"Let's search all personal care items – perfumes, aftershaves, air-fresheners, scented pens, perfumed lighters, et al – for any connection with 666. In other words, anything devilish!"

The 666 Story

Manufactured by Daikar Brothers, 'The Devil' is an expensive perfume, exclusively made by order for niche customers. A 100 ml bottle costs over a lakh of rupees! A wood fragranced unisex perfume, it is neither distributed in merchant shops nor available at retail stores. Orders for this perfume could not be placed online either.

Morena's ability to identify fragrances was commendable. Even in her state of drowsiness, she had the presence of mind to write '666' on the newspaper, instead of 'The Devil', the real name of the perfume. There was no doubt now that Morena's assailant was wearing this perfume. Possibly, when Morena scribbled that note, the killer was inside the house.

The perfume could not be traced in Morena's house, nor did any of the suspects seem to have it. Mili got a sample of 'The Devil' from Mr Daikar. She also got a list of customers who had bought the perfume since January 2012. Morena's name was there, but none of Mili's other suspects featured on the list.

"The killer also had an affinity for perfumes or was someone who received it as a gift from Morena," Gatha stated.

"Morena had interacted with the murderer before she was drugged. Naturally, with her strong sense of smell, she had enough time to identify the perfume the killer was wearing," said Mili.

"Should we barge into people's homes and start searching their belongings?" asked Anubhav.

"That's a pathetic idea. Our first task is to ensure that no one else is harmed now. So we will arrest our culprit today," Mili said confidently.

"*Whaatt?*" Gatha and Anubhav said in chorus, shock written large on their faces.

"I will meet you all at 3.00 p.m. today at Trehan's office. I am asking ACP Trehan to gather all suspects at the police station at 3.00 p.m. sharp," Mili replied.

"Isn't that a traditional detective's approach to solving a case, much like crime-fiction detectives?" asked Anubhav. "They like to gather all suspects in a room and announce the name of the culprit. It is spooky!"

"Interesting. Can you name such a detective?" Mili retorted.

"How about Byomkesh Bakshi?" replied Anubhav on his way out.

▼

"There is good news, Ms Mehta! We have found the murderer. Please come to the police station at 3 p.m.," ACP Trehan declared.

"Why me?" asked Sheena.

"Well, we are calling everyone so that we can close the case now," replied Anubhav when Rounak asked the same question.

"Why can't you give me the name over the phone?" asked Varun.

"Today, attendance is compulsory in ACP Trehan's office at 3.00 p.m. See you!" said Gatha, keeping it crisp.

Morena's best friend Rashi was also summoned to the police station.

"Are we calling Saahil too?" asked Gatha.

"Yes, Mili will call him. He is being discharged from the hospital today."

One by one, Amar Kerkar and the rest of the Kerkar family, Morena's parents, Sheena's husband, Vicky Sharma, Gopal, and few others from Zarine were summoned to the police station.

Mili grinned as she thought about the impending drama that was about to unfold at ACP Trehan's office.

Police Station

3.00 p.m.
10 July 2014

"Do you like perfumes, Ms Mehta?" asked Mili.

Sheena got a jolt. "Sorry?"

"Well, we see that Mr Anil Daikar is your uncle. Incidentally, he manufactures a rare perfume brand. Am sure you are aware of it?"

"I… er… yes. Anil uncle is my mother's cousin brother. But I have never bought fragrances from him," defended Sheena.

"I never talked about buying anything. I understand that you like to pick up things you fancy," replied Mili.

"What do you mean?" screamed Sheena. "I am not a kleptomaniac."

"It's okay, Ms Mehta. The sample that you flicked was the one that went missing from your uncle's store last week. What did you do with the five ml bottle of 'The Devil'? Morena wrote 666 on the newspaper to lead us to the culprit. Our investigation points to this perfume called 'The Devil'. Morena's assailant was wearing this perfume on the evening of her attack. Did Morena share her love for perfumes with you during your Geneva trip, Ms Mehta?"

Sheena froze in her seat and did not utter a single word. Her husband looked at her, spellbound. Suddenly all eyes were on Sheena.

"I...me...I know nothing about this," said Sheena. "Yes, I lifted that perfume. But I did not kill anyone. I gifted it to Saahil for his birthday." Sheena was in tears.

"When did you gift it to Saahil?"

"I...I gave it to him on Friday, the 4th of July. I was supposed to be on leave from the 7th of July. Since I would not be meeting him on his birthday on 8th July, I decided to hand over the gift in advance," said Sheena, in one breath.

"We did not find the perfume at Saahil's house! So how did you plan to disappear after committing multiple murders?" asked Mili.

"Excuse me, ma'am," Saahil interrupted. "I think I have already given my statement that Morena attacked me that night. Sheena has nothing to do with it. She is my friend."

"Shut up, you liar!" Varun Kulkarni shouted. "My wife is innocent. She considered you her friend. But you ruined her life, and mine too. I wish you were dead. Why the hell did you recover?"

"Mr Kulkarni, please do not be abusive. In a few minutes, we will have the culprit with us. You are right, Saahil. Sheena could not have attacked you. After all, you two were in love. But she had enough motive to kill Morena," declared Mili.

Saahil blushed and looked at Sheena, who was wiping her tears and crying uncontrollably.

"If it happened in your family, you would know how it feels, detective. I have no interest in your crap story," said Varun.

"I really did not kill anyone," Sheena whimpered.

"Varun Kulkarni, you never liked Saahil. Why?" asked Mili.

"I hate him. I have tolerated his lecherous streaks," yelled Varun.

"We have evidence to believe that you were in Mumbai on 4th July, Varun, and not in Delhi, as you claim," ACP Trehan interrupted the conversation.

"Yes, fine. But I did not kill anybody," replied Varun, without overreacting to the statement.

"You said the murderer is here. I want to know who killed Farzad," Saahil Kerkar demanded.

Mili knew this was coming. She turned to Anubhav.

Anubhav stood up almost mechanically and walked towards Saahil. "Come, let's take a walk."

"No, I want to hear it all," Saahil protested.

Mili started, "On the evening of the 4th of July, when Saahil Kerkar left office, Morena's husband Varun was following Saahil. He was aware that Saahil had dropped Rounak and Farzad at the railway station. He also knew that Morena was with Saahil. What made him angrier was the fact that Saahil and Morena had spent a considerable amount of time in Saahil's car inside the Manor Jungles. That park, styled as a jungle with all its beautiful landscape, is no less than a jungle at night."

Saahil's face grew red when Mili mentioned this. Sheena looked at Saahil, surprised. Varun was unaffected and maintained a straight face.

"My car was stuck, ma'am," Saahil whimpered.

"I am just narrating the course of events, Saahil."

"Anyway, Varun waited with baited breath for them to get out from Manor Jungles. Morena got off on the highway, despite Saahil's offer of a home-drop. She went home, kept her phone and came out, ensuring that she was safe if the police decided to track the location of her phone! She was in touch with Varun, who was still following Saahil according to the plan. Varun informed Morena that Saahil was heading towards the bus stop near her home. So within half-an-hour of dropping Morena, Saahil offered her a lift again, when he spotted her at the bus stop. What Saahil failed to notice was that Varun Kulkarni, Morena's husband was also present at the bus stop," said Mili, clenching her fists.

Saahil's face turned red.

"Varun created a perfect alibi to prove he was in Delhi at that time. You planned the murder like a seasoned criminal!" added ACP Trehan.

Varun kept his head lowered as Morena's parents and sister looked at him in astonishment.

Mili continued, "Once Morena was in Saahil's car, she looked for an opportune moment to nip the injection in Saahil's shoulder," said Anubhav, in a voice befitting an army officer.

"As soon as Saahil lost consciousness, Varun climbed inside the car. Then the husband-wife duo had the perfect plan in place to kill Saahil and Farzad."

Varun was silent. Saahil Kerkar was restless and he whispered something to his brother Amar.

ACP Trehan continued, "Varun Kulkarni and Morena then drove to the highway near Farzad Mistry's house. Morena called up Farzad and asked him to meet her. What Morena did not know is that the CCTV camera near the mall where she met Farzad was capturing her discussion with Farzad. We received the photographs from the mall authorities, and understood that Morena did meet Farzad on the night of 4th July."

"Varun was Morena's accomplice in the crime. The duo drugged Farzad and then pushed him in front of the truck. We know what happened after that. All this while, Saahil was inside his own car, unconsciousness and unaware of the crime being committed," said Mili and looked at Saahil.

"Did you not invite Farzad's family here? They should meet these ruthless murderers," Sheena suddenly spoke up, happy to have her name cleared from the crime.

"No, I will convey the news to them once I arrest the culprits. I am yet to narrate how Saahil was attacked, how Nirmal Kanitkar was killed, and finally Morena too," said Mili.

"Didn't Morena commit suicide?" asked Sheena.

"No."

"Why would she kill Farzad?" asked Sheena.

"Saahil can answer that for us. Will you Saahil?" asked Mili.

"I am feeling extremely unwell. I want to leave," said Saahil.

"I want to take him home," added Amar. "He has recovered by God's grace and Saahil's health is of utmost importance to us."

"You are right to be protective about your elder brother," ACP Trehan told Amar. "Sure, you can take him home."

Saahil and Amar Kerkar walked out with their mother, Suhasini Kerkar.

Colonel Kerkar waited back. "I will listen to the whole story, Ms Ray. After all, you are fighting for justice. This is in my son's best interest."

"Thank you, sir," Mili said. "Varun and Morena then drove to Saahil Kerkar's garage, made him eat prawns when he gained consciousness but was drowsy, and finally slit his wrist. Next, in the dead of the night, they parked the car outside the Blue Lime Residential complex, shifted Saahil to the driver's seat and left. They thought he was dead."

Morena's parents stared at each other in disbelief. "Why would Morena kill anyone?" asked Morena's mother.

"I did *not* kill anyone, nor did Morena," said Varun.

"Really?" prompted Mili. "So for all of you who thought Varun was in Delhi on 4th July, let me give you a taste of the truth.

"Mr Varun Kulkarni travelled to Delhi on the 3rd of July. He was scheduled to take the first flight back from Delhi on the 5th of July. But he was back in Mumbai on the 4th. How did he do that?"

"I really did not kill anyone," cried Varun.

Mili continued, "Coincidentally, Varun Kulkarni has a musician friend named Varun Kumar. You all may know pop star VK. His full name is Varun Kumar. VK had a live performance in Delhi on 3rd July, and his return ticket to Mumbai was for the 4th of July. Morena's husband Varun was aware of VK's itinerary. In Delhi, he checked in at the same hotel as his friend. For his office party, Varun requested VK to be the guest performer on the 4th of July. VK was a bit reluctant. Moreover, he already had return tickets for the 4th. Varun pleaded that this was an issue of his prestige in office and if VK declined to perform, it would be a real let down for Varun. VK finally agreed to help his friend. Varun promised to take care of the ticket reschedules.

After VK's live show at another office on the night of 3rd July, Varun was waiting for his friend at the hotel lobby. After the performance, Varun met VK and explained his urgency to go back to Mumbai on the 4th of July. VK was a tad embarrassed and said it would be very funny if Varun were missing while he performed at Varun's office function!

Varun pleaded again and VK hesitantly agreed to exchange flight tickets with his friend. Names were printed on both their boarding passes as Varun K. So, nobody suspected Varun Kulkarni when he showed his own photo ID against Varun K's ticket, and vice versa. Further, Varun convinced VK to keep the ticket swapping bit a secret. Since VK was a public figure, he agreed to do that to avoid any trouble. So when VK was performing at Varun's office function in Delhi, on the evening of the 4th of July, Varun was already back in Mumbai. Varun's colleagues thought he was unwell and resting in his room. So nobody bothered him. He was carrying minimal luggage and no one in the hotel had any inkling when he walked out. Besides, he was a frequent traveller and a corporate guest; nobody would suspect him. On the morning of the 5th of July, VK checked out from the Delhi hotel for both Varuns."

Varun Kulkarni looked at Mili and did not know what to say. He turned towards ACP Trehan and said, "I agree about the ticket swapping. But honestly, I did not kill anyone. How did you find out about VK?"

"Well Varun, VK told us himself. VK knew Saahil quite well and they had played guitar together a few times. When he heard about the attack on Saahil, VK called to tell us that he had met Saahil on 2nd July," said Trehan.

"It was a responsible gesture from VK. Usually celebrities shy away, fearing a controversy. VK was all praises for Saahil's singing style. When we probed further, he told us about his performance in Delhi and the stay extension, courtesy good friend Varun Kulkarni. The rest is history," said Mili.

"No wonder you readily had boarding passes, tickets available when we questioned you. Just to make it realistic, you said they were in office for claiming expenses," said Gatha.

"I did not kill anyone!" Varun screamed.

"Your biggest mistake was to ask your friend VK to perform at your office function," said Mili.

"It doesn't end here. You killed an innocent taxi driver and finally, you killed your wife!" said Anubhav.

"You guys are crazy!" said Varun.

"You helped Morena attack Saahil and kill Farzad. That was her revenge. But you had to fulfil your own revenge too. You killed the taxi driver first so that I would suspect Morena. Finally you killed Morena and made it look like suicide," said Mili. "Besides, you made the terrible mistake of attacking me!"

Rashi spoke in a broken voice, "I should not have listened to Varun when he called me on 8th July. I was at the door and kept ringing the bell wondering why Morena was not opening the door. I tried entering with the spare keys I had but the door was locked from inside. I called Morena but she did not take the call. Just at that moment, Varun called me. It was so sudden! I was taken aback as he never calls like that! He asked me to buy a bottle of wine to cheer up Morena. I happily obliged. I had no clue that he was calling me from inside the apartment itself and was busy killing my friend," Rashi stated, crying bitterly.

ACP Trehan said, "Relax Rashi. Thank you for reporting this phone call."

Varun looked at Rashi with tearful eyes. "You too don't believe me, Rashi? This detective has messed up everything. But the fact remains – I did not kill anyone."

"Time up, Varun Kulkarni! You are under arrest for the murder of Farzad Mistry, Nirmal Kanitkar, and Morena Dave," said ACP Trehan.

Morena's parents sat still for some time. They could not come to terms with the betrayal yet. Why would their son-in-law want to kill their daughter?

"Thank you everyone for your attendance. None of you should leave Mumbai in the next forty-eight hours," announced ACP Trehan.

"But you said the case is solved?" asked Rounak Arora.

"Just do as you are told, Rounak," said Anubhav.

One by one, the Daves, Zarine employees and Colonel Kerkar left the police station. The sky was a deep orange. The sunset had left fiery orange imprints across the sky.

"Thank you Varun," Mili said under her breath as the cops were taking him away.

"I can do anything to nail the bastard who tried to kill my wife," Varun replied. "I hope you will beat him to death."

"Your support has led us to the culprit. I will talk to you soon," said Mili and patted Varun on his shoulder.

Anubhav and Gatha stared at Mili while she spoke to Varun in whispers.

▼

Kwest office

9.00 p.m.
10 July 2014

"What were you telling Varun today, Mili?" Gatha asked.

"Varun Kulkarni did not kill anyone," said Mili, munching on a juicy apple.

"What? Why did we get him arrested then?" asked Anubhav.

"I cannot risk any more lives. He will be safe in police custody," Mili replied matter-of-factly.

"Why didn't you tell us?"

"What would I tell you?" Mili shot back.

"That Varun is innocent! Who killed Farzad Mistry then? Or is that still a mystery?" replied Gatha.

"We are very close, just not there yet."

"What are you saying, Mili? I don't understand anything," said Anubhav.

Silenced

*

9.00 a.m.
11 July 2014

"Welcome ACP," said Mili. "How is our guest in the prison doing?"

"Varun is doing well. But he is staying at my place," said ACP Trehan.

"Thank you, ACP. I am sure he is safer there," said Mili with a smile.

"You know, it is strange when you call me ACP or Trehan. How about changing that to just Purab?" asked ACP Trehan.

"Purab it is then. By the way, my name is Mili, in case you were wondering!" Mili added teasingly.

"Thank you Mili," came the quick reply.

"Does anyone else know about the surveillance camera yet?" Mili inquired.

"No, I have printed the blow-ups for you. Even DIG sir doesn't know yet," replied Trehan.

"Indeed a picture speaks a thousand words. Had I not met Farzad Mistry's wife the other day, I would have never found out, perhaps," said Mili.

ACP Trehan nodded, "I am still in a daze. But we have to give them full marks for the planning."

"You bet!" said Mili.

Gatha and Anubhav entered office. Mili quickly hid the picture.

"Oops, we will come later if there is a secret discussion going on here," Gatha said, cynically.

"Breaking news! We just received the CCTV camera footage revealing the face behind Farzad's attack on 4th July," declared Mili.

"Ah, but you had the footage yesterday itself," said Gatha. "You told everyone at the police station. Remember?"

"I lied, Gates. We got the print just now, thanks to Purab. Here you go!" Mili shared the pictures.

"Purab?"

"That's how ACP Trehan wants to be addressed, Anubhav."

As Anubhav looked at ACP Purab Trehan, the latter smiled in acknowledgment.

"So there is no way Morena was innocent," mourned Gatha.

Even Anubhav, who was expecting some more drama after the trailer he witnessed at the police station the day before, was dull.

"This conversation with Farzad Mistry clearly happened. We got these pictures from a video clip."

"What happened? You two are not happy that we finally have our murderer?" asked Mili.

ACP Trehan started laughing.

"What now?" asked Gatha. "Suddenly you two are a team, is it?"

"Now, listen to me carefully," Mili said in a voice that demanded immediate attention.

"I want you guys to see some other pictures. Look at them carefully."

"Hmm...nice. But what is the point now?" Gatha said, looking at the pictures that Mili spread over the table.

"Yuvika Patil," said Mili, introducing the person in the pictures. "Upcoming model, singer, and struggler. A resident of Goa, Yuvika shifted to Mumbai a couple of years back to become a model."

"Context?" Anubhav asked.

"Just take a look at her pictures. Oh and one second – I want to show you some videos too. Wait, I'll just get my laptop," said Mili.

"What are you saying? How can this be Yuvika Patil?"

"Farzad's wife identified her from this photo," Mili said, handing over a photo to Gatha.

"Oh my god! I can't believe it," said Anubhav.

"So we have established one fact. Farzad Mistry knew Yuvika Patil. They were good friends," said Mili, while opening the video files on her laptop.

"Did Saahil and Morena know her too?" asked Anubhav.

"Perhaps Saahil did, going by his popularity among women, but I'm not sure about Morena."

"We may want to check with Varun?"

"No, he doesn't know her," ACP Trehan added confidently. "I showed him the videos this morning and he too was zapped."

"Okay guys, now look at this video from 2013 first and then this new one from last week. See how her hairstyle and nose are completely different in the most recent video?" asked Mili.

"I understand that a model can change her hairdo every day. But why the nose job? She looked good in her earlier avatar too," commented Anubhav.

"Several people go for cosmetic surgery these days. What's so surprising about that?" commented Gatha.

"If you closely look at these two pictures, you will understand why the surgery was done," Mili replied, placing two photos on the table. "Now tell me who is who?"

Gatha's jaws dropped. "This is insane! I always thought Morena was innocent."

Mili said, "I know what you are saying Gatha. But people are unpredictable."

"What next?"

"ACP...I mean Purab, you go and talk to the beautiful lady. Please take good care of her," Mili smiled at Trehan. He had done stupendous work on this case so far.

Gatha looked at Mili from the corner of her eye while examining the photographs.

"At your service ma'am," said ACP Trehan. "Are you planning to visit the Kerkars anytime today?"

"No. The Daves first. You have the family history with you Anubhav?" Mili asked.

"Yes, I do."

"Oh, I forgot to update you about something really important. Remember the attack on me last week?" asked Mili.

"Who can forget that?" Gatha said, in a frustrated tone.

"Nirmal Kanitkar, the taxi driver who died, was a resident of Dharavi."

"Right! I waited for you at the bus stop for an hour the other day Mili and you did not turn up. We had to go to Dharavi," said Gatha angrily.

"Sorry, I got caught up, Gates. Incidentally, I met my childhood friend Snigdha on the same day. She is Morena's psychologist, as you know. After talking to her, I got more insight into Morena's life, especially her history of depression, you know," Mili said.

"How is that connected to the murder of Nirmal Kanitkar?" asked Anubhav.

"Oh, I lost track again. So, coming back to the point, Nirmal, our taxi driver, was a resident of Dharavi. Amar Kerkar, Saahil's younger brother, has business clients in Dharavi and is a frequent visitor there. Saahil's laptop bag is purchased from Salim's shop in Dharavi. The shoes Saahil was wearing on 4th July are also from Dharavi. In fact, Saahil buys most of his leather goods from the area where Nirmal lived," Mili reckoned.

"How can you be so sure, Mili?"

"Shame on me if I cannot recognize something purchased from the flourishing leather industry in Mumbai that we call Dharavi," Mili contended.

"I ask because you abhor leather products," Gatha said, curiously.

"I don't like animals being killed to beautify myself or my house. But that is a separate discussion," Mili replied. "The bag Saahil was carrying on the 4th of July and the shoes on him – both were purchased from Salim's at Dharavi."

"Interesting!" said ACP Trehan.

"Hold your breath now as I announce my stalker to you," Mili said, enthusiastically.

All eyes were on her.

"Amar Kerkar?" Gatha asked, making a guess.

"Love you Gates. Yes, it was Amar Kerkar. He hit me on the head with a hockey stick. He sent his friend Nirmal Kanitkar to pick me up. I dragged myself into the cab and fainted after sometime. In that dungeon-like garage, Amar killed Nirmal and left that note in Nirmal's pocket. He knew I would discover it."

"How can you be so sure that it was Amar Kerkar who was following you that day?" asked Anubhav.

"From his footsteps. I remember every detail about the footsteps behind me on the 7th of July… the sound of the shoes hitting the ground, the walking pace, the thrust of every step – I know the pattern just so well," Mili accounted. "So when I heard them again at the hospital the very next day, when we left Saahil's room, I knew my stalker was in the hospital."

"Oh my God!"

"When I thought harder," continued Mili, "I realized that I had heard these steps earlier that morning too…just before entering Saahil's room."

"When Amar said that he wanted to take his parents to the hospital café?" asked Anubhav, appalled.

"Yes, you got it! His eyes were deep red that day, though not from tears. After attacking me just the night before, it was obvious that he didn't want to face me. When he walked away with his parents, my mind must have recorded his footsteps!"

"But how do you know Amar wrote the note?"

"I sent that paper to the handwriting expert," said Mili. "I also went to Dharavi, to Salim's main shop. At least four people saw Amar with Nirmal Kanitkar on the day he was killed, which also happens to be the day I was targeted – 7th July 2014."

"So, Amar Kerkar attacked Saahil and then you?" asked Gatha.

"Wrong! Amar Kerkar attacked me and killed Nirmal. His role ends there. He did not kill Farzad, nor did he attack Saahil or Morena," said Mili.

Mili's phone rang. "One minute guys, I must take this call."

"That's wonderful news, Dr Dighe. Is Varun there too? Please don't inform anyone else yet."

Mili came back smiling. "We have come to the last phase of our case folks. I have good news for you."

"What happened?" asked Anubhav.

"Morena Dave is out of danger. Her husband is by her side now. But we are not declaring this to anyone before tomorrow."

"Whatt?" shouted Anubhav. "Morena is alive?"

"Yes, without her, we will not be able to close the case logically. Let's go meet the Daves and the Kerkars in the meantime."

"Oh my God, this is wonderful news! But why didn't you tell us that Morena was alive?"

"We weren't sure that she would survive, Gates. The doctors are magicians."

"But Morena won't have any memory of that night, right?" asked Gatha. "Considering that the drug she was given will erase the memory of that day from her life?"

"That is right. However, I hope she can tell us what happened before she was drugged," Mili answered.

"I'll go get Yuvika Patil till then," ACP Trehan said.

"Thanks, Purab. Please don't forget to arrest Amar from his office tomorrow. Until then, nobody should know that he killed Nirmal Kanitkar," said Mili.

"That goes without saying, Mili! My men are keeping an eye on him anyway. We won't let him get away," assured Trehan.

Meeting Morena's parents

11.00 a.m.
11 July 2014

The police had released Morena and Varun's apartment the previous evening, following which Morena's parents had shifted to their daughter's house. Their younger daughter Divya, who flew in from Delhi, also joined them.

"Thank you for your help, Dr Dave. And I am sorry we had to arrest Varun. There was no other way we could save him," said Mili.

"Nothing matters now. We lost our daughter," Dr Dave sat down on the sofa, disdain written all over his face.

Mrs Minakshi Dave walked in and took a seat beside her husband.

"What I am going to tell you now will uplift your spirits," said Mili.

"When will the police release my daughter's body? Does it take so long to do a post-mortem?" Mrs Dave could not hold back her tears.

"They are calling her a murderer and what not. Can we at least complete her last rites?" Mrs Dave folded her hands and requested Mili.

"Sir, ma'am – the good news is that you need not worry about all those things," Mili said, beaming.

The Dave couple shot a betrayed look at Mili.

"We don't appreciate your joke, detective! Nobody expects sensitivity from law enforcers, but this is the limit!" Dr Dave said, enraged.

"Your daughter is alive. She is out of danger and under police protection."

"Whaatt?"

Mili loved the change in expression on their faces. Priceless!

"Yes, we had to declare her dead as we were apprehensive that the killer would try to harm her again," Mili said.

Minakshi Dave hugged Mili. "I want to see my child."

"You can meet Morena tomorrow. We have to arrest the culprits before that," Mili said.

Dr Dave nodded. "Who are they?" he asked.

"You will get to know everything tomorrow, I promise. In the meantime, I have to ask you some questions about Morena's childhood," said Mili.

"Ask anything you want."

"In 1996, did you and your family visit Alibaug, Dr Dave?"

"We have been there quite a few times. I cannot recall. Do you remember Minakshi?" Dr Dave asked his wife.

"I think we did. Divya clicks many pictures. She will know. Divya is our younger daughter," said Mrs Dave.

"Yes, I know. Is she here?"

"She is taking a bath. I will call her."

As they waited for Morena's younger sister Divya, Mrs Dave walked towards Morena's wardrobe to look for family albums.

"Here you go. This one is from the nineties," Mrs Dave smiled, happy now that she would be able to meet her elder daughter again.

Looking at Minakshi Dave's enthusiasm, Mili did not have the heart to tell her that the Kwest team had already sieved through all the albums, but had found nothing from Alibaug.

Morena's face had not changed, Mili thought, as Mrs Dave drew her attention to one of the photographs. Morena looked almost the same as she did twenty years back. The smile was her biggest asset.

"Hi," said Divya as she shook hands with Mili.

"Hi Divya! I was looking for some details on your Alibaug trip in 1996."

"In 1996? I was a kid then."

"Do you remember anything from that trip? Any accident or anything peculiar?" Mili asked.

"Mmmm. I cannot be sure. But now that you mention accident, I think somebody got drowned in the sea," Divya said.

"Oh yes, I remember," said Dr Dave suddenly. "We read in the papers about a girl who lost her life due to the water currents. It was a small news item but caught my eye perhaps because we had just returned from Alibaug, and the trip was fresh in our minds."

"I still feel a shiver down my spine thinking it could have been our daughters too; they were playing in the sea," Mrs Dave said, worriedly.

"Did you know the girl who died, Dr Dave? Or may be anyone in her family?" asked Mili.

"No idea," Dr Dave replied.

"Divya, do you have any photographs from that trip?" asked Gatha.

"I have plenty of them. But none in Mumbai."

"Would you have any over the Internet?"

"No, it was a long time back. Let me check if Morena has an album."

"No, she doesn't. We have searched all her belongings," Anubhav said.

"I want to ask you one more time, just to be sure. Please try to remember – Did anything else happen? Did Morena do anything that surprised you guys at Alibaug?"

The Dave family sat together, looking at one another, trying to think hard. Then, they finally said 'no'.

"Divya, I know that was a long time back. But please try to think. May be Morena hid it from her parents but didn't she confess anything to you at least?" Mili asked desperately.

Divya looked concerned, but she shook her head after a while.

"Okay," Mili said. "I will show a photo. See if you know this girl."

Anubhav handed over the photo to Divya Dave. The Dave family looked intently at the picture of the sixteen-year-old swimmer.

Finally, Divya said, "She looks very familiar. But I just cannot remember."

"Let me refresh your memory. You met her at Alibaug," said Mili.

"Oh yess! How could I forget? Her name is Kashi. She is a swimming champion. We met at Alibaug and I became her fan instantly. We even clicked pictures together. We met for about ten or fifteen minutes. She was so ambitious, focused... and inspiring! She promised to keep in touch but obviously, that did not happen. She must be an established swimmer now."

"Unfortunately, she died," said Mili.

"What? When? How?" Divya asked, appalled.

"This happened minutes after you met her at Alibaug. She was swimming against the current and could not hold on. She drowned," Mili added.

"Oh my god! That is terrible. She was very young, almost my sister's age!" Divya said.

"Her family believes that somebody pushed her into the waters. Do you have any idea who that could be?" Mili asked the Daves.

"How do we know? We did not even know that she drowned that day. This is so unfortunate," said Divya.

"Let me ask you straight – did Morena have anything to do with Kashi's death?" Mili inquired.

Minakshi Dave couldn't hold back her tears.

Yuvika Patil

❦

Police Station

1.00 p.m.
11 July 2014

"Hello, Purab," Gatha greeted Trehan and looked at Mili. She was blushing.

"Hi…hi Gatha," Trehan fumbled, surprised by Gatha's emphasis on his name. He also looked at Mili.

She returned a 'what' expression and pulled a chair.

"How is our guest doing?" Mili asked.

"She was crying. She is waiting to meet you," replied ACP Trehan.

"Oh, why waste any time then?"

Mili, Gatha, Anubhav and ACP Trehan walked up to Yuvika's cell. Yuvika sat in one corner of the dingy cell, hugging herself tightly.

"Hello Yuvika," said Mili.

Yuvika looked up at Mili, her deep blue eyes overflowing with tears.

"Contact lenses?" Mili asked ACP Trehan.

"No, these are real. She was wearing the brown contact lenses all this while," said Trehan.

"Not just that. You were right, Mili. She got the nose job done last month. I have the details of the surgeon. She has also styled her hair to match the character she was playing. Luckily, she did not have to bother about the height or weight."

"Incredible," said Gatha. "I would have never believed it, had I not met Yuvika Patil in person."

Anubhav was quiet. He was stunned and kept staring at Yuvika.

"Separated at birth?" he wondered.

"Well Yuvika, you must have guessed that we have cracked your story. Out with the motive now," ACP Trehan said, coldly.

"I already told you Inspector, I did not kill anyone," she said, sniffing.

"Strange, isn't it ACP?" added Mili. "No one kills anyone, yet people die. Why did you kill Farzad Mistry? He was a family friend, right?"

"I didn't kill Farzad. I just called him to the highway. I had no idea he would be killed. Believe me, please!"

"Stop lying. What did you tell him when you called?"

"I identified myself as Morena Dave. I said it was urgent and I needed help. He was shocked to learn that Morena was calling him. Before he could ask me anything else, I pleaded with him to meet me at the highway as I was in deep trouble. Within five-seven minutes, he reached the spot, which was right opposite to the Horizon Mall. He was not happy to see me at all. He was annoyed," Yuvika paused.

"What exactly happened on the 4th of July?" Mili asked, raising her voice.

Yuvika quivered. Then she started narrating the course of events.

Farzad: *What kind of stupidity is this, Yuvika? Look at the weather. Go home.*

Yuvika: *I thought you would be surprised to meet me Farzad.*

Farzad: *Why did you take Morena's name? How do you know her?*

Yuvika: *(Lying) You mentioned her so many times. I was just pulling your leg.*

Farzad: *This is not funny. It is past 11.00 p.m. and you do not even have an umbrella. Here, take mine and leave. Or, come with me and stay at my place tonight. Everyone will love to see you.*

Yuvika: *Oh, no no. I have to go. Let us sit under that tree for a while. Just five minutes. I have something very important to tell you.*

Farzad and Yuvika sat under the tree in front of them to keep the rain at bay. Farzad's temper had cooled off by then.

Farzad: *Guess what? Today only I was thinking about you.*

Yuvika: *About me?*

Farzad: *Yes, I was asking my colleagues Rounak and Saahil if they know you. Saahil finds similarities between people all the time. So, I wanted to ask him if he knows you.*

Yuvika: *Oh God! Why did you say that? Why did you take my name? What did he say?*

Farzad: *A cat came in front of his car and our conversation ended abruptly.*

Yuvika: *Anyway, I am very thirsty. Let me finish my drink. You want some?*

Farzad: *Okay, one sip.*

[After a while]

Farzad: *Nice drink. What is it?*

Yuvika: *Apple juice. You can finish it. I have to go now.*

Farzad: *What did you want to say?*
Yuvika: *Nothing important.*
Farzad: *You came all the way to give me this apple juice?*

"That's all we spoke about," said Yuvika. "Farzad got a headache. He had never consumed alcohol in his life before that day."

"And he never will, you b****," screamed Mili. "On top of that, you mixed the sedative in his drink?"

"And then you just pushed him in front of the speeding truck and put the blame on Morena," Gatha said angrily.

"*I did not!*"

"You are equally at fault as your accomplice. You could have had a flourishing career in modelling. Look at what you have done to yourself!"

"How did you bring Saahil to Yarawada? How did you manage to shift him to the driver's seat?" asked ACP Trehan.

"Amar helped me," said Yuvika.

"Amar Kerkar?" Anubhav gulped.

"Did Amar push Farzad in front of the truck too?"asked Mili.

"No. Farzad was walking like a drunkard. He had to cross the road in order to reach home. He lost balance and the truck hit him. It was an accident, how many times will I tell you?" shouted Yuvika. "Let me go!"

"And you guys waited and watched? Wasn't he your friend?" asked ACP Trehan.

Yuvika kept quiet.

"How did Amar Kerkar enter the scene?" Gatha asked, astonished.

"When I drove to Saahil's home, he was still unconscious. Amar was waiting inside the garage for us. He has duplicate keys to Saahil's house and the attached private garage space," said Yuvika.

"Whoa! Saahil is Amar's own brother?" Anubhav asked.

Yuvika threw a dirty look at Anubhav.

"You deliberately hit the tree before pulling the brakes in front of my house. Then both of you pulled Saahil on to the driver's seat. You ensured his head hit the steering. But before that you created the 'screeching' noise that woke me up," said Mili.

"You got that sound from the Internet, isn't it? It's part of the prelude music of the first song in the Riverine Specials album. Right?"

"Yes," said Yuvika, startled. "It was a rare album. We didn't think anyone would suspect us. Besides, it is just a six-second audio."

"Perhaps I was lucky there, Yuvika," said Mili. "When I was busy searching 'car screeching sounds' over the Internet, the radio played this number, out of the blue! It didn't take me less than a second to understand that you guys had lifted the sound from this song!"

Trehan stared at Mili in silent admiration.

"You had it stored on your mobile phone. Using Bluetooth, you played it on the car stereo in full volume. The noise gave you time to put Saahil's head on the steering, get off from the car, and walk away. Is that how it happened?" asked Mili.

Yuvika nodded hesitantly.

"But Amar Kerkar was home attending some neighbour's function, right?" asked Gatha.

"No, he left early, citing a headache. I spoke with his neighbour. Amar did not have dinner with them. His wife knew that he was outside, but she did not disclose anything. His parents were not aware of his absence," answered Mili.

"How much money did you make, Yuvika? I don't see any other motive for you to commit a ghastly crime like this!"

"Ten lakhs."

"Each murder – five lakhs, is it?" asked ACP Trehan

"I did not kill anyone."

"How did you attack Morena?" asked Gatha.

"It was easy to get into her building. Nobody suspected me."

"How shameless!" Anubhav whispered to Gatha.

"Morena was surprised to see me. I was equally stunned as we had never met before that day."

"Since you drugged her already, why did you slit her wrist?"

"That was the plan. I did not ask questions. I just got my money."

"You put your nursing training to good use, Yuvika. Instead of saving lives, you procured the drugs to harm people," said ACP Trehan.

Yuvika was rubbing her eyes. She looked at ACP Trehan, traumatized.

"We know about your nursing background. A nurse-turned-model-turned-murderer. Quite a career graph, that!" said Gatha.

"Why were you wearing a black dress? To confuse Saahil?" asked Anubhav.

"That was the plan," Yuvika said, defiantly.

"What else was planned?" Mili asked, cynically.

With a straight face, Yuvika replied, "I was supposed to drag Morena to the bedroom after slitting her wrists. But the doorbell rang and I became nervous."

"Yes, that was Rashi," Mili said. "Had she entered the house, you would have killed her too."

"I did not kill Morena. I was only asked to injure her. Not kill her," Yuvika added, crying. "I don't know how she died."

"You must have used the refuge area to walk to the other wing of the building and exit from the gate of Wing B," said Mili. "No wonder the security guards didn't see you leave the building."

"Yes, I knew the refuge area would let me to go from Wing A to B in a jiffy," said Yuvika.

"Why did you wear 'The Devil' perfume?"

"To confuse Morena. It was her favourite perfume."

"Did you help to kill the taxi driver also?"

"No, it was just Amar. I was nowhere in the picture."

"I thought as much!" said Mili.

"Why don't you arrest them?" Yuvika screamed as Mili and team left the police station.

The Perfect Plan

Amar Kerkar's residence

9.30 a.m.
12 July 2014

"Stop thinking about it now, Saahil," Suhasini Kerkar said. "You have to eat well and get fit soon."

"Where did Papa go in the morning?" Saahil asked his mother, while helping himself with another spoonful of the apple pudding.

"He went to the bank. Don't worry, Amar is dropping him on his way to work."

"I am happy that Muskaan has resumed school too," said Saahil. "I will go back to my flat today."

"You are not going anywhere till you heal completely," Mrs Kerkar said. "You must rest."

"How can I rest until she rests, Aai?" Saahil said, and hugged his mother.

"We would never be able to forgive ourselves if you didn't come back Saahil," Mrs Kerkar said. "I am so happy that you are home. Your father does not say much. But at this age, we won't be able to survive another shock."

"I am here, right in front of you. Why are you worried? The guilty has been punished. Now she will rest in peace, finally."

Saahil garlanded the photograph that he had hung on the drawing room hall of Amar's home in the morning.

"She looks so pretty, Aai," Saahil said.

"Yes, prettier than ever."

The doorbell rang.

"I'll answer it, Aai. You see why Jyoti is calling you," Saahil replied, as he heard Amar's wife calling out for his mother.

Saahil opened the door and his jaws dropped. He stepped out, looked right and left. Then he retracted back to the threshold of his apartment, and gently closed the door behind him.

"What are you doing here?" he whispered, furiously.

The visitor did not say anything but continued to stare at him.

"I told you, we cannot meet now. This is risky. Go now. I will call you when the time is right."

The visitor continued to stare at Saahil, one teardrop making its way from her eye down to her cheek.

"What drama is this now Yuvika? Please go," Saahil whispered in her ear.

"You don't even recognize me, Saahil."

Saahil looked at her in disbelief when he heard those words.

"Morena Dave, Senior Project Manager, Zarine Software," Mili announced as she came out from behind the staircase.

"What's going on here?" Saahil managed to say nervously and pushed the door that was right behind him. He tiptoed back inside his flat.

"We deeply regret your twin sister, Kashi, I mean, ace swimmer Enakshi Kerkar's untimely demise."

Mili's low-pitched voice startled Saahil.

"What happened, ma'am?" Saahil said in his charming, gullible style. He was looking excessively handsome, even with the pale green baggy T-shirt hanging over a paler pair of pajamas.

Mili started to walk towards Saahil and entered his apartment.

She looked at the garlanded photo on the wall and said, "For almost two years, you didn't go to college or mix up with people. You underwent psychological treatment. You could not study Medicine. There was so much unrest in you."

Saahil did not understand what was going on.

Mili continued, "Brigadier Rawat, your grandfather, made a 'will' with strict clauses. I wondered why? But after we reviewed your history, it became clear."

"There must have been a mistake, ma'am," Saahil said politely.

"No, Saahil. I know that you were shattered after Enakshi's death. Brigadier was worried if you would ever recover. So, he promptly transferred the Nasik land in your name. Known to be domineering, Brigadier had deep faith in Colonel Kerkar, your father. So, he gave the power to make any amendments to the will only to him."

"Ma'am, you are crossing the limit now," Saahil warned. "Yuvika, what is all this nonsense?"

Mili continued, undeterred, "Since you had suicidal tendencies, Saahil, and because the psychiatrist had advised that your wound might take decades to heal, Brigadier created those strict clauses, to protect you."

Saahil and his mother kept staring at Mili, shaken!

Mili turned towards her team, who had also entered the apartment following her.

She continued, "Saahil Kerkar met Yuvika Patil online. Initially, he thought Morena was playing a prank on him. But when he met Yuvika in person, he knew the time was right to avenge his twin sister Enakshi Kerkar alias Kashi's death. Am I right or am I right, Saahil?"

Anubhav tightly gripped Saahil's hands while Mili spoke. Saahil's sister-in-law came to the drawing room hearing so many voices.

Mili said, "Saahil knew Yuvika was an aspiring model. He promised her a sum of ten lakhs rupees and a modelling contract once she completed this special assignment. Yuvika was a trained nurse, and that was a bonus for Saahil."

Morena continued to cry as she heard Mili speak.

"Yuvika Patil, the perfect Morena lookalike. Even Saahil was confused today. He mistook Morena for Yuvika."

Anubhav pitched in now. "But when Saahil had met Yuvika for the first time in January this year, it was not so easy. Yuvika's eyes were blue. So Saahil bought brown contact lenses for her, matching Morena's eyes. Yuvika's nose was different too! So, Saahil paid for her nose surgery. Saahil's attention to detail is mind-blowing. He worked on Yuvika's hairstyle, posture, mannerisms, etc., until he was cent-per-cent sure that she looked like a carbon copy of Morena Dave."

"Stop playing this game now, Ms Ray. Morena is dead. She tried to kill me. You all are trying to fool me. Come on Yuvika, tell them," Saahil shouted.

Morena came forward and extended her hands. He saw the bandage on her wrists. He looked at her face. The kindness in her eyes was difficult to miss. Saahil lowered his head and closed his eyes.

"Tell us your story, Saahil."

There was absolute silence for a moment. But in that moment, Saahil's mind travelled a thousand miles. Morena, Kashi, parents, Nasik, Yuvika, Zarine, Singapore....

"We are waiting," Mili said, losing her patience.

Saahil looked at the faces staring at him and took a deep breath. "Where is Yuvika now?"

"In jail. Your brother will soon be joining her there. ACP Trehan has reached Amar's office."

"Noooooooooooo," screamed Jyoti, Amar's wife. "Please leave Amar out of all this."

Gatha put an arm around Jyoti's shoulder and helped her sit on the sofa. This was her eighth month and so much tension was not good for her.

"Yuvika's passport has never been stamped. She should go to Singapore. She has not killed anyone," Saahil said.

"Oh yes, how did I forget to mention this? Saahil has got Yuvika enrolled for an advanced modelling course at Singapore. What perfect timing! Any guesses who is sponsoring this?" Mili asked her team.

"Saahil's grandfather?" asked Gatha.

"Precisely! Before his thirty-fifth birthday, Saahil sold a part of the ancestral land at Nasik to a businessman. He has received the payment too," said Mili.

"Saahil, what are they saying?" Mrs Kerkar asked. Saahil did not say a word.

"You killed Farzad only because he knew that Yuvika Patil looked like Morena?" asked Mili, aghast.

"He was a simple man, just playing on with your lookalike game. He made the mistake of taking her name in your car on the 4th of July. Before anyone else could find out about Yuvika, you killed him. You are insane!"

"How did you accommodate the last minute murder?" asked Anubhav.

"Oh, he was already flirting with Yuvika and coaxed her to call up Farzad, posing as Morena. He allured Yuvika with his charm and asked her to meet Farzad at a place where the surveillance camera could capture the meeting – bang opposite the CCTV camera at Horizon Mall. And who did you all see in the video clip from that camera?" asked Mili.

"We saw Morena, of course," said Gatha. "How would we know that Yuvika even existed?"

"Crime never pays, Saahil," said Mili. "You know how I discovered that it was Yuvika in the camera footage?"

Saahil looked at Mili in dismay.

"I had shown Morena's photo to Shireen Mistry, Farzad's wife. Shireen immediately identified Morena as Yuvika. I was lucky that she knew Yuvika. Or perhaps you were unlucky, Saahil. Or is ill-prepared a better word?" Mili said, irritated.

"Farzad's family knew Yuvika?" Morena asked, breaking her silence.

"Yes, much before Saahil met her. She is a family friend. Yuvika never shared that with Saahil though," replied Mili.

"Did you not ask Yuvika how she knew Farzad?" Anubhav asked Saahil.

"She said he was an acquaintance," Saahil replied coldly.

"What did you tell me at the hospital when I asked you if Farzad's dad had come to see you, do you remember, Mr Saahil Kerkar?" asked Mili.

Saahil looked at Mili blankly.

"You told me that you had seen solace in Cyril Mistry's eyes, assuming that he was at peace after Morena's death but you also said that he met you during the visiting hours, between 4.30 and 6.30 p.m. Now you tell me Saahil, how did Mr Mistry know at 6.30 p.m. that Morena would die later that night? I did not expect such a silly mistake from a mastermind like you!" said Mili.

Saahil tried to release his hands from Anubhav's grip.

"Oh, and there is more, Saahil. While giving your statement on the 8th of July, you said that Farzad was a teetotaller! Why did you give me that information? Nobody had told you that the police found alcohol in Farzad's body."

Saahil did not know where to look, or what to say.

"What I do not understand is why you chose such a complex process to fake the murder attempt on you?" said Mili.

"After dropping Morena home, you picked up Yuvika from the bus stop near Morena's house. What you missed to notice was that Varun, Morena's husband was waiting at the same bus stop. Next, Yuvika injected you with that sedative. You moved from the driver's seat and Yuvika took over. That made sense because she knew where Farzad lived. You did not. But then, if she had drugged you, how did you help her pull Farzad's body into the bushes?"

Saahil was silent.

"Come on Saahil, we want an answer," said Anubhav.

Finally, Saahil spoke. "That was a rehearsal. Yuvika pretended to pierce the needle at around 10 p.m. and I was acting as if I had been drugged. Only after we moved Farzad's body into the bushes did Yuvika give me the injection."

"What a sick sadist! You gave a lift to this colleague in the morning and dumped his body in the bushes at night. You acted like a seasoned criminal," said Gatha.

Mili continued, looking at Saahil, "Varun had been stalking you on the 4th of July. Varun had decided to spend the night at the bus stop, had he not spotted you near his house, for a second time! Varun told me, *'I saw Morena taking a lift from Saahil again that night.'* Varun was so shocked that he called Morena from his pre-paid Delhi number, which was mapped to his Delhi hotel number. Morena received the call. Just to be sure that his wife was at home, Varun asked Morena to open his wardrobe and check if his black shirt had been ironed. He even asked her to click a selfie and send it to him. Morena instantly obliged.

But because Varun's cell was switched off, he could not view her photo. When he saw it the next morning, the first thing he noticed was the timestamp. Morena was very much at home that night," said Mili.

Saahil's face was emotionless, expressionless now.

"Can I get a glass of water, please?" Mili asked. She walked to the dining table and poured herself a glass of water from the bottle that stood still at the centre of the table.

"Okay, so where was I? Yes, after getting rid of Farzad, Yuvika finally injects you with the sedative. You get drowsy and Yuvika continues driving your car. She reaches your home and waits for you to regain consciousness. Once you are in your senses, the two of you spend a good time together and perhaps even laugh over the murder!" Mili said harshly.

Saahil's face grew red. "Arrest me. I do not want to hear anymore."

Mili continues, ignoring him. "Then, you gorge on prawns, to get the desired allergies. That was a big risk, which saw you fighting for your life for the next three days. Had Dr Shah not started your treatment on time, you would have been dead by now."

Suhasini Kerkar looked more shocked than ever.

"Amar arrives at your place on time. Next, you, Yuvika, and Amar head towards your garage. Amar has already cleaned your car by that time. Per your instructions, only the outside of the car is cleaned and the floor. Why? To confuse us, obviously. As for us, we got four set of fingerprints from your car – those of Saahil, Morena, Farzad, and Rounak. Amar was cautious but Yuvika was not. Unfortunately, for you, we also recovered a fifth set of fingerprints – Yuvika's."

"Why did you do all this? I cannot believe this!" cried Suhasini Kerkar.

Ignoring her, Mili continued, "Then, the three of you sit inside the car. You instruct Yuvika to slit your wrist. I can understand how painful it must have been for Amar to watch the scene! But with revenge in your eyes, both of you execute the dangerous plan. You prefer to be in your senses when your wrist is slit. Our trained nurse Yuvika's experience comes in handy here. She knows exactly when to stop! When the allergies get worse, Amar and Yuvika drive you down to my house, at rocket speed. After shifting you to the driver's seat, they leave, confident that you will get help. This was nothing less than a suicide attempt, Saahil Kerkar!"

"We all know what happened after that. You were half-dead. The crowd gathered, I spotted you, and then the ambulance transferred you to the hospital. You took a huge risk. So much for revenge? You didn't think about your parents, even once?" asked Mili.

"Yuvika had the anti-allergy medicines with her. But Saahil, you refused to take them. You could have died!" snapped Gatha.

Saahil flared up. "I didn't care. Whenever Morena made a mistake, she would say, *'Nothing can get worse than this. Nobody will send me to jail, right?'*" Saahil said mimicking Morena's voice. "So I decided to send her to jail. Morena killed my twin sister. She committed a heinous crime and deserved the punishment."

"Your twin sister?" Morena looked at Saahil, shocked. "I didn't even know you had a sister! Is that why you distanced yourself from me? You thought I killed your sister? Saahil?" Morena screamed at the top of her voice.

"This was a project that had to be executed. Like an astute project manager, Saahil implemented his deadly plan," added Anubhav.

"I loved Kashi more than my life. Someone who killed Kashi had to suffer," said Saahil. "Yes, she was my twin – a reflection of my own self."

"You attacked Morena on the basis of an eighteen-year-old picture? And you claim that she was your friend?" asked Gatha.

"Nothing was more important than avenging my sister's murder," said Saahil.

"Why didn't you kill Morena then?" asked Anubhav.

"I was shocked when I heard about Morena's death. The plan was never to kill her. I wanted her to suffer in jail. Yuvika informed that Morena's hand had moved a little after the wrists were slit and there were tears in her eyes. That's what I wanted – I wanted to see remorse in her eyes," Saahil started laughing viciously.

"You are disgusting! I cannot believe you did that," said Jyoti, Amar's wife.

"The Morena I have known would have never given Saahil's name to the police," Saahil added, still laughing.

"Stop it Saahil," yelled Morena.

"I saw you, Morena, you were running away from the beach with your sister. You were screaming – 'I did not do it, I did not do it'," said Saahil, hysterically.

"Alibaug, 1996! I don't even remember!" Morena said, holding her head.

"It was the 4th of July 1996. I will never forget that day, nor your face on the beach," Saahil said with hatred in his eyes.

"Let me throw some light here," said Mili, interrupting the heated exchange between the estranged friends.

"In 1996, the Dave family was visiting Alibaug for a holiday. Coincidentally, Saahil Kerkar and his twin sister Enakshi Kerkar were also in Alibaug at that time with a group of friends. Enakshi, or Kashi as she was better known as, was a national-level swimmer. On the 4th of July, Kashi was enjoying her swim in the sea. Despite requests from her friends and warnings from the lifeguards, Kashi refused to come out of the water. In 1996, the safety measures in place were not as advanced as they are today. Kashi was unable to resist the water currents and drowned in the sea."

"No, that's not true," screamed Saahil. "Morena and her sister pushed Kashi into the water to save themselves from drowning. They ran away like cowards while she was fighting for her life."

Morena kept looking at Saahil in disbelief. She did not know why he was saying what he was.

"I can't believe you can talk like this, Saahil," Morena muttered.

"No Saahil, you are wrong," said Mili.

"On the day Kashi died, Morena and her younger sister Divya were standing near the sea-shore. Their father had given them his wallet while he went for a swim in the sea. Morena and Divya were standing in ankle-deep water and chatting. Suddenly, a big wave came and swept the wallet away from Morena's hand. They could see it go away from them, tagged to a sunhat, which I believe, belonged to Kashi. They pointed to the wallet and ran towards the shore. While Morena was scared thinking what her dad would say, Divya tried to comfort Morena," said Mili.

"Oh yes, I remember," said Morena. "We had met a terrific swimmer at the beach that day. She was such a bright person, I suddenly remember her face," said Morena. She turned around to look at the picture on the wall. Everything fell into place now.

Morena walked up to Saahil, held his hand and said, "I did not kill your sister, Saahil. She was an angel. Divya was constantly talking about Kashi after we returned to Pune. That day, we were running on the beach, as we were scared that Dad would scold us. Trust me."

Morena continued, "Your sister was a national level swimmer, Saahil. Do you think if a frail teenager pushed her, she would drown in the sea? Why didn't you talk to me about it? How could you assume that I killed her?"

Saahil looked at Morena, covered his face and sat down. His mother was sitting on the sofa too. His pregnant sister-in-law could not take the tension and stepped back to her room.

Colonel Kerkar was back from the bank. He was standing at the door, appalled.

"Saahil, how did you know that Morena was in Alibaug in 1996? When did you realize she was the girl?" asked Gatha.

"Kashi has a photo from the beach. I recognized the girls who were running on the beach from that photo. I have looked at the photo every day, for the last eighteen years. I was always on the lookout for those two girls. One day, in 2013, Morena showed me her childhood photographs. I immediately recognized her as the older girl on the beach. I asked Morena if she had been to Alibaug in 1996. She confirmed that she did go there with her family. I told her that I was there too, in 1996. She said, *'I wish we had met then only. We'd be childhood pals then'*. I wanted to kill her that very day. But I had to plan this right. I wanted my sister's murderer to suffer for eighteen years, just the way I did... my family did," Saahil said angrily.

"You dragged your younger brother in this too. He has a family. Did you not think about your parents? They have lost Kashi already. Will they want to see you and Amar behind bars? You spoiled it for everyone, Saahil Kerkar," said Mili.

"Kashi was Amar's sister too. Like any other brother, Amar also wanted justice for her."

"My sons are my pride. I am proud that they tried to get justice for Kashi," said Colonel Kerkar suddenly to everyone's surprise. He had been standing at the hallway and watching this drama unfold.

"After serving in the Indian Army, I am astonished that you could make such a statement, Colonel," flared up Suhasini Kerkar. "This is not the man I married."

Colonel turned towards his wife with pain in his eyes. Saahil looked at his father, excited like a child.

"Is Sheena aware of your plan? Was she an accomplice?" Mili asked, interrupting the emotional outburst.

"No, not at all. Sheena and I were good time-pass for each other. That is all. I knew she was jealous of Morena," said Saahil, with a wicked laugh.

"She gifted you 'The Devil' perfume that she flicked from her uncle!" said Mili.

"Yes, as a birthday gift. I didn't want to keep it as it reminded me of Morena," said Saahil.

"How did that reach Yuvika?"

"Yuvika likes perfumes. So I gave it to her on the same day that I received it – 4th July."

"Wow, what an amazing set of people. Someone flicks something and gifts to her beau. He in turn gifts it to his bait," remarked Anubhav.

Saahil looked dreamy.

Relying on his army man's instinct, Anubhav anticipated that the situation might get out of control. He wanted to move Saahil to police custody immediately. He was quick to take advantage of Saahil's emotional state of mind.

"Saahil Kerkar, you are under arrest for the murder of Farzad Mistry, for planning your own murder, and for attempting to kill Morena Dave. The police have arrested your brother Amar Kerkar for the murder of Nirmal Kanitkar," announced Anubhav.

"Oh really? Is the police in such a sorry state that private detectives are arresting people? Don't try to fool me," Saahil said violently.

ACP Trehan's team had not yet arrived.

Before Anubhav could reply, Saahil suddenly jumped and reached for the drawer on his study table. He pulled out a pistol and put it against Morena's head.

"Let me go, else I will shoot her," he said. His swift acrobatics stunned everyone. "To the world, she is already dead. So this won't count as murder," Saahil continued in a slurred voice.

"You cannot get away with this, Saahil Kerkar. The police have surrounded this house. If you shoot now, you have no idea how many bullets will bring you down in no time. So, be a sensible man and drop the gun," Mili said calmly.

"*Shut up!*" Saahil screamed back and pulled Morena by the arm. With the pistol against her forehead, he started walking to the door. "I will kill Morena if you don't let me go."

"Everyone! *Step back!*" ordered Mili.

"That's like a good girl," smirked Saahil.

Saahil stepped out of the flat dragging Morena along and reached for the elevator. He entered the elevator with her and pressed the button for the ground floor. Mili and team followed by the stairs.

Once on the ground floor, Saahil ran outside the building. A taxi stopped in front of him. Saahil hit Morena on the forehead with the back of his pistol and pushed her. She collided against the lamppost on the road and fell on the ground. The pistol slipped out of Saahil's hand. Instead of going back to fetch it, Saahil boarded the cab and asked the driver to go as fast as he could. The cab moved a little, and then stopped.

"Drive, else I will kill you!" threatened Saahil. But the driver was not able to move the cab. It was stuck.

The police had reached. ACP Trehan's team surrounded the cab.

Mili opened the door and dragged Saahil out by the collar.

"You see Saahil, you are not the first criminal who tried to run," she said and punched him so hard on the face that he fell on the ground.

"All yours, ACP," Mili concluded as ACP Trehan handcuffed Saahil Kerkar.

Afterthought

❧

"I hate to think that Saahil committed this crime. I remember him as that carefree singer on the train who was in love with life," Mili said.

Gatha added, "His mother was telling me the other day how bright Saahil was as a kid. At seven, he could solve the Rubik cube in minutes, though nobody had taught him the trick."

"You know when I met him at the hospital, I found it weird that the window was always shut and covered with curtains, despite such amazing sea-view. Now I know why he hates the sea!"

"I noticed that too, Mili! His twin sister's death shattered him. She was just ten minutes younger to him," said Anubhav, thoughtfully.

"Some people believe that the lives of twins are intertwined. If one dies, the other may not survive for long," said Gatha.

"Oh yes, I have heard that one," Mili said.

"I feel really bad for Farzad and Nirmal. They had nothing to do with anything and yet they were killed," said Mili.

"I am happy that we could at least save Morena Dave," Gatha said with a feeble smile.

"Though she has lost her faith in friendship," said Anubhav.

"She will make new friends and move ahead in life," Mili said optimistically.

"When did you find out that Morena was innocent?" asked Gatha.

"I always knew she was innocent. But I needed facts to substantiate my gut feel. Besides, you were overtly defensive about her!"

"Hahaha, you're too funny, Mili."

"By the way, if you guys think Amar helped Saahil only to avenge his sister's death, you are mistaken," said Mili.

"Anything to do with the land?" asked Anubhav.

"Yes, Saahil had sold part of the land and had decided to transfer the other half to Amar. The lawyer informed Purab," said Mili, with a smile.

"Oh yes, ACP Trehan has been excellent!" said Anubhav, with music in his voice.

"What do you say Gatha?"

Gatha laughed. Mili wore a smirk but did not react to the comment.

"Our police officers are a tough lot, Anubhav," Mili finally said. "I agree that there are the corrupt ones. But they do not make up our force. We have heroes who guard us during periods of crises. If you look at the houses where constables live, you will think that we live in heaven! They are in a profession where they can never bring their personal tension to work or take a half-day if they do not feel like working."

Mili lit a cigarette.

Gatha immediately snatched it from her. "We have a role model with us here – *you*! How can you smoke while talking about something so inspirational?" Gatha shot back.

"You said you will quit smoking once we are done with this case," Anubhav said.

"Did I?" Mili asked, scratching her head.

"How about Tequila tonight?" proposed Gatha. "This calls for a celebration."

"I am asking Purab to join us too," winked Anubhav.

Mili's phone rang.

"Congratulations! Well done."

"Thank you, sir. Team effort! ACP Trehan has a promising future ahead," Mili added.

As Mili disconnected the phone, she realized that Trehan had a strange resemblance with her martial arts teacher in college.

Indeed, every individual has at least one exact lookalike in some part of the world, she thought.

Recommended Reading

An Invitation to Death
Anil Thakraney

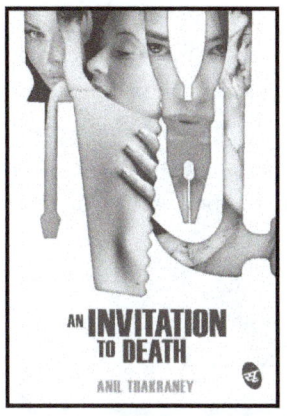

Darius Irani is a hyper-intelligent young man who puts his mind to the dark path – he becomes a serial killer. He targets young, beautiful, urban women, who fall prey to his easy charm, sense of humour and innate madness. He does not rape them, but the brutalization is savage-like. Will the police be able to end the cat and mouse game?

Anil Thakraney is a senior journalist based in Mumbai. Experience in covering real-life crime stories adds a dash of thrill to this book.

ISBN: 978-93-82665-43-4; Price: ₹ 195; Pages: 160; Binding: Paperback

Happily Murdered
Rasleen Syal

The radiant new daughter-in-law of the influential Mehta family dies mysteriously on the very next night of her wedding. Since the police is certain that it's an inside job, the suspects turn into amateur detectives, hunting for clues, delving into hidden secrets of others, coercing, prying and even blackmailing to get to the bottom of the mystery.

A mystery addict, *Rasleen Syal* designs homes to make a living and reads to make her life worth living.

ISBN: 978-93-82665-18-2; Price: ₹ 195; Pages: 256; Binding: Paperback

Nothing Lasts Forever

Vish Dhamija

A fire incident in Mumbai's posh Worli Sea Face apartment kills Raaj Kumar. Police officials are convinced that this isn't just an accident; it could be hefty insurances and adulterous relationships too. It's when a close friend of Raaj dies in mysterious circumstances and the share market nosedives that the police start digging old graves.

Vish Dhamija works in digital marketing and his nomadic inclinations have made him live in several parts of India and UK.

ISBN: 978-93-80349-24-4; Price: ₹ 150; Pages: 272; Binding: Paperback

Googled by God

Pulkit Ahuja

This is a fast-moving financial thriller that takes the reader on a journey to the dark realms of entrepreneurship and technology. Revolving around the ever changing worlds of stock markets, investments and money, the reader soon finds himself in the middle of a dangerous game of emotions and karma.

An MBA gold medallist in Finance, *Pulkit Ahuja* is a serial entrepreneur with experience in founding and running disruptive technology start-ups in education, ad-tech and transportation domains.

ISBN: 978-93-82665-44-1; Price: ₹ 195; Pages: 178; Binding: Paperback